Mind Games
by
Toi Moore

TM Publications
Colton, California, USA

Mind Games
by: Toi Moore

All Rights Reserved. Copyright 2003, Toi Moore

COVER ARTIST:
Eric Olsen
eosart@aol.com

COVER DESIGN:
D'Graphics Publications, Inc.
dgraphics1@juno.com

ISBN 0-9713221-1-2
First Printing, October 2003
10 9 8 7 6 5 4 3 2 1

Copyright Toi Moore, 2003
Printed in the United States of America

Published by:
TM PUBLICATIONS
P.O. Box 443
Colton, CA 92324
http://www.ToiMoore.com
TMPublications1@aol.com

PUBLISHER'S NOTE:

This is a work of fiction. Names, characters, places, and incidents either are the products of the author's imagination or are used fictitiously, and any resemblance to actual persons, living or dead, events, or locales is entirely coincidental.

All rights reserved. No part of this book may be reproduced, stored in or introduced into a retrieval system, or transmitted, in any form, or by any means (electronic, mechanical, photocopying, recording, or otherwise), without written permission of both the copyright owner and the publisher, except in the case of quotes used in critical articles and reviews.

DEDICATION

I dedicate this book first to my husband **Greg**, who always stands by my side. You have always encouraged me to believe in myself, while assuring me that I can do anything I put my mind too.

I love you!

Toi

I would also like to dedicate this book to my two handsome sons,

Kenan and **Amon**.

You two are very special and make me very proud! A mother could not ask for more. You have assured me that children are definitely blessings from God. You are truly my blessings! You have made my job of being a mother wonderful and worthwhile!

I love you both very much!

Always be proud of who you are!

YOU ARE GREAT AND POWERFUL MEN!

Never allow others to guide your faith, look within your heart, it's already there!

Mom

SPECIAL THANK YOU'S
TO MY CHARTER MEMBERS

Thanks to you, it's book number two! I would again like to give a special thanks to those of you who believed in me when I only had a dream. All of you put your money where your mouth was when it was needed the most. Due to your love, kindness, encouragement and contributions I was able to fulfill my dream by self-publishing my first book and now I'm on number two. I want all of you to know that I will always hold a special place in my heart for each of you, knowing that you were there in the beginning of a journey that will exceed distances I never imaged. I wish each and every one of you peace, love, happiness and the joy of also fulfilling your greatest dreams and desires. My prayers will always be with you. Don't let anyone tell you that you can't! Let the word **can't** be totally eliminated from your vocabulary. Always know that the sky is our only limit and God can give us the world if we work hard and aim toward our dreams and goals!

Gregory Moore, Kenan Moore, Amon Moore, Harriette and George Parker, Wilma Westmoreland, Muriel Darling, Evonte Moore, Michele McDowell, Michael Minor, Eric Anderson, Stanley and Ivy Westmoreland, Rhonda Shaw-Beard, Candy King, Donovan and Diane Carter, Tefere and Jan Hazey, Evelia Sands, Bruce Gordon, Sheila Glenn, Lillie Anderson, Rita Jackson, James and Charles Etta Jackson, Frances Wilson, Alan and Lekili Hubbard, Sheryl and Land Richards, Lori Parker, Jamille Goodall, Robert and Cynthia Hooks, Edward and Noreena Ramos, Brenton Woods, Florence and William Parrott, Betty and James Daniels, Jane Luper, Patricia Blake, Sonya Parker, Jeannie Wahsington, Christine Bias, Charles McVay, Erma Stanncil, Lori Robinson & Erlinda Garcia

In loving memory of those very precious to me and have gone on in search of the light, I miss you!

'Grandma,' Idora Cook, 'Nana,' Willie Mae Watson, 'Daddy,' James R. Blake, 'Uncle,' Gerald Blake, 'Nanny' & 'Granddaddy,' Gladys & Sam Blake, 'Cousin,' Stanley Westmoreland II

ACKNOWLEDGMENTS

God is definitely GOOD! When I didn't think I could do it again, here I am, still going strong with more determination than ever! Thank you *God!* I am very grateful that you have given me the strength, power and faith to realize that you are the source of all my blessings. Without your love, I have nothing, nor am I anything! I thank you for giving me a wonderful family and friends who mean the world to me. To have family and friends who truly love you is a blessing within itself. I cherish each and every one of them. Thank you *God!* Thank you *Mom* and *Niko* for your love, I love you back. Thank you *Mom* in Detroit for your continued love and support, you're always there! *Evonte* you're a great brother-in-law. *Harriette* and *George*, what can I say, you're always there, I love you both! *FloParrott* and *Michele McDowell*, thanks for being my true friends all these years, I value our friendship. *Eric Olsen* thanks so very much for designing such a creative and touching book cover, you should be very proud. *Tanisha Rodrigues, Jamille Newell, Penny Andrada, Fredia & Billy Morris, Durell Coleman, La Vetta Buchana, Ed Ott, Julie Johnston, Courtney Phillinganes, Monica Brogdon* and *Vonda Brown,* thank you so very much for your editing skills and great suggestions of my work. *Councilmember Parks, John Bryant, Synthia Saint James* and *Jackie Kallen,* thanks for your encouagment. *Pat Blake*, thanks for being a great aunt and always offering words of encouragement. Thanks for also being the best salesperson I could have. Your help and support means the world to me! I know that Atlanta has my back because of you! I love you! *Uncle Stan* and *Ivy*, all I can say is I love you, you've always been the very best, never changing! *Sister Shah'Keyah,* thank you for always being only a phone call away. I am VERY grateful for all your help, support and friendship. We have a speical bond. *Cynthia Hooks & Lori Robinson*, we'll always be the Three Musketeers. *Yvonne, Howard, Christina & Stephen*, welcome to our family. *Courtney,* I look forward to enjoying our new friendship and lunches. *Pat Tobin*, I look forward to our new working relationship and friendship. *Gina Green*, thanks for hooking up my hair for my cover, you're the best! *Cherise Bracamonte, Jamile Newell, Patrice Reed, Vanessa Brown & Monica Brogdon*, thanks for all of your help, you're always there when I need you. To those of you who have volunteered your time and services to me, I truly appreciate you! To all of you who have loved and encouraged me throughout my life, know that I thank and love you back with all my heart and soul!

Joi

ABOUT THE AUTHOR

Toi was born and raised in San Diego, California. If you hear the sound of her voice, you'd swear she was from the south. Nevertheless, she's just a plain ole' city girl. She has been a wife for over 19 years. She is the mother of two teenaged sons. Her interest in writing started at a very young age. She would write notes of inspiration to friends and family members on birthdays' or holidays. During that time, Toi did not take her writing seriously, nor had she recognized her gift, which was given from God.

While a senior in high school, she wrote a poem titled "I Remember." After writing this poem, she put it away, too afraid to show anyone. Ten years later, that very poem became published in the high school memory book, in honor of her ten year class reunion. This was the first time her work had been published. After seeing her work in print, she was encouraged to pursue writing more seriously, which lead to her writing more poems and stories.

Her genuine interest in writing immediately occurred after hearing the words of famed romance writer Judith Kranz. On a popular television talk show, Ms. Kranz spoke words of encouragement and how anyone could write if they just put their mind to what they are doing. At that very moment, Toi decided to farther her skills in writing by creating a short story. This story was a steamy romance titled "No Words Were Spoken." After its completion, Toi shared it with several family and friends. Their overwhelming and positive responses assured her that she was on the right track. In fact, their response confirmed she was on the track, inspired by God. However, after reading Terry McMillan's book, 'Waiting to Exhale,' she was farther encouraged to write with an added ethnic cultural and sassy flair.

After this confirmation, she went on to write

several short stories, along with becoming a staff writer for many newspaper and magazine publications. She has also written for Billboard Magazine. Her talents also lead to her interest in writing her first novel, with others that have followed. Since the awakening of her gift to write, her talents have allowed her credits to include over 200 published articles in various newspaper and magazines throughout the United States and Canada. She also adds to her credits several short stories and six novels. Toi has also worn the hat of publisher, as she published her own magazine titled *"Mini Romances."* This magazine was designed to allow a voice for new and unpublished writers. She also successfully published her first novel; *Momma, Please Forgive Me!*, which received rave reviews from many and helped a lot of people who were afraid to address domestic violence.

Toi has several bylines to her credit in which she has authored and/or interviewed, including a variety of well-known celebrities as: *Oprah Winfrey, James Ingram, Vivica A. Fox, Jermaine Dupri, Leila Ali, Synthia Saint James, "Sugar" Shane Mosely, Boney James, Regina Belle, Marilyn McCoo & Billy Davis, Jr., Jaheim, Patti LaBelle, Patrice Rushen, Lamont Dozier, Howard Hewett, NAACP Chairman Kweisi Mfume,* and *Barry White* to name a few. While composing these stories, she has covered a wide range of subjects such as: entertainment, health, religion, politics, sports, education, and children's issues. Her experience, faith and hard work make her an experienced and well-rounded writer.

Today, she continues her writings, while realizing and accepting her gift from God. She realizes that discovering your gift is precious within itself, therefore, grab onto it and hold tight until you've made your way to the top. The love and support from her family and friends motivates her in her continued journey, while never accepting no for an answer.

INTRODUCTION

Mind Games, the sequel to *Momma, Please Forgive Me,* explores the after effects of how a woman, who has been separated from her family for over ten years, comes back into society and tries to live a normal and happy life. La Vonne desperately seeks love, but will she be able to find true love while feeling guilty for killing her husband? There are many twists and turns in this story as La Vonne tries to be the perfect mother to her now teenage children.

This story explores the daily lives of how La Vonne's children treat her and how their classmates treat them after finding out the hidden truth of what their mother did, and why she hasn't been a part of their lives for so long. This book will send readers on a thrill ride as they try to figure out if Jonathan is in fact dead, or just playing *Mind Games*.

Now, sit back and get comfortable as you explore the journey you're about to venture into.

The author welcomes your thoughts and comments on this book. If you're interested in an appearance by the author in your town, or discussing *Mind Games* with your book club, please email: tmpublications1@aol.com.
Enjoy!

You are now entering the journeys of

MIND GAMES
by
TOI MOORE

Mind Games

CHAPTER ONE

"Oh shit! La Vonne, La Vonne!" Jay yelled as he opened the door of his black BMW and ran toward La Vonne. She was lying on the wet grass next to the grave site of her twins. She had fainted and Jay didn't know why. "La Vonne, wake up! Wake up!" He yelled as he lifted her head, kneeling beside her. He gently shook her limp body as he tried to revive her. The night was dark, cold and windy. A setting that would make the perfect mystery story come to life.

"What happened? Where am I?" She said, as she slowly looked around confused.

"What happened?" Jay asked and explained what he saw, "One minute you were on your knees praying. Then you stood up while looking at the grave site. After that I looked up and you were laying on the ground passed out. Are you feeling alright?" He was confused and concerned as to why she reacted in such a strange way.

"I think so. What happened? Why am I on the ground?" she asked.

"You must have fainted." Jay was holding her cold body in his arms, trying to console her while she laid helplessly against his warm body. La Vonne was a petite, light-skinned woman who had a well-proportioned figure. While in prison, her shapely body attracted many of the male guards. It even got Jay's attention, without her knowing.

La Vonne was still confused as she looked around the dark woody area. Suddenly she became agitated and broke away from the safety and warmth of his arms. "Where is he? Where did he go?" She looked around petrified.

"Where is who?" Jay said. He was trying to see who she was searching for. "I don't see anybody. Who do you think you saw?"

"It was Jonathan."

"It was who?" Jay was totally blown away by her comment.

"It was Jonathan! I know it was! I saw him standing right there, behind that weeping willow tree!" She pointed as they both looked toward the large tree that stood in the darkness about five feet away.

Jay helped La Vonne stand up. "Can you stand by yourself?"

"Yes, I'm fine." she pushed him away, dusting herself off.

Not wanting to lose La Vonne's trust, Jay found it hard to believe her theory, but attempted the impossible. "Okay, stay right here. Let me check around," he whispered. He picked up the flashlight that she had taken from the car in order to view the darkened spot and walked toward the tree. He slowly looked around to see what she was talking about. He shouted as he walked back toward her direction, "I don't see anyone. I think you're just tired. You've had a very long day. Maybe you just saw the shadow of the tree or some leaves fall and assumed it was a man. Come on, let me take you back to your mom's house so you can get a good nights rest."

La Vonne became hysterical. "I know what I saw, it was Jonathan standing right there smiling at me! He was wearing a dark trench coat with a dark fedora brimmed hat on his head. He had a single red rose in his hand and said, "Welcome home La Vonne, I've been waiting for you." La Vonne snatched the flashlight out of Jay's hand and ran toward the exact spot of where she saw Jonathan and looked around herself. "I know I saw him. I just know I saw him. He was standing right here!" Hysterically, La Vonne pointed to the very spot she thought she saw Jonathan. The very same man she had just spent ten years in prison for killing.

Mind Games

La Vonne suddenly began crying and walked toward Jay. He held her tight in his arms and again, attempted to console her. "It's alright. Everything is going to be alright. Come on, let me take you back home. All you need is a good nights sleep and you'll feel much better tomorrow, I promise. I'm sure that after spending ten years in prison can make anyone believe that even shadows are real. So come on, let me take you home." They walked toward the car that was parked down a small hill from the grave site.

After hearing Jay's comment, she was beginning to doubt herself and what she saw. "Okay, but I could have sworn I saw him standing right over there beside that tree. Then again, I don't know what I saw. Maybe I'm seeing things. Maybe I'm just losing my mind. Like you said, its been a long time since I've seen anything outside of prison walls. So it could have been anything. It could have been a shadow like you said. I guess my mind is just playing games on me." But I could have sworn he was standing over there, she thinks.

Today was the first day La Vonne had come home from prison. She had spent the last ten years of her life in the Hallsworth, Louisiana State Prison for killing her husband Jonathan for abusing her and her children. Before coming to the grave site, she had been in good spirits after the welcome home party her mother, Gloria, gave to her that was shared with family and neighborhood friends. However, La Vonne still felt empty because she was not allowed to say her final goodbyes to the twin babies she lost on that dreadful night, due to Jonathan's rage, and the fact that she was locked away for his murder.

Before they got into the car, she looked again to the spot where she thought she saw Jonathan and noticed something laying on the ground. She immediately ran toward the object, leaving Jay behind. "Wait a minute, what's this?" After reaching the very spot, she noticed a freshly cut red rose. She picked it up and held it high in the air so Jay could see it. "See, this is what he had in his hand. This is what I saw him holding, this red rose right here!" She carefully examined the rose and smelled it to make sure it was real.

Jay walked over to La Vonne and looked at the rose more closely. "Yes, this is a red rose. But La Vonne, this is a grave site. I'm sure someone just dropped it on the ground, or maybe the wind blew it over here. I don't know, but I sure don't think it came from Jonathan." He was beginning to also question her strange behavior, but kept those thoughts to himself.

La Vonne became agitated, "Don't you believe me? This is the red rose Jonathan had in his hand when he smiled and spoke to me while standing behind that tree!" Her voice calmed down and trembled, "Jay, you have to believe me. You can't just think I'm tired or losing my mind. You just can't! Come on, let's look around. I don't think my mind has gotten the best of me this soon. I'm too happy for anything like that to happen. Let's look some more, he has to be around here somewhere. I'm sure he didn't get away that fast. He's probably watching us right now. Come on, let's look again, but this time let's look more carefully."

La Vonne started looking around the immediate area. Jay followed her closely, searching for any sign that would lead to Jonathan, or a sign that would solve her dilemma. However, after looking for over fifteen minutes in the dark, cold cemetery, with the small dimly lit flashlight, no one was found. The entire area consisted of Jay and herself, the grave markers, and the many trees that surrounded the gloomy, moonlit area.

After searching, La Vonne became weary and wanted to leave. "Come on, maybe it was my mind just playing games on me.

Mind Games

I have to accept that Jonathan is dead. I killed him. I saw him laying on my living room floor bleeding from the gunshot wound in his chest. I know he's dead. I know he is!" She fell to her knees on the wet ground and began crying as she thought back to that dreadful night.

Ten years previous, an abusive fight began when Jonathan, La Vonne's husband, beat her until her body became weak, badly bruised and bloody. After several years of putting up with his abuse, La Vonne knew she could no longer take anymore. After their eight-year old son, Jonathan Jr., tried to stop the fight, Jonathan Sr. hit him in the face causing his nose to bleed. While watching the blood that ran down the face of her son, and the tears her six-year-old daughter shed from watching the fight caused her to lose it.

As La Vonne gained enough strength from her weakened and bruised body, she saw Jonathan on the couch. He was sleeping peacefully while wearing a smile of contentment. The look on his face, the pains that came from her body, the tears from her daughter, and the blood and tears that ran down the face of her son played over and over in her mind, making it harder to handle. So she slowly crawled to the couch, where she reached for the shotgun that laid hidden away from their children. She rose to her feet and shot him in the chest. The powerful force of the gun caused him to fall off the couch, onto the floor. As he lay on the floor bleeding to death, La Vonne ran out the house and down the street screaming as loud as she could. Later, after she was arrested, she sat handcuffed in the back of a police car, watching her children cry, knowing they didn't understand what was going on. Their tears admitted that they wanted her to return to protect them from the confusion. It was at that point that she regretted her act. It was also at that point that she felt a sense of relief by knowing that Jonathan would never hurt them again. As she slowly rode away in the police car, she wondered if his death was worth the pain and suffering she would experience in prison locked away from her children.

After crying for five minutes, Jay put his arm around La Vonne, helped her up and quietly walked her back to his car. As he pulled away to take her back to her mother's house, she sat in silence, constantly looking out the window. Her mind was totally focused to the sight of the weeping willow tree with hopes of seeing Jonathan re-appear. La Vonne could hardly move. She never took her eyes off that tree, or released the red rose she found that was tightly clinched in her hand. The rose served as proof that her experience was real. It also seemed to have power, a negative power she hoped she would never relive. However, through it all, she tried to assure herself that Jonathan's presence was only a figment of her imagination and that her mind was just playing games with her.

As Jay continued the drive to take her home, La Vonne remained quiet while totally glued to the darkness of the night. After being incarcerated for over ten years and finally being released, this was a night when she should have been the happiest. However, she was feeling totally depressed. All she could do was focus on the negative things that happened in her life. Her mind would not let her escape the fact that she killed a human being, even though she had been abused for years. Her mind took her back to the days she spent with Jonathan, as his oversized body towered her petite frame, causing her to become helpless to his violent attacks. His mental and physical abuse damaged her self-esteem and pride. However, her guilt of killing Jonathan was embedded so deep within her soul that she lived with her guilt every night when she went to sleep.

After La Vonne was asleep, her mind began working over

time, causing her to toss and turn in her seat. Jay watched her strange and unusual motions, but left her alone, knowing that she was exhausted. It had only been less than twenty-four hours since she was released. He knew that sleeping peaceful was something that would take time getting accustomed to.

After seeing who she thought was Jonathan, La Vonne's mind took her to the possibilities of him actually being alive, back to that dreadful night, where she imagined things that could have happened, wondering if he was in-fact for real. "Oh my God, Jonathan is still alive! He had a few shady friends on the police force who were mad at me because I kept sweating him about hanging out with them. I bet that's why the police came so quick when the neighbors called for help. Normally, they didn't come in our neck of the woods, and when they did come to answer distress calls, which I made several, they took their sweet time. But this time they were at my house before I could even get down the street. I bet his police friends heard on the radio what was going on at our house and immediately came. They picked him up and took him to get help before anyone else could investigate. So that means Jonathan could still be alive, he didn't die!"

Her mind continued to race, "I know I saw him at the grave site. His friends took him away and hid him. He was already in trouble for killing his so-called friend Ryan Dennison after they got into an argument. After the police found Ryan's body buried in a sunken grave in the baseball park they started looking for Jonathan. I remember how he started acting really strange a few weeks before I shot him. I thought his strange behavior was because he had taken more drugs than normal. I bet his crooked police friends found out that he was getting ready to get locked up and came to our house to hide him so he wouldn't go to jail for Ryan's death. They knew that if he went to jail they could be busted and their drug cover would be lost. But I shot him before they got to the house and ruined their plans. They couldn't take the chance of him living, getting locked up and uncovering their business. Yeah, that's what happened, that's what happened! Now I know I'm not crazy, he is still alive!"

The more La Vonne slept, the more her dream continued, getting wilder by the minute. She found herself thinking about the situation so hard that she was bound to believe whatever her mind told her was true. However, she was still troubled, wondering if in-fact her story was true, or just make-believe. Due to her dilemma, she questioned herself, "Why did I go to prison if they couldn't find his body? If his friends took him away before anyone could get to the house, why did I have to suffer? Did they get to my house and find his blood on the floor and think I hid the body myself? Or did they replace Jonathan's body with someone else's dead body and blame me? I don't know what to think. All I know is that I went to prison, and now my mind is playing games on me because I know I saw him standing under that tree." La Vonne was so confused that she didn't know what to think. Her thoughts were locked so deep within that she would never remember her dream once she awakened.

Once in the driveway, Jay was careful to not awaken La Vonne, so he carefully opened the car door, picked her up and carried her to the front door. After reaching the front door, he knocked with his foot and Gloria directed him to the spare bedroom that was made up for La Vonne, the same room she would now call her own. Jay laid La Vonne down on the bed and pulled the blankets over her cold and tired body. She was still holding on to the red rose. It was clutched so tight in her hand that he didn't want to take it from her, fearing he'd awaken her from her deep sleep. Jay laid La Vonne

Mind Games

down in her bed, whispered goodbye to Gloria and left to go home.

After serving as La Vonne's lawyer for eight of the ten years she spent in prison, Jay could understand her feelings and suspicions. He wasn't surprised that her thoughts would wander back to Jonathan, a man she once loved, but killed to protect herself and her children. Jay knew that it would take time for the healing process to begin, because while in prison, he knew that her thoughts were mainly focused on survival, not freedom and relaxation. He also knew that this wouldn't be the last time her thoughts would revisit Jonathan.

CHAPTER TWO

"Jonathan, I don't think you should be hanging around with those thugs. They ain't nothin' but drug addicts and dealers. If you continue hanging with them you're gonna end up just like them or worse, dead!"

"La Vonne, mind your own damn business. You ain't gonna tell me who I can or can't hang out with. I'm a grown ass man. I know how to handle myself. You just handle the kids and I'll handle everything else. Besides, I've been handling things around here this far just fine, so get off my back and leave me alone. Lately, it seems that all you do is complain about what I do, and nag me about who I'm hanging with. If you'd mind your own damn business as much as you mind everybody else's, yours would be better off." La Vonne was in a deep sleep, safely tucked away in her bed at her mother's house. She was reliving the argument between her and Jonathan that started the nightmare that ruined her entire life.

"Oh, so I need to mind my own damn business. Well, I'll just do that and leave! And when I'm gone you can take care of the kids and cook them something to eat, since all I do is mind everybody else's business. And you need to get your lazy ass off the couch and clean up around here." She grabbed her purse and keys and stormed toward the car in a fury. "Mommy, don't go. Don't leave us here with daddy!" Stacy and Jr. yelled and cried as La Vonne continued walking toward the car. They didn't want to be left alone with their mean, abusive father.

"Shut up you little brats and let her go." Jonathan told the kids as they stood on the front porch watching La Vonne get in the car. "Besides, it'll be much quieter around here if she leaves. Take your little asses back in the house and go play in your room so I don't have to see you. Don't let me hear a word out of either of you or your asses will be mine. And stay out of grown folks' business, because you ain't grown. Besides, your momma ain't going too far, she'll be back when she cools down. Now go on back in the house and cut out all that damn crying," Jonathan warned the kids, who were only six and eight years old.

He yelled out to La Vonne as she started up the car, "We won't miss you while you're gone anyway, so take your time!" She backed the car out of the driveway, leaving skid marks in the street. As she put the car in drive, she sped away, leaving only the smell of gasoline fumes and a cloud of thick black smoke in the air. Jonathan smiled and shook his head as she disappeared down the street. He walked back into the house and closed the door. He got an ice cold beer out of the refrigerator, lit up a marijuana joint, and sat comfortably in his favorite run-down lounge chair, located in front of the television set with the remote control clutched tightly in his hand. "Now, peace and quiet," he said with a smile before he fell fast asleep.

Two hours had passed when the telephone rang. "Hello,"

Mind Games

Jonathan faintly said as he picked up the receiver.

"This is Martin Luther King Memorial Hospital. Is Mr. Jonathan Brown there?" asked the unfamiliar female voice on the other end.

"Yeah, this is him. Who's this?" He slurred. He wasn't totally awake or conscious to understand what the caller said or wanted.

"Mr. Brown, your wife, La Vonne has been brought to the emergency room at Martin Luther King Memorial Hospital. She was in a car accident and she's in very bad condition. We need you and any other family members to get here right away."

Suddenly Jonathan sat straight up in his chair and awoke from his sleep and his high and panicked, "What? La Vonne? She's where?" The beer he tightly clutched in his hand before he went to sleep fell to the floor, draining the remaining liquid onto the dirty carpet. As he tried to gain his balance to get out of the chair, the ashtray that sat on the nearby table joined the beer on the floor, spreading ashes on top of the liquid.

"Sir, she's in the hospital and she's not doing very well. We need you to come down here right away! We don't know if she's gonna make it much longer."

"I'm on my way!" Jonathan slammed down the telephone and called Gloria to tell her the bad news. He took the kids to the next-door neighbor's house and waited for Gloria to pick him up since the vehicle La Vonne sped away in was the only one they had.

CHAPTER THREE

"Where am I?" La Vonne asked as she quickly opened her eyes and nervously looked around the room. She had been asleep for over fifteen hours in a big bed that was warm and comfortable. Everything in the room represented purity and safety. It was so unlike the prison where she came from, dark and dingy, representing corruption and dismay. As she calmed down, she thought, "Oh, I'm at Momma's house. I didn't know where I was or who's bed I was sleeping in. I almost forgot that I was released from prison yesterday. Thank God the dog next door barked loud enough to wake me up from my bad dream. I guess dreams really do seem real when you eat late. What did I eat before I went to bed anyway? My dream seemed so real. I could have sworn I was arguing with Jonathan about him hanging out with some drug addict thugs. Then again, I also dreamt I saw him holding a red rose in his hand while I was visiting the twin's grave site last night. Oh well, thank God it was only a few bad dreams. At least I'm not locked up anymore because that was a nightmare in itself."

La Vonne sat up in her bed yawned and looked around the room, admiring what was now her safety zone. She was ready to start a new and exciting day of freedom when she looked down and noticed a red rose firmly clutched in her hand. She was uncertain where it came from. "What's this?" she thought as she looked at the rose tightly embedded in her hand. Suddenly she became frightened, dropping it to the floor and shaking her hand as fast as she could in an effort to get rid of its meaning and purpose. But she didn't want to let her family know what she had been thinking. So she got out of bed, put on the worn-out pink house-slippers that were on the floor, the fluffy robe that was on the foot of the bed and walked into the living room.

"There's my sleeping beauty," Gloria smiled and said to La Vonne as she walked into the living room where everyone was watching television. Gloria put down her Bible, got out of her rocking

Mind Games

chair and hugged and kissed her daughter, welcoming her back home. Jonathan Jr. and Stacy, who were now sixteen and eighteen years old, ran to their mother and also hugged and kissed her. They had stayed home from school to share their mother's first day of freedom with her.

"I slept so good but when I woke up, I didn't know where I was."

"Well, now you know exactly where you are, and don't you ever forget it," Gloria said. "Now, sit right down on this couch and I'll have you something to eat in a few minutes," she walked toward the kitchen. Gloria cared for La Vonne's children while she spent time in prison. The full figured caramel colored, grey-hair lady had a warm and loving personality, which was a welcome for La Vonne to come home to. Even though she was warm and loving, Gloria had a firm demeanor which everyone knew and respected. She was also a devoted Christian who attended church at least three days a week. Gloria's strict and religious upbringing insisted that Jr. and Stacy attend church with her, even though they went unwillingly.

La Vonne's arrival home was sweet and serene. The scene in her mother's house was as if she'd never left. Gloria was still wearing the same type of full-length dress that tied in the back with bright flowers throughout it. This was the same type of dress that a kid could cuddle under to stay warm, or feel protected from anything harmful. Gloria's warm smile and the mole on the right side of her face, under her eye supported her round shaped glasses, allowed anyone to spot her in a crowd. She was a very attractive grandma. Her faith in God is what always kept the family together.

"How did you sleep?" Stacy asked her mom.

"Very good!" La Vonne responded as she sat on the couch. While sitting there, she admired her children's appearance. Jr. stood 6 feet 2 inches high, with medium brown colored skin, marked by pimples that don't take away from his handsome and youthful appearance. His black hair is in a short, but neat style. He has a sweet disposition that is admired by everyone he meets. Jr. is an honor student and very respectable. Often times he wears gear that displays his favorite clothing line, *Sean John*, and his shoes stretch to a size 16. He is popular and his personality is one that any girl would love to be associated with.

Stacy is a petite brown skinned girl who wears her black curly hair in fancy styles of braids, ponytails and flips. She has an attractive figure, which La Vonne knows boys watch very carefully because they used to watch her when she was Stacy's age. Stacy's shapely behind resembles the same form of what La Vonne has worked very hard to keep in check. Stacy had such a shapely body, nice personality, and attractive appearance, that La Vonne knew she needed to be guided well in order to protect her from the many guys who would want her as their trophy prize. While in prison, La Vonne was happy knowing that her children were in good hands with her mother.

La Vonne began talking to her children in an attempt to get to know them again and regain their trust in her as a mother. "What were you guys doing?" she said.

"Watching a movie," they said in unison

"What's the name of it?"

"*Double Jeopardy*," Stacy said.

"Oh. So what's it about?"

"It's about a lady who killed her husband and went to jail, but she found out that he wasn't dead. It's almost the same thing that happened to you mom, but the only difference is that our dad is really dead. So you don't ever have to worry about that," Jr. said with a very serious look.

Mind Games

Suddenly La Vonne's mouth fell wide opened. She began thinking about what she thought she saw last night while at the grave site. She also thought about the single red rose that was on the ground where she thought Jonathan stood, the very same rose that was found in her hand when she awoke. She remembered how Jonathan always brought her a single red rose each week during their happier days together. "Oh my God!" she said with great panic.

"What's the matter mom?" Stacy said.

La Vonne didn't want her children to know what had happened at the grave site. She knew that at age sixteen and eighteen they were old enough to understand her concerns. However, she didn't want them to think she was losing her mind, especially since she had not regained their unconditional trust. "Oh nothing, I was just thinking about what you said, you know, the movie. That's awful something so cruel happened to that lady."

"Mom, you don't ever have to worry about anything like that," Jr. said with confidence. "But if this movie is making you feel bad we can watch something else." He began looking through the TV guide.

"Yeah Mom, do you want to watch something else?" Stacy asked, "We can turn the channel. We have a satellite dish, so there are several shows we can watch." Stacy hugged La Vonne and she smiled.

"That's alright, I'm fine. You guys watch whatever you want. I'm gonna go in the kitchen and talk to grandma." La Vonne got off the couch and walked into the kitchen. "Hi Momma, how are you doing?" she hugged Gloria and sat at the small kitchen table.

"I'm just fine, especially since you're back home with us. Me and the kids missed you so much. Now that you're back we can put that ugly past behind all of us. Everyone can start a new life and be happy."

"Momma, I couldn't agree with you more. That's exactly what I want to do, start over. So, what ya' cooking?" La Vonne got up and started smelling around the pans that were covered on the stove.

"I'm making you some homemade blueberry pancakes, bacon, sausage, fried potatoes with green peppers and onions, and fresh squeezed orange juice. How's that sound?" Gloria smiled as she watched the excited expression on La Vonne's face as she licked her lips.

"How does that sound? Momma, the smell of everything is making me want to pinch myself to believe that it's all for real."

"Well, get used to it baby, because I'm gonna take real good care of you and my grand-babies. I want to do all I can to help you get on your feet and get your life together. Besides, you could use a little fattening up anyway, you're too thin girl." Gloria sized up her daughter's figure by looking above of her glasses.

La Vonne smiled, knowing that was her mother's way of making her point. "Thank you Momma, and thank you again for watching Jr. and Stacy for me while I was gone. You did a wonderful job. I'm really proud of how you raised them and I'm really proud of them. They've grown up to be such beautiful, handsome and well-mannered children. Momma, thank you again, you did very good!" La Vonne began to shed a few tears as she looked at her children watch TV.

"Thank you baby. Those are my Grand-babies, I'll do anything for them." Gloria said and hugged La Vonne before going back to cooking. Then she asked, "Do you want me to put your rose in some water?"

La Vonne froze. She didn't know how her mother found out

Mind Games

about the rose and declined to reveal her the truth. However, she didn't know how to explain the rose so Gloria would understand. "What rose?" she asked with denial.

"The one you had in your hand last night. Didn't Jay give that to you?"

La Vonne looked surprised by Gloria's response. "Ahhh, yeah! That's where it came from, Jay."

"Well, do you want me to put it in some water or not?" Gloria repeated.

"No thank you. It's kinda dried up now. I already threw it away. So, is breakfast almost ready?" La Vonne said trying to change the subject.

"In just a minute." Gloria said as she put the finishing touches on La Vonne's plate. Shortly after, she brought the homemade blueberry pancakes, bacon, sausage, fried potatoes with green peppers and onions, and fresh squeezed orange juice to the table for her to eat. "Here you go baby. Now, eat up. Like I said, you need to put a little meat on your bones. You got skinny while you were gone. I need to fatten you up because ain't no good man gonna want a skinny woman." La Vonne laughed while wearing a look of excitement as she gazed at the plate full of food. Her mouth watered just looking at the well prepared meal. This was the first real meal she was going to eat since she had been locked up in prison, and remembering how her mother cooked, she knew it would definitely be a meal worth having. Before the food could get a degree cooler, La Vonne dove right into eating. Gloria laughed while watching her. La Vonne's actions were those of someone who had never eaten before. Gloria loved every bit of what she was watching.

After she finished eating, La Vonne was ready to get out of

the house and see everything she had missed over the last ten years. "Come on, let's go somewhere." She gleamed.

"Where do you want to go Mom?" Jr. asked.

"Anywhere! I just want to get out of the house and go somewhere where there are no walls or ceilings. I want to get in the open sky and feel the cool air blow through my hair. I want to buy an ice cream cone, or some popcorn, and see people walking around in colors other than bright orange and gray. I want to see dogs running around chasing balls. I want to see people throwing Frisbees in the air and kites flying high in the big blue sky. I want to see things that most people take for granted!" The simple things in life that La Vonne imagined, the very things that justified freedom while she was locked up, were the things she missed most.

Gloria looked at La Vonne and the kids and smiled, "Okay, let's go to the park. The park around here is real nice, you'll enjoy it. La Vonne, there's some clothes for you in my room. Stacy picked out some of hers for you to wear until we get yours out of the garage and get them cleaned. We'll wait while you take a shower. I'm sure that'll be something you'll also enjoy."

La Vonne went into the bedroom and found a crisp pair of blue jeans, tee-shirt and tube socks on Gloria's bed. She went into the bathroom to take a nice long shower. "Boy, this water feels good," she thought as she stood in the shower and let the warm water run down her entire body. "This privacy feels too good to be true. It feels so good that I don't ever want to get out." She slowly lathered her body with a vanilla scented soap, taking all the time she needed to make her body feel refreshed.

Everyone watched TV while she took her shower and got dressed, which lasted a little over an hour. She came out of the

Mind Games

bathroom, feeling clean, refreshed and ready to go into the open world, "I'm ready!" she gleamed, "Let's go!" The cool day caused everybody to grab their jackets before heading for the door.

"I got the front seat," Stacy said while racing Jr. to the car.

"No, I'm older, I got the front seat," demanded Jr.

"Jr., quit teasing your sister. You're too old for all that nonsense. Besides, neither of you are getting in the front seat because your mother is sitting there from now on. So both of you get in the back and be quiet," Gloria said with authority.

La Vonne looked at her mom, then at the kids and everybody laughed.

"Okay," Jr. moped. "Well, can I drive then?" he asked with an ounce of hope.

"No, I'm gonna drive," Gloria responded.

"Grandma you never let me drive. I have my drivers license, so why won't you let me drive?"

"Jr., you already backed my car into a pole while watching some fast tail girl walk across the street, which cost me $500.00 in damages that the insurance company wouldn't pay. I had to spend money from my savings account to fix this car. I could have donated that money to the church instead of paying for unnecessary car repairs. Do I need to say more?"

"No Ma'am. I get your point," Jr. smiled and walked toward the car with his head down.

Everyone laughed as he pulled the front passenger seat up and climbed into the backseat, allowing La Vonne to take the front seat. Gloria backed out of the driveway and they were on their way. As they drove around town, La Vonne constantly looked out the window admiring the town she once knew. She was amazed at how things had changed so much. "I can't believe all the changes that have been made in this little town since I've been gone. When I was a child, nothing ever changed this much, everything always stayed the same."

"I don't know what you're talking about, things changed a lot when you were younger. You just didn't notice the changes as much because you watched them happen right before your eyes," Gloria said while she continued driving. Gloria's entire family was born and raised in Hallsworth, Louisiana. The entire population of the small town consisted of about twenty-thousand people. Since the city was so small in size, everyone knew most of the residents, which caused gossip to spread quickly.

As they took the scenic route around town, La Vonne felt so relaxed, happy and free. She still couldn't believe she was out of prison. This was going to be the first time since her incarceration that she could let her guard down and enjoy life. As Gloria drove down the street, La Vonne could not believe her eyes when she saw a familiar face. The face she thought she saw was Jonathan, standing along side of a storefront in an area that was shaded. The darkened passageway made it hard for her to see in the mid-afternoon shadow.

"Are you alright?" Gloria said, after noticing how La Vonne began to abruptly tremble.

Startled by Gloria's reply, because her mind was totally focused on the shadowed figure, La Vonne replied, "Yeah, I'm fine." Then she took another look, searching for Jonathan. But this time she didn't see anyone. "I thought I saw an old classmate. But when I looked again, it was someone who just looked like a guy I knew back in high school. I'm sure it was just my mind playing games on me. Don't worry, I'll be fine. Let's just get to the park." She sat quietly as

Mind Games

Gloria continued her drive.

Shortly after they reached the park, everyone jumped out of the car and enjoyed the rest of the day. La Vonne enjoyed her newfound freedom while putting the thoughts of Jonathan out of her head.

****

"Boy that was nice!" La Vonne said as they got into the car. Her day was so fulfilling that she felt as happy as she did yesterday, after hearing the words of the judge tell her that she was free. "I can't believe I can still run that fast," remembering back to when she was a child full of energy. "It felt so good to be able to run and not stop, or to not have a wall or a guard stop me in my tracks. Just to see the wide open blue sky with nothing but trees in my path was great! What an experience that was! What an experience! Momma, thanks for bringing me here." La Vonne smiled from ear to ear, as if she were a kid visiting the park for the very first time.

"You're welcome baby. I'm glad you enjoyed yourself." Gloria was pleased that she was happy. She felt that her family was now on track toward getting their lives back in place.

Everyone in the car was enjoying La Vonne's happiness. "Momma, you can run fast! You even beat me and I can beat a lot of my friends in school," Stacy bragged.
"You can't beat anybody. Your friends are just slow." Jr. teased.
"Grandma, tell him to stop. He's always teasing me."

La Vonne looked at her mom, who didn't say a word, only giving her an eye signal that allowed her to handle the situation herself. So La Vonne turned to the backseat and spoke, "Stacy and Jr., I'm back now and if anyone needs to be disciplined, I'll be the one doing it!

Your grandmother was nice enough to put up with you two for the last ten years, but now that I'm back, I'm taking over. You're my children, not your grandmother's. Therefore you come to me and not her when there's a problem, do you understand?" La Vonne knew that eventually she had to put her foot down, she just didn't know she was going to have to do it so soon.

The smiles immediately disappeared as they looked at each other with disbelief. "I said, do you understand me?" La Vonne repeated sternly.

"Yes, we understand," they mumbled in unison.

"Good. Now, Jr., you're too old to be teasing your sister. You guys need to grow up and act your ages. You're almost grown, but you're acting like little kids with all that teasing. That's not necessary and I don't want to hear it anymore," she warned.

Jr. and Stacy were not used to hearing their mother speak to them in that forceful tone. Every time they saw her in prison she was always very nice. They didn't know how to handle her harsh words and demanding attitude. They were so used to teasing each other that it just came naturally. They never meant any harm to one another with their words. That was just their way of showing affection. So they sat quietly, thinking about their mother's comments. They wished they could hurry up, get home and close the door of their rooms for safety.

La Vonne's comments caused the ride back home to become quiet and uneasy for everyone. Gloria was trying to let her resume her motherly duties by staying out of the conversation. However, she didn't want her grandchildren to stop speaking, or have bad thoughts toward their mother before understanding her theory. So she decided to break the ice, "Look, there's an ice cream shop ahead. Let's get some,"

Mind Games

Gloria said as she changed lanes and turned her car into the driveway.

Suddenly, the silence was broken and everyone was happy. "Ice cream sounds so good!" La Vonne said. Jr. and Stacy were happy, but remained quiet. They were unsure about their mother's previous response and didn't want to trigger another round of lectures.

"Come on, let's go in," La Vonne said with the reaction and expression of a child. She hugged Jr. and Stacy and pulled them close to her as they walked into the ice cream shop. She knew that they were feeling uneasy about her comments. However, at that very moment she wasn't sure how to make things right.

After everyone got their ice cream, they sat at a nearby table. "This tastes sooooo good!" La Vonne said as she ate the chocolate mint ice cream cone that was starting to drip down her hand. "How's your ice cream?" she asked Jr., trying to make him feel at ease and start a conversation.

"It's good," he said as he kept eating, keeping any additional comments to himself.

"Stacy, how's yours?" La Vonne asked.

"It's good too," she said as she continued enjoying her ice cream, also keeping any additional comments to herself.

La Vonne finally decided that it was up to her to break the silence, "Jr. and Stacy, I'm sorry!" They looked at her, then at each other. They were still unsure about what she was going to say.

"Look, I'm sorry for snapping at you guys, but things have been really hard for me over the years. I love both of you and I want to start being your mother again. I know I can't make up the lost time, or the hurt feelings and thoughts you may have experienced while I've been gone. But please know that I love both of you and I don't ever want to hurt you. I know that I just got home. I also know that you don't expect me to simply come home and take over, but I'm your mother and it's my job to discipline you, not your grandmother's. Your grandmother was just stepping in for me while I was gone, but now I'm back. All I want is for you to acknowledge me as your mother, that's all. Don't leave me out. I want you to come to me with your problems so I can try to help you work them out. I want to gain your love and respect. I want you to know that you can trust me and come to me with anything, but I can't do any of that if you don't let me. I know I'm asking a lot, and I also know that it will take some time for you to open up to me, but please try, and please start now. I promise I'll be the best mother I can, but I need your help to do that. So please forgive me for snapping at you earlier, and try to understand that I'm only doing it because I love you. I guess snapping at you is the only way I know how to handle things, but with your help I'll learn how to handle things more calmly. Please help me be your mother again." After she was finished, she had tears running down her cheeks as she held her ice cream in her hand that was now dripping down her arm.

 Stacy leaned over the table and hugged her mother. "Momma, I love you and I forgive you. I guess me and Jr. aren't used to you being here and telling us what to do."

 "I know, but I want all of that to change, and I can't change anything without the help of both of you. Do you think you can help me be a good mother?" La Vonne hoped for the best.

 "Sure, we can. We love you Momma," Jr said as he also hugged his mother. She hugged both of them while Gloria smiled. Everyone finished eating their ice cream and went to the car to go back home.

Mind Games

CHAPTER FOUR

"Hey Sherri, what's up?" Trina the prison guard said to La Vonne's ex-cell mate. Trina was the only prison guard who looked out for La Vonne while she was locked away. She always had her back. She didn't think La Vonne was treated right when the judge locked her up for protecting herself and her children against her abusive husband. Trina believed that La Vonne got railroaded when it came to being sentenced. She always believed that if it hadn't of been a Mayoral election year, La Vonne would have received a fair and sympathetic trial and gained her freedom. Trina had worked as a prison guard for over nineteen years. She had seen several prisoners come and go, but got close to very few. La Vonne was the exception because she too had been abused by her former husband. While La Vonne was locked up, Trina offered words of encouragement to her on a regular basis, inspiring her to be strong and hang in there. Now that La Vonne had been released, Trina had taken to Sherri since Sherri's valuable information about Jonathan killing Ryan helped free La Vonne.

"Nothings up with me but the same ole thang, it's just another day to do it on," Sherri laughed as she did her daily prison chore of mopping the kitchen floor after breakfast. While La Vonne was in prison, Sherri lived in the cell next to her's.

"I heard that. I'm also doing my job and trying to keep you guys out of trouble and make sure no one tries to kill anyone." Trina said as she did her routine prison check, making sure everyone was getting along and doing what they were supposed to be doing.

"Well, staying out of trouble is my middle name," Sherri said while mopping. "I hope that by staying out of trouble will let me get out of this joint soon. I'm sure La Vonne's enjoying her freedom now. I'd give anything to be in her shoes. Hell, I'd give anything to just sleep in a soft bed with a fluffy pillow and soft sheets all around me right now." She shook her head while thinking about a soft bed.

"I heard that. But your time will come, just hang in there a little longer. You'll be out of here before you know it. Hey, I also wanted to tell you that what you did for La Vonne was real cool. It's good to know that people are still willing to go out on a limb to help someone other than themselves, especially when they aren't getting anything out of it. Hopefully what you did will be considered as something big in the parole board's eyes when it's time for your next hearing." Trina told her.

"I sure hope it does too because I have much love for La Vonne, she's a cool sista'. We really bonded while she was in here. I'm glad what I had to say helped her get out. Hell, if anybody has the chance to get out of this dump I'm glad for them. Even the folks I don't like, I'm glad they got out. I just wish I would have been able to help her sooner. She could have been out of here a long time ago if I would have thought about the connection between my no good ex-boyfriend Sonny and Jonathan fuckin' around with those drugs and killing that guy. The damn fool! Why didn't I think of telling La Vonne earlier? She could have been home years ago!" Sherri was really upset that she didn't help sooner.

"Girl, don't beat yourself up. I'm sure that if you would have known that the information you gave La Vonne would have helped her gain freedom, you would have given it to her sooner. So, just be grateful that you helped her when you did. Just think, if you wouldn't have thought of the connection between Sonny and Jonathan, she would still be in here. So be thankful that you were able to help at all."

Mind Games

"I know you're right. Well, for what it's worth, I'm glad the mutha' fucka' is dead because he shouldn't have been beating on La Vonne in the first damn place. Hell, no man needs to put his hands on a woman to make his point. It's always about power, that's all. A man always thinks that the only way to get his way with a woman is to overpower her with his hands or mouth. I guess Sonny, thought he had power in his fuckin' dick when he slept with my best friend in MY fuckin' bed! The bastard! I guess I showed him who had the power when I shot his dick off with his own damn shotgun. Now the nigga's crippled because of my good ass aim. I guess he'll think twice before bringing a gun into the house if he's gonna be fuckin' around. It's too bad that he didn't get shot while his ass was running around in the streets with Jonathan, because it would have kept me out of prison. Hell, it would have also kept La Vonne out of prison if Jonathan would have got shot while in the streets hanging out with Sonny and all those drug addicts. You know it's a damn shame that niggas think they can just play sistas and get away with that shit. That is until they run into sistas like me and La Vonne who have no problem putting a piece of lead in their asses to teach them a lesson."

"Girl, stop it! You're killing me!" Trina was laughing so hard that her stomach started to hurt while Sherri laughed with her and continued.

"Well, I'm here to say that we showed them assholes that they can't do a sista' wrong and expect for her to just turn her head the other way and forget about what they've done to hurt us. Hellllllll NO! It just ain't happenin' like that! All that forgive and forget me shit ain't what sista's are all about! You better believe that the bullet I put in Sonny's black ass didn't feel so good after a good fuck in my damn bed with my best friend. I can also bet that the bullet La Vonne put in Jonathan's black ass didn't feel so good after he slapped the shit out of her that one last time. That's one black ass nigga' that ain't around no more to tell his side of the story. Payback is a mutha' fucka. So don't tell me that both of them niggas didn't get what they deserved, because I know they damn well did. All I have to say now is that I'll have to just do my time in this damn dump and hold my head up high while doing it, because I'd do it again if I had too. After brotha's realize that there's some crazy ass sistas out there like me and La Vonne, and recognize that we don't play that shit, tell me that they'll think twice before they fuck with any sista' again." They both fell out laughing, with Trina holding her stomach.

"Girl, stop it! You're too funny! You need to get back to your mopping because I gotta get back to work. If I stay around you any longer I'll be peeing in my pants. So take care and stay out of trouble," Trina told Sherri as they both went back to work. Trina always knew that she was in for a laugh when she visited Sherri. Sherri was all the way ghetto and didn't care what people thought of her. All she cared about was doing her own thing and getting out of prison. She also thought about sex and often had men friends visit to take care of her needs.

"Like I said earlier, I stay as far away from trouble as I can, unless I have to prove my point," Sherri smiled and continued mopping while Trina walked away with a smile. While Sherri mopped, she thought about La Vonne, "La Vonne sure is lucky. I'm sure she's enjoying the hell out of her freedom. I wish I could get out here sooner, rather than later. I wish all I needed was another motive as to why I shot Sonny to justify my actions. La Vonne said that she would see if her fine ass lawyer friend could get me out of here. I sure hope he can. Well, whatever happens, I sure hope the next two years go by fast so I can get the hell out of here. The last ten years have been pure hell and I sure miss my daughter! So for now, I'll just have to do what I need to do in order to keep things cool by staying out of trouble and being ready when it's my time." She continued mopping the floor.

CHAPTER FIVE

The telephone rang at Gloria's house, "Hello," Gloria answered. Stacy stood nearby in case the phone was for her. "Hi Peaches. How are you doing?" After realizing that the telephone was not for her, Stacy walked back to her room with a disappointed look. She hoped the caller was the new friend she had her eyes on, Joseph.

"I'm fine Ms. Johnson. Is La Vonne there?" Peaches asked. Peaches and La Vonne were very good friends when La Vonne lived at home with Gloria, before she married Jonathan. After La Vonne was married, Jonathan did whatever was necessary to keep her away from her family and friends, especially causing argumentative conflicts so no one wanted to be in their company.

While La Vonne was in prison, Peaches provided Gloria with a telephone number and address to Sonny Moore, who helped La Vonne gain her freedom.

"Sure, let me get her for you, hold the phone," Gloria walked back to the bedroom. After opening the door and realizing La Vonne was sleeping, Gloria attempted to quietly close the door to avoid waking her. However, before she could close the door she overheard La Vonne talking in her sleep.

"Go away! Why are you back in my life? I killed you. Why are you here?" La Vonne was tossing and turning in her bed, struggling with her dream.

Gloria was surprised by what she heard and listened closely to hear more. However, La Vonne's voice quickly became quiet, causing Gloria to go back to the phone.

"Peaches, La Vonne's sleeping right now. It sounds like she's having a nightmare. So let me go so I can make sure she's alright."

"Alright Ms. Johnson. I hope she's alright. I'll stop by tomorrow to see her," replied Peaches.

"That'll be good. I'll see you tomorrow." Gloria hung up the telephone and went back to check on La Vonne. As she peeked in, La Vonne was sound asleep, apparently not dreaming anymore. Instead, she wore a smile. Gloria closed the door and walked back to the living room.

****

The next day when La Vonne woke up and came into the living room, she noticed her mother sitting in her favorite rocking chair reading the Bible. Jr. and Stacy were not around because they had left for school. La Vonne and Gloria were all alone. La Vonne quietly walked over to Gloria and kissed her on the forehead, catching her off guard, "Good morning Momma."

Gloria jumped. She wasn't used to anyone being in the house with her after her grandchildren left for school. "Ooh, you scared me. Girl, don't sneak up on me like that again." Gloria said as they laughed. "So, how did you sleep last night?" She asked with a suspicious tone.

"I slept fine," La Vonne said as she sat on the couch next to Gloria's chair, looking at the newspaper on the table.

Gloria looked at her with confusion. She wanted to know why her daughter was talking in her sleep. She was waiting for

Mind Games

La Vonne to tell her what her dream was about instead of asking questions. "So, you slept fine, huh?"

Smiling, "Yes Momma, I slept just fine. That bed is so comfortable. Sleeping in a warm and fluffy bed like this is one of the extra comforts of being out of prison."

"That's nice. Did you have happy thoughts while you were sleeping? Did you dream about anything?" Gloria asked, not wanting to tell La Vonne what she overheard.

"I don't remember dreaming at all. But I do remember sleeping like a baby, safe and warm."

"That's good baby. I'm glad you're back at home with us and happy. Now, if anything bothers you, make sure to tell me. I want to help you all I can, but I can't help you if you don't tell me what's going on, Okay?" Gloria was hoping that her invitation would encourage La Vonne to open up and share her dream.

"Okay Momma, thank you. Is there anything to eat?" La Vonne casually said as she got up from the couch, walked toward the kitchen, and looked on the stove for any sign of warm food to eat.

"No, I was waiting for you to get up. So go sit back down, watch TV or read the newspaper, and I'll have something special for you in a few minutes."

"Thanks Momma," La Vonne said as she walked back to the couch to read the newspaper.
"By the way, Peaches called you last night, but you were sleeping."

"Oh, I need to call and thank her for helping. The information she gave you was a lifesaver. I hate that she wasn't able to come over when I came home. I know she had to work. I'm gonna call her right now, where's her number?"

"It's in your telephone book on the table next to my chair."

Gloria was hoping that Peaches didn't mention to La Vonne that she had a nightmare. She wanted La Vonne to confess the information herself.

"Thanks Momma." La Vonne got the phone book and made the call. "Hi, is Peaches there?"

"No she's not, she's at work," the unenthusiastic voice said. "Can I tell her who called?"

"Yes, can you tell her La Vonne Brown called?"

Suddenly the voice became friendly and alive, "La Vonne, is that you?"

Surprised by the response, "Yes, it's me. Who's this?"

"This is Ms. Jean, Peaches' mother. Welcome home. How are you doing? We missed you girl."

"Hi Ms. Jean, I'm doing fine." La Vonne was happy to hear an excited and welcoming voice.

"La Vonne, it's been a long time. But thank God you're back home where you belong."

"Thank God is definitely right!" La Vonne responded. "I'm so glad to be home. There were plenty of days when I thought I would never return, but God is definitely a good God!" La Vonne said with pride.

"Yes he is! Well, it's good to have you back. You have to come see me when you get a chance. I'd love to see you. I'm sure you've changed since I last saw you."

"I'm sure I have too, Ms. Jean. I'll come by as soon as I can. So, do you know when Peaches will be back home?"

"She'll be home after six. So call back later, or I'll have her call you when she gets in. Well, let me get back to taking care of my bad ass grand-kids. I can't leave them alone too long, or they'll get into trouble. Since I've gotten on the phone, their bad asses started running all over this house like they're crazy. They're getting ready to get a good butt whipping if they don't settle down. So, you take care and I'll talk to you soon. Bye La Vonne."

"Bye Ms. Jean." Ms. Jean had hung up the phone before La Vonne was able to get her words out. La Vonne hung up her line and looked at her mother. "It sounds like Peaches has some bad kids over there. How many kids does she have anyway?"

"I'm not sure. We never talked about her kids, just about her helping you. You'll have to ask her that when you talk to her. Hopefully she'll leave them at home with her mother when she comes to see you, because I heard them making all kinds of noise in the background while I was on the phone talking to her. Now, here's your food, and after you eat you need to call Jay. He mentioned something about getting you a job so you can get back on your feet."

"I know, he told me a few details about it yesterday. I'll call him after I finish eating."

Gloria had fixed La Vonne some country-style biscuits and gravy, sausage, hash brown potatoes with green peppers and onions, and fresh squeezed orange juice. After seeing her plate, La Vonne smiled and her mouth watered as she picked up her fork and began eating like she had never eaten in her life. Gloria smiled, knowing that her cooking was making La Vonne very happy, healthy and would put more meat on her petite body.

After La Vonne finished eating, she called Jay to confirm their meeting and got dressed.

****

"Hi La Vonne," Jay said when she opened the door. He came to La Vonne's house to pick her up and take her to a job interview. To his amazement, La Vonne's new appearance was acceptable from his view point. After representing her case for over eight years, he was used to seeing her wearing no makeup, an orange prison jumpsuit with arm and leg chains, and her hair pulled back in a simple ponytail. Now, she was wearing a navy blue knee length dress that fit her well-proportioned body. Her black shoulder-length hair was curly and hung down freely. Her face was beautiful with touches of makeup worn just right to complement her smooth brown skin. Her lips were colored with a touch of pale rose lipstick that seemed to be calling his name.

"Hi Jay, thank you for coming to pick me up," La Vonne said as she moved with confidence throughout the living room, hoping to keep his eyes on every inch of her body. "Let me get a jacket and I'll be right there." As she walked to the back room passing Jay, she left a whiff of her vanilla scented perfume in the air, causing him to smile as he admired the sweet smell. Jay watched her closely as she walked out of the living room. He was overwhelmed by her beauty.

"Hi Jay," Gloria said as he quickly turned toward her direction. "I'm so glad you're still helping La Vonne. I thought that after her release, you'd be too busy to help anymore. I actually didn't think we'd ever see you again."

"Normally that's how things go with other clients. However, over the years I grew very close to La Vonne while working on her case. I couldn't just forget about her that easily. Besides, I know that she needs help to get back on her feet and I want to help her as much as I can."

"Well, that's mighty nice of you to do that. She's very lucky to

Mind Games

have you on her side. I know that she'll be alright with you helping her. And something else."

"What is it Ms. Johnson?"

"Now, just between you and me, I want you to watch her closely," Gloria whispered. "She was having a nightmare last night and it worried me. I know it's going to take her some time getting used to being home, but I'm worried. I guess that's a part of being a mother. So, just keep an eye on her and let me know if she's acting strange because if she is, I may need to have her talk to Pastor George. He'll know how to help."

"Okay, I'll keep an eye on her for you," Jay responded. "But you have to remember she's only been home for two days and she's been in prison for over ten years. It's going to take some time for her to get used to being at home. It's just her being on guard. So don't worry too much. She'll be alright. I'm sure she's just adjusting to being home."

"I'm ready," La Vonne said as she walked back into the living room. "What were you two whispering about?" she looked at them with curiosity.

Gloria and Jay looked at each other like nothing was said, shrugged their shoulders and together said, "We weren't whispering."

Jay changed the conversation, "Come on, let's go. I have a ten o'clock appointment set for you to meet a friend of mine. She wants to talk to you about possibly working for her. You don't want to keep a possible employer waiting. So, let's go so you're not late."

Jay and La Vonne walked out the door and got into his shiny black BMW and drove off. "How did your first full day of freedom feel?" He asked as they rode down the street with the sunroof opened, absorbing the warm sunlit sky.

"They've been better than great. They've been wonderful!" exclaimed La Vonne. "But it's really too soon to enjoy or believe that I'm free, especially since I've only been home for two nights. Actually, the entire ordeal of me being released is almost too good to be true. I have to keep pinching myself to believe that I'm free and at home. The first night that I was at home I woke up wondering where I was. I woke up looking around the room, wondering if I was dreaming or not when I found myself in a warm and comfortable bed with soft pillows around me. It was far from the dark, cold and hard room I was used to waking up in."

"Well, I don't think you'll have to pinch yourself much longer because with a little more time, you'll get used to being free. For now, just take it all in, one day at a time."

La Vonne smiled, "I'm definitely taking it all in one day at a time and enjoying every minute of it," she winked.

Jay smiled and winked back, keeping all comments to himself while listening to the sounds of his CD playing *James Ingram's, '100 Ways.'*

His pleasant response shocked her. He had been so distant and cold to her advances while being locked up. She often wondered if a man with his style, professional status, and good looks would ever be interested in her. As she sat there feeling encouraged, she began to check him out with good and hopeful thoughts, "Umm, umm, um! His body looks so good I could eat it up right now! I'd love to just pull this car off the road and make love to him so good that he breaks down and cries. Umm, umm, um, look at his chest. The way his shirt tightly fits his masculine body shows how everything is very well proportioned in all the right places. The short black curls on his head are neat and stylish, just like him. I would have fun running my fingers through them all night long. His flawless coco brown skin makes me so excited that I'm getting hot by just looking at him."

La Vonne's body was warming up to levels unmeasurable as she continued to observe him. "Ummmm, and his strong and manicured hands are holding onto the steering wheel just the way I would want them to hold my body. Look at those luscious lips, umm, umm, ummmmm, I can lick them up like I'm licking on a sweet lollipop. And to top things off, his personality is very polite and calm, just like I'm sure the stroke of his hot body would feel on top of mine while I'm rocking his naked body all through the night. He's definitely a dream come true for any woman who lays eyes on him." La Vonne was slightly smiling, while trying to not let on that she was admiring him.

Her thoughts suddenly soured, "I wonder if he already has a lady in his life, because he has never tried to hit on me over the last eight years." Soon after, her thoughts reversed, "Damn, as good as he looks, who cares if he has a lady, because hell, after I'm done making love to him she'll be history in his books anyway." She silently laughed as her thoughts gave her the hope of someday being Jay's lady, which was also another reason to be happy to be back home. She continued to smile as she listened to the sexy and smooth sounds of *James Ingram*, while enjoying the sun, thinking about what could be between her and Jay and enjoying the rest of her ride.

****

"Hi Sandra," Jay said to the attractive sixty-something year old woman who was standing at the counter, as they walked into a bridal shop named '*Sandra's Wedding Boutique.*' She had gray-black hair that rested in a ponytail, laying on the middle of her back. Her beautiful Carmel-colored skin was makeup free. She stood about 5 feet tall and wore about a size 10 in clothes. Since this was not the busy season, Sandra was trying to fix up her shop. She was dressed very casual with blue jeans and a white tee-shirt. She had a no-nonsense, straight-forward personality. People either liked or disliked her because she didn't bite her tongue. Her bold personality was warm and friendly and she had many friends. Since last years death of her husband, Frank, who she was married to for forty-two years, she remained alone, spending little time with anyone, mourning in silence. However, she'd managed to keep herself busy and preoccupied by handling the duties of her boutique alone.

As she looked up from her glasses and noticed Jay standing at the door. His presence excited her, "There's my other son," she said. "Come over here and give me a hug and kiss," Sandra hadn't seen Jay since the funeral. She was an old friend of his family. They used to be next door neighbors when he was a small boy. Although, years later, she and Frank moved to a better neighborhood with a bigger house. Jay had always been very close to Sandra, Frank and their four children, that they considered him as a part of their own family.

"It was good hearing from you yesterday," Jay said to Sandra. "It's been a long time since I've seen you and you're still looking good," he kissed her on the cheek, making her blush.

"I was looking through my phone book, ran across your name, and decided to give you a call. When you were growing up, you were like one of our sons. Boy, I used to clean your butt when you were a baby." Everyone laughed as Sandra continued, "We loved you very

Mind Games

much. After you grew up and we moved away, Frank used to always ask about you and call to check on you. But now that he's not with us anymore, I decided to call and see how you were doing myself."

"I often think about him," Jay began to reminisce, "Especially since my father has passed on, too. I miss both of them." Suddenly his happy mood went somber, along with Sandra's. La Vonne patiently stood there, waiting to be introduced, not knowing what to do. She did not want to interrupt and appear rude.

Sandra tried to brighten the mood by changing the conversation, "Well, how's your Mom doing? I haven't seen her since the funeral."

"She's doing fine. She just asked about you the other day and wanted to know if I'd spoken to you since Frank passed. I was really glad when you called because I've been so busy with work that I hadn't gotten around to calling you. But that's no excuse, since we should never be too busy to call family."

"I agree," she smiled with looks of sarcasm on her face.

"Well, all that's gonna change today." He gave her another big hug and she smiled. "Now, I would like for you to meet the lady I told you about." He turned and looked at La Vonne. "La Vonne, this is Ms. Sandra, Ms. Sandra, this is La Vonne Brown."

Sandra was very open and secure. However, La Vonne was very different. She was still uneasy with her emotions and who she could trust. La Vonne held out her hand to shake and smiled, "Nice to meet you."

Sandra looked at her strangely, walked close to her, and gave her a big hug, "Girl, put your hand down. If you're a good friend of Jay's, you're family. So, give me a hug."

La Vonne was caught off guard by Sandra's friendly warmth,

while timidly hugging her back. She tried to feel at ease, although she wasn't totally comfortable with the exchange.

"Jay tells me that you just got out of prison for killing your husband and now you need a job. Well, I need someone to help me around the shop with cleaning and assisting the customers. So, is that you or not?"

La Vonne was confused by Sandra's boldness. She looked at Jay and back at Sandra. She couldn't believe that Sandra knew about her prison life and was not afraid or nervous.

"Child, don't act shy around me, I said we're all family around here. So tell me, do you need a job or not? I ain't got no time to be playing games with folks, cause if you're willing to work hard I got work for you. But if you're playing games I gotta move on. So, what's it gonna be?" Sandra folded her arms and stared at La Vonne, waiting for her response.

Suddenly, La Vonne had no other option but to let down her guard and feel at ease, "Yes, I'd love to work for you. I guess I'm just a little surprised by your offer. I didn't think someone would offer me a job or trust me right away, especially knowing that I was in prison for murder. So yes, I'd love to work for you if you'll have me!" La Vonne was all smiles. Jay and Sandra were smiling as well.

"Baby, if you killed your husband, the bastard probably deserved it because you don't look like you'd hurt a fly. Anyway, like I said earlier, if you're a friend of Jay's, you're family. I used to babysit him when he was a small boy. Our families were so close that you couldn't pull us apart. So, if he put a good word in for you, you're in, because his word is all I need. He said that you're good people and will work hard, and right now I need someone to help me keep this store together. When Frank died fifteen months ago,

Mind Games

I didn't know what I was going to do without him. That man was in my life for over forty years. God, do I miss him somethin' awful! But when the Lord calls for you to come home, you have to do what he has called you to do. Ever since my Frank left this good earth, I've been trying to keep things together at the shop by myself. But I'm getting too old for all of this work, I need help. None of our four children are interested in working in the shop with me. They help me when I need them, but they have their own careers and their own lives. I can't expect them to just drop the things they're doing to help me because their father died."

La Vonne was hanging on to every word Sandra was saying as she continued, "La Vonne, if you want to work here I'll need you to do a little sweeping and cleaning. I'll also need you to help some of the ladies try on their wedding dresses when it gets busy. The work is very easy and it'll put a little change in your pocket and help you get on your feet until something better comes along. You see child, I don't believe in judging people. I believe that everyone makes mistakes and everyone needs someone to trust them. Jay said I can trust you, so you're the help I need if you want it. When can you start? Is tomorrow too soon?" Sandra had been rambling on for minutes, not allowing anyone to break her thoughts.

With tears in her eyes La Vonne gave Sandra a big hug and smiled, "No, tomorrow isn't too soon at all! What time should I be here? I'm sure my mother will see to it that I make it here on time everyday."

"That's my girl," Jay said, showing his big bright smile.

"Okay," Sandra smiled, "I'll see you tomorrow at ten. You'll work Monday through Friday, except during the busy season, when I keep the store open on Saturday's. Now when you come tomorrow, don't wear anything fancy, just something comfortable like what I'm wearing, jeans and a tee-shirt. Make sure your clothes are old, something that can get dirty because I have a lot of rearranging to do around here. Later I'll have you doing some painting, nothing too big, just touching up a few dull areas. When the busy season gets here you'll have to get some nice clothes to wear since you'll be assisting customers. By then you should have made enough money to be able to afford a few nice things, or have your mom take you to a thrift store to buy you a few nice things. So, can you handle that?" Sandra asked.

"Yes ma'am," La Vonne said as she smiled at Jay, knowing that life was finally looking good.

"Okay, thanks Sandra. We're going to get out of here. I'll tell mom to call you. You guys should get together more often. Mom said she tried to call you a few times, but only got your answering machine, but she understands. She figured that you just needed time. She knows what you're going through now that my dad is also gone. Both of you are alone now, so you'll have something in common to talk about. It's been eight years since Dad passed away, boy time flies," shaking his head in disbelief. "It would do both of you good to just talk," Jay said while hugging Sandra.

"You're absolutely right. We do need to get together. After Frank died I didn't want to talk or see anyone, I wouldn't even pick up the telephone and I closed the shop for several months. I'm just now able to talk about my loss. I'm sure with time, I'll be better. But you're right, I do need to get with your mother. Your dad has been gone for a long time. I'm sure she can help me get through my pain. Your dad and Frank were the best of friends, they were like brothers. I'm sure her words will give me the strength I need to get by. Tell her I'll definitely call soon, or have her call me."

Mind Games

"I'll do that. I'm sure she would love to hear from you. Her words can help you get stronger. So don't forget to call her. Her number is still the same. Let me get La Vonne back home so I can get to the office. I just wanted to bring her in to meet you myself. I knew you two would hit it off. My work is done for the day with you two pretty ladies. Now I need to get some legal work done. Love you and be strong." Jay kissed Sandra on the forehead, gave her a bear hug and turned to leave.

"Go on boy, you're gonna make me cry," Sandra said while trying to stay strong. She grabbed some wedding books that were on the counter and handed them to La Vonne, "Here, take these books with you. Look them over and see what wedding dresses are in style just in case some of the ladies ask your opinion."

"Okay, I will. Thank you. I'll see you in the morning. Thanks again for your trust." La Vonne said as she gave Sandra one last hug. Sandra waved as they got in Jay's car and drove off.

"That was really nice of you to help me like that. Why did you do it? You don't owe me anything," La Vonne asked Jay as he drove her home.

"True, I don't owe you anything, but I wanted to help. I hope it was alright. I hope I didn't overstep my boundaries."

"Oh no, that was great. I just wasn't expecting Sandra to show me so much love and compassion. Thank you very much!"

"You're very welcome. Everybody needs somebody to help and believe in them. I was able to help you, so I did. And you know I believe in you. Who knows, maybe you can help me with something one day." Jay smiled.

La Vonne smiled back, "Maybe I can. Just ask and I'll be there." She took his hand and blushed as they continued their drive.

****

Fifteen minutes later they arrived at Gloria's house. "Thanks for the ride and the job hook up. I'll talk to you soon," La Vonne said as she got out of the car. "I owe you."

"Dinner would be nice," Jay said.

"Oh yeah, you do still owe me dinner. That was the promise you made while I was locked up. Just let me know when and where."

"How about celebrating your release and new job tonight?" Jay replied.

La Vonne displayed a large smile, "What time? Because it can't be too late. You know I have to get up early in the morning and go to work," she said proudly.

"Let me call you in a few hours. I need to go to the office and see what I need to do, I'll have a better idea of a good time. How's that?"

"That's fine. I'll be waiting for your call. See you tonight." La Vonne walked toward the door and waved goodbye.

As Jay drove away, Gloria came outside and noticed La Vonne's big smile. "So, where did you go?"

"I got a job, Momma! I got a job!" La Vonne was beaming with joy.

"Oh thank God! Where at honey, where?" Gloria also became excited. They walked toward the house as La Vonne began telling her mother about her new role.

"Jay took me to meet a friend of his family. The lady's name is Sandra and she has a dress shop. She wants me to start working tomorrow at ten. Can you take me please, can you?"

"Sure I can baby, sure I can. Congratulations honey. I'm so

Mind Games

happy for you. See, I knew the Lord would watch over you," Gloria beamed and gave La Vonne a big hug.

"But you haven't heard the best part yet." La Vonne was beaming with even more excitement.

"Well, are you going to tell me or do I have to tickle it out of you? You know how you hate to be tickled."

"Oh no, please don't tickle me because I'm weak when I get tickled. Anyway, Jay asked me out tonight for dinner, I think he likes me." La Vonne was blushing like a teenage girl who was going on her first date.

Gloria frowned. She wanted to protect her daughter's feelings by expressing her true thoughts, "I don't want to bust your bubble, but don't jump to any conclusions. Jay is just being nice. Besides, what makes you think he likes you?"

"I can just tell, that's all. Now Momma, you must remember that I haven't been away that long where I can't tell when a man is interested in me." La Vonne did not want to hear any more negative words from her mother.

"Well, that would be nice if he was attracted to you, you're an attractive young lady. But all I'm saying is don't get your feelings hurt by hoping for something that isn't there. Now, let's drop the subject and get you some lunch. You should be hungry by now." Gloria walked to the kitchen while La Vonne took off her shoes and sat down on the couch.

"Yeah, I am hungry." They quietly ate their lunch while La Vonne fantasized for a miracle with Jay.

****

A few hours had passed when Stacy arrived home from school. Shortly after she walked in the house, the telephone rang. She raced to answer it, "Hello." A masculine voice responded, "Can I speak to La Vonne please?"

Stacy was surprised by the call because she wasn't used to her mother being at home, let alone receiving any phone calls, especially from a man. Most of the calls were for her. Therefore, her curiosity peeked knowing that very few people knew her mother was home. "Uhhh, yessssss, she's here. Who's this?"
"This is Jay. Is this Stacy?"

"Yes it is. Oh hi Mr. Mitchell, I'll get my mom for you, hold on," she yelled, "Mommmm, Jay's on the phone for you," she teased.

La Vonne smiled and quickly took the telephone from Stacy and walked in the other room. "Hello Jay."
"Hi La Vonne, how are you doing? Long time no hear," he joked.

"No kiddin.' What was it about three hours ago since I last spoke to you?" she joked back. "I'm fine and you?"

"I'm fine too, thanks for asking. Well, if you still want to go out tonight, I'd like to hold up to my offer and take you to dinner."

La Vonne blushed while listening to his words. "Sure, I'd love to go out tonight. What time should I be ready?"

"Well, I don't want to keep you out too late. Therefore, I can pick you up early so we can eat and enjoy each others company. That way you can get home and get a good night's rest. Then you won't be to tired to start your new job tomorrow. So, is six o'clock alright with you?" he asked.
"Six is great for me."
"Good, I'll see you at six."
"I'll be ready," she blushed.

Mind Games

"Okay, let me get back to work. I'll see you at six, goodbye."

"Goodbye." La Vonne hung up the telephone, came out the room and yelled, "Oh my God! I'm actually going on a date with Jay. I can't believe it! I've wanted this man for eight long years and now I'm finally going out with him!" La Vonne was so excited that she began to tremble.

Everyone laughed. "Don't get too excited, it's just a simple date, nothing more. Don't try to make it into something that it's not and get your feelings hurt." Gloria said, spoiling La Vonne's good mood.

"I'm not Momma, but you have to realize that this is a date I've been waiting for from the first day I set eyes on Jay. I can still remember the very first day I met him. He was so fine with his tall and handsome chocolate body that looked good enough to eat," she licked her lips while wearing a large smile.
Stacy looked at her mom, "Mommmmmm." she laughed.

"Excuse me baby, but your momma hasn't had a man in her arms for a longggggggggggg time and you just don't understand how I feel. Then again, you may understand because you're a young lady now. You should understand how it feels to be in the arms of a handsome man that you care about. And don't tell me you're still a virgin. As pretty as you are, I'm sure you've had a few boyfriends who you've gotten close to." La Vonne looked at her daughter who's measurements would make most women jealous, 36-22-36, and smiled.
Stacy blushed, "Yeah I have."

"Stacy! Girl, don't tell me that you've had sex already. You ain't married yet and I've been keeping a close eye on you since you started fooling around with that crazy boy, Teddy. I sure hope he didn't talk you into doing something you didn't need to be doing." Gloria said with a roar of anger.

Stacy looked at her Grandmother with fear. She knew that Gloria was very strict and it would break her heart if she knew that she had sex before she was married. Stacy also knew that Gloria would have been extra mad if she knew that she ditched school several times to have sex with Teddy, who convinced her that she was doing the right thing. "Grandma, I just kissed Teddy, that's all." She crossed her fingers and quietly asked God to forgive her for lying.

La Vonne could see right through her daughter's lie. Stacy was showing the same expression she showed Gloria when she lied about having sex with Jonathan. "Momma, leave her alone. She's a beautiful young lady and she's eventually gonna have sex one day, so just get used to it." La Vonne looked at Stacy and candidly smiled.

Stacy quickly changed the subject to avoid any trouble. "What are you going to wear for your date tonight, Momma?"

"I don't know. It's been a long time since I've shopped." she sarcastically grinned. "All my clothes are still packed away in the garage and I sure don't have any money to go out and buy something new. So, do you have any suggestions?" La Vonne looked at Stacy and Gloria.

"Don't worry Momma, you're about my size." Stacy was a size 5. "Come in my room. I'll find you something really nice to wear." La Vonne smiled as Stacy took her hand and lead her to her bedroom. This was the first real sign of acceptance by Stacy. Gloria smiled as she realized her family was going to be alright.

CHAPTER SIX

It was 5:40 in the evening as she put on the finishing touches of her makeup and began getting excited, "Oh my God, finally, a date with Jay. I can't believe it!" she thought again. "I've been waiting for this night for eight long years." While making herself look beautiful, shortly after La Vonne looked at the clock and began to panic as she noticed the passing time, "Oh my God, it's 5:55. Jay will be here any minute. He's never late." La Vonne's mind was working overtime as she finished applying her makeup and looked over her clothes. Suddenly, the doorbell rang. She stopped in her tracks and continued touching up her makeup. She also looked around the room to see if she missed anything.

Gloria walked to the door and opened it, "Hi Jay, right on time as usual." His promptness was something they learned to depend on. "La Vonne will be out shortly, so have a seat," she motioned to the couch. "I'll go get her." Gloria walked to the back room to check on La Vonne with Stacy following close behind. She knocked on the door and said, "Are you ready yet? Jay's here."

"Come in Momma," La Vonne answered. Stacy was right behind Gloria looking over her shoulder smiling. "I'm ready. How do I look?" La Vonne was wearing a knee-length lavender dress that had a circular mid-length neckline. The tightly fitted dress hugged her body so well that it showed every inch of her well proportioned curves. She had on black spaghetti-strap shoes that circled her ankle with a low spike heel. Stacy had freshened up her Mother's hair with curls that laid onto her shoulders. She wore her favorite vanilla fragrance perfume that added the final touch for her special date.

When Gloria and Stacy first saw La Vonne their mouths

fell to the floor. "You look beautiful baby. Just like a princess! I'm so happy for you." Gloria said as she hugged her daughter. This was the first time in over ten years that she had seen her look so beautiful. "You sure do Momma. You really do," Stacy added with pride.

"La Vonne, you look so pretty. I need to get my camera so I can remember this day." Gloria added as she began to search for her camera. "Well come on now. You don't want to keep your date waiting." La Vonne, Gloria and Stacy walked into the living room where Jay and Jr. were patiently waiting, while Gloria looked for her camera.

"Mom, you look beautiful! I need to be taking you out so I can keep a close eye on you." Jr. teased and kissed La Vonne on the cheek.

"You sure do look beautiful!" Jay added as he glowed at the sight of La Vonne. "But Jr., keeping a close eye on your Mother will be my job tonight," Jay proudly said.

"Thank you," La Vonne blushed. She was not used to getting so many compliments.

"Okay, I have my camera now. You two get together so I can take a picture." Gloria said. Jay and La Vonne got closer and posed. "Say cheese," she added. Before Gloria could snap the picture, the door bell rang. "Now who can that be?" she asked with an attitude.

"I'll get it," Stacy said as she went to the front door. "Hello," she said as she greeted the stranger, barely opening the door, while looking through the metal protective door.

"Hi, is La Vonne here?"

"Stacy who is it?" Gloria said before Stacy could answer.

"I don't know," she said. She turned to the strange lady and asked, "What's your name?"

"Peaches," the lady answered.

Mind Games

"It's Peaches. She wants you Mom."

"Let her in child." Gloria told Stacy. "Peaches is that you?" Gloria was happy to see her.

"Hey girl," La Vonne responded and gave her long time friend a big hug as she walked in. Gloria also hugged Peaches.

La Vonne looked at Jay, who was waiting patiently to take the picture and go to dinner. "Jay, this is Peaches. My friend who got Sonny's telephone number for you. Peaches, this is my Lawyer, Jay."

Suddenly he was excited. "Hi, it's nice to finally meet you. Thank you for your help. You saved the day," he told her while extending his hand.

"Nice to meet you too, and I'm glad I could help. I've always had my girl's back. So I'm glad the little I did do made a big difference."

"It made more than a big difference. It helped set me free! So thank you from the bottom of my heart," La Vonne told Peaches and hugged her again.

"And is this Jr. and Stacy?" Peaches was surprised by their appearance and growth. They smiled, acknowledging her greeting. "They've gotten so big since the last time I saw them and I'm ashamed that I haven't seen them since you got locked up. Especially since I live just blocks away. You guys please forgive me. My job and my kids keep me so busy that I don't have much time for anything else." Peaches felt badly over her admission.

"Don't worry about it girl, they were fine. Momma saw to that," La Vonne reassured her.

"I'm sure she did because Ms. Gloria took care of a lot of stuff when we were growing up." They laughed, remembering their younger days.

"And how many kids do you have? I heard them yelling in the background when I called your house," La Vonne asked.

"Girl, I have five hardheaded little brats. The youngest is five and the oldest is twelve," Peaches responded.

"Five? Girl, you've been busy," La Vonne said.

"Did you ever get married?" Gloria boldly asked.

Peaches put her head down, "No Ma'am, I didn't."

"Well, where is their daddy and who is he? Does he help you out with the kids?" Gloria wanted all the juicy details.

Peaches was ashamed to answer, but knew Gloria wouldn't let up. "Well, they all have different daddies." Everyone in the room looked at her with their mouths wide open, speechless. Stacy was counting on her fingers as Peaches continued, "After La Vonne left, I got lonely and kinda wild, that's when I began doing drugs. I started hanging out with a few friends who smoked weed and they encouraged me to try it, so I did. At first it started off with me simply smoking pot, then the pot wasn't enough, so I went to stronger drugs that would make me feel better or ease any pain I was feeling. I thought the drugs would make the pain go away faster."

La Vonne looked at her friend, but didn't say a word. After her ordeal with Jonathan, she knew what the drugs could do to someone's mind. She was surprised that Peaches would even indulge in drugs, especially after knowing how Jonathan's habit changed her entire life. Peaches continued, "Eventually, every man who said he loved me got me pregnant and left me. Before I could put things back together I was left alone with five little babies and no job or money to take care of them. I soon found myself selling some of the drugs that I wasn't using in order to survive, along with selling my body."

"You got THAT lonely?" Gloria asked.

Mind Games

"Yes Ma'am, I thought I was," Peaches answered as she put her head down. Everyone remained quiet as she continued. "That's exactly what my Momma said after I had my fifth child while living in a one bedroom apartment. I would leave my babies with who ever would watch them while I got high, sold my body for drugs, or sold the drugs for a little money to keep my rent paid. You see, I had stayed away from my mother for years. She didn't even know I had all those babies. She couldn't help me even if she wanted to. All I wanted to do was get high and have sex. I thought I knew it all until one day a good friend of mine overdosed on some cocaine while getting high with some of our friends. That was the day I opened my eyes and realized just how bad things really were and called my mother for help. Thank God she came. Because if she hadn't, I don't know what I would have done. But everything is alright now and I'm cool! I've been sober for five years, three months and ten days. I've gotten myself together now. I have a good job and momma helps me with the kids. Everything is much better now. I even talk to teenagers about my problem every once in a while so that they don't go down the same road I went down."

Peaches looked directly at Jr. and Stacy as she continued, "The reason I told you guys everything is because I don't ever want Jr. and Stacy to do anything stupid like I did. You guys please be careful out there. Don't let your friends talk you into doing something you know isn't right, I knew what I was doing wasn't right, but I still did it. At the time I just didn't care. Don't ever get to the point where you just don't care. It's too hard to come back and get yourself together after you fall, that is if you do come back. People like my girlfriend didn't get a chance to come back. So, don't be a fool like she was."

La Vonne looked at Jr. and Stacy, then at Peaches.

La Vonne hugged her friend, "Well, I'm happy to see that you're getting on with your life," she told her.

"Yes I am! It's been hard, but I'm doing the best I can." Peaches said with pride.

"Good," La Vonne said as she hugged Peaches tighter. She could see Peaches was about to cry. She knew if Peaches started crying, she would cry with her, which would mess up her makeup and she didn't want to have to start over, so she broke a loose from her hug.

"Well, it looks like I came at a bad time? You two look so nice," Peaches said.

"We're just on our way to dinner to celebrate my release and new job." La Vonne told her.

"You already got a job?" Peaches was happy and surprised to hear the good news. "You go girl!" She gave La Vonne a high five.

"Yeah, thanks to Jay, I'm going to be working in a bridal shop across town. I start tomorrow."

"That's real good. I'm happy to see that things are finally looking up for you. You definitely deserve to be happy. Well, I don't want to hold you guys up any longer. I just got off from work and wanted to stop by and say hi before I went home. I knew that once I got home I wouldn't leave again until it was time to go back to work," Peaches told everyone.

"I understand that," Gloria said. "Before you leave let me get a picture of you too. But let me get La Vonne and Jay first. Let's take these pictures so you guys can get out of here before it gets too late." La Vonne and Jay quickly got in place for the picture.

Gloria prepared for the picture. "Say cheese." Everyone in the room laughed as they hugged for the picture and said, "Cheese."

Mind Games

"Okay, Jr. and Stacy, get over there with your mother so I can get you guys in a picture too." They got close to their mother and everyone again said, "Cheese" as Gloria snapped the entire group. The sight of the happy foursome made Gloria shed a tear. "You guys look so nice together as one happy family," she added.

"Okay Grandma, you get over there with Mom, let me take one of you two," Stacy said as Gloria stood close to her daughter and hugged her, while trying to fix her hair. "Cheese," they said as the flash went off.

"Ms. Gloria, let me take one of you, La Vonne, Jr. and Stacy." Peaches said while taking the camera from Stacy as everyone got in place.

"Okay, one more," Gloria said as she took the camera from Peaches. "Peaches you get over there with Jay and La Vonne." Peaches rushed to get in the picture as they said, "Cheese."

"Okay, that's enough pictures for one night. You kids better go on to dinner before it gets too late." Gloria was trying to rush La Vonne and Jay out the house. "La Vonne, you know you have to get up early in the morning. I'm sure you don't want to be late on your first day. So go on now." She opened the front door.

"Okay, let's go because I don't want to be too tired in the morning either," La Vonne said as she walked to the couch to get her jacket. After getting her jacket, Jay helped her put it on and they walked toward the front door. Jay took her hand, put it inside of his folded arm and escorted her to his car. Jay and La Vonne were off to celebrate La Vonne's freedom, while Gloria, Stacy, Jr. and Peaches stood at the front door waving and smiling goodbye.

Peaches turned to go home, "Bye Ms. Gloria."

"Bye Peaches, it's so good to see you. And I'm glad to hear

that you're doing better. You tell your mother I said hi."

"I will. Talk to you soon." She left as Gloria, Stacy and Jr. waved goodbye.

****

At the restaurant, Jay had the car valet parked. La Vonne was escorted out of the car by the attendant and treated with class, just like a princess. This was treatment she wasn't used to receiving. Jay got the valet ticket and proudly escorted La Vonne into the restaurant on his arm with her blushing every step of the way. Once they stepped into the restaurant, Jay gave his name to the hostess and they were immediately ushered to a table that was located near a window with a lake view that shadowed the sunset. La Vonne felt like she was in heaven. "Oh my God, this is beautiful!" she said with excitement.

"So, I take it that you like it here?" Jay responded.

"No I don't like it here, I love it here! This restaurant is beautiful! I've never been to any place as beautiful as this in my life. Thank you for bringing me here." La Vonne was so amazed that she felt like a kid seeing *Disneyland* for the very first time. As she sat silently in awe, her thoughts were clear and happy while looking at the beautiful sunset sky.

"Hello, my name is Janet. I'm going to be your server tonight. Would you like to start your evening off with a drink?"

Jay looked at La Vonne and signaled for her to give her order first. "Sure, I'd like a coke please."

"And I'll have an iced tea. Can you also bring us a bottle of sparkling apple cider, we're celebrating tonight, thank you."

Mind Games

Jay ordered and the server walked away to fill their request. They purposely didn't order alcohol because drugs and alcohol is what resulted in La Vonne's husband being abusive to her and her children. She vowed to stay away from any type of alcohol and asked that anyone around her refrain from drinking alcohol as well. "What would you like to eat pretty lady?" Jay was staring directly into La Vonne's eyes mesmerized.

She blushed and responded, "Well, I'm not sure what I want, everything on the menu looks so good. It's been a long time since I've had this many choices." Jay was staring so hard at La Vonne that she buried her head in the menu from embarrassment. La Vonne tried to avoid any direct eye contact. She could not believe Jay was looking at her with such emotion and what appeared to be passion. This was something she had dreamed and hoped for from the very first day she set eyes on him. However, now that Jay's emotions were showing, she wasn't sure how to react.

Jay noticed how uncomfortable La Vonne was to his stares. He took his hand, placed it under her chin and lifted it up so her eyes would meet his, "La Vonne, you look so beautiful tonight. Thank you for being my date." he said.

She was so nervous that she thought she was going to pee on herself. "Thank you and you're welcome." She quickly buried her head back in the menu.

Her shy gesture caused Jay's hand to slide down from her chin, causing him to smile before returning to his menu.

Suddenly the server came to the table with their drinks and put a basket of homemade hot dinner rolls on the table. The smell of the rolls made La Vonne's mouth water. The server gave them their drinks. "Here you go. A coke for the lady, an iced tea for the gentleman and a bottle of chilled apple cider with two chilled glasses."

"Thank you," they said.

Janet asked, "Are you ready to order?"

Jay looked at La Vonne, "Do you know what you want?"

"Ummmm, I'm not sure. There are so many things to choose from, I don't know what I want. Can you order for me please?"

"Are you sure?"

"I'm sure, I trust you. I think you know this menu better than I do so go ahead."

Jay looked at the menu and began ordering, "Okay, we'll have the filet mignon and lobster dinner with fresh vegetables and a baked potato. Add the works on top of the potatoes, please." Jay gave the waitress his menu.

La Vonne's entire face lit up and her mouth watered like Niagara Falls after listening to his order. "That's what I call a good meal!"

"I'm glad you approve of my choice. Now, let me make a toast." Jay poured both of them a glass of sparkling apple cider and they held their glasses up high while he made his toast. "La Vonne, I'm very glad you're finally free. Your case was very difficult and timely. I learned a lot about domestic violence and your struggles during the last eight years. I also understand why you did what you did. You should have never had to kill your husband in order to protect yourself and your children. No man should ever have to put his hands on a woman in order to settle a disagreement. That's why I want to help you get back on your feet, this whole ordeal was not your fault.

She was glued to his words as he continued, "Now that it's all behind you, you can start a whole new life of happiness for yourself and your children. Today life has begun and God has shined on you.

Mind Games

I want you to know that I'm very proud of how you handled yourself. I also want you to know that I've admired you throughout the years for being strong and fighting for your freedom. Tonight I make this toast to you for your strength and determination. I also make this toast to celebrate your release and the chance to start your life over again. Your freedom will allow you to give your children back their mother. The very mother they've lived without for over ten years. May the rest of your life be wonderful and give you back the things that life took away from you. To freedom." They raised their glasses to seal the honor.

Tears fell from La Vonne's eyes while listening to his words. "Those were some of the nicest words anyone has said to me in a very long time. They made the toast very special. Now it's my turn" Jay held his glass back up and listened. "Jay, I thank God for you. I'm so glad you came into my life. I don't know what I would have done if you weren't there encouraging me to go on and be strong. I thank you for that. You gave me the courage I needed to be strong and hang in there till the end. God gave me the strength and faith to know that one day I'd be released. I know it took ten years to happen, but during the time you've been my lawyer, you've always believed in me and encouraged me to never give up. For that, I thank you. Now, I make this toast to being thankful and blessed, along with having good and lasting friendships." They toasted again. The sparkle in La Vonne's eye was almost as bright as the bubbles floating in the glass.

"Now tell me something special about you. I got to know a lot about your case, but not about the personal side of you. So, tell me about your childhood. How was it growing up?" Jay asked.

La Vonne blushed and answered, "Well, I wasn't a bad person that's for sure. But ever since I killed Jonathan I feel like bad things always seem to happen to me. Why did I have to kill him? Why couldn't he have just left us alone and went away? All I wanted to do was protect me and my babies." La Vonne became sad.

"Please don't beat yourself up for what happened in the past. You've paid your dues for that mistake. Tonight is supposed to be a happy time, a time for celebrating, not a time of regret. So, finish telling me about the good times of your past and forget about Jonathan, he's history." Jay said.

La Vonne smiled and continued, "You're right. Okay. Well, I grew up in a Christian home with two loving parents who always taught me right from wrong. My father was a strong and proud man who was a hard worker and a firm believer of 'do unto others, as you wish them to do unto you.' Boy do I miss my Daddy, God bless his soul in heaven."

La Vonne became quiet and held her head down. A tear fell from her eyes as she reminisced about the good times she had with her father. In spite of her painful loss, Jay understood more than ever. So he held her hand to give her the needed strength to carry on. She smiled and gained her composure and continued, "Well, because of my parent's upbringing, I always tried to do what was right to make them proud. In fact, I did it so well that everyone called me Little Miss Perfect, a name I grew to hate. Momma had a real hard time after losing Daddy from that car accident, as well as losing Suzie, my baby sister, to SIDS. Susie was the only other child Daddy and Momma ever had. After Suzie's death Momma just couldn't seem to pull herself together to try for more children, so I grew up alone. After Daddy and Suzie died our house was never the same. Momma seemed to cry every time she saw a baby girl that resembled Suzie, or if she saw a loving couple together that resembled her and daddy. Through her pain she still managed to raise me with dignity and pride."

La Vonne was feeling really bad. However, Jay continued holding her hand, reassuring her that he was there for her. Feeling lost in sorrow, she shared, "I know I said I wouldn't talk about Jonathan, but I have to get it out." Jay could not say any words to cheer her up. He knew that she needed to get her pain out, so he sat in silence reflecting on her words as she continued, "No wonder she had such a hard time accepting the fact that I killed Jonathan. Killing someone is one of the commandments in the Bible and Momma lived her entire life by the powerful words of that precious book. I'll never forget the pain I saw in her eyes at my first court hearing. She never gave me a chance to explain. It took two years before she finally opened up and read one of my letters that explained why I killed Jonathan. It also took two years before she forgave me, or before I saw my children. That picture will be embedded in my heart forever. That was a day I never want to see again. Thank God she eventually forgave me, and thank God for prayer. I believe that her strength and prayers helped release me from prison, along with your help. But growing up as an only child with one parent, who was always depressed, made my life really hard. I always wished that I had someone to talk to. Especially when I was going through the hellish trials and tribulations with Jonathan. I wish someone would have been there for me, because if someone had been, I might have made better choices in my life and not ended up in prison." She put her head down in remorse. After realizing that she was spoiling a perfectly good evening. La Vonne put her head up high and smiled, "Now, I want to know about your life, since you know so much about mine."

Jay smiled. "Well, I grew up in a poor family. My parents worked hard every day. My mother cleaned houses for white families and my father was a janitor for my middle and high schools. Everyone used to tease me because they knew my father worked at the school and he would always keep me in line. My friends used to tell me that they would tell on me if I messed with them, or if I messed up in school. I guess in a way, I also had to be perfect. Anyway, I have two sisters and one brother. We're a very close family. However, everyone is so busy with their careers that we have to make appointments with each other in order to have family gatherings. But we always get together for Easter, Thanksgiving and Christmas because our mother can cook like no one I've ever known. We never pass up a home cooked meal prepared by Momma." A big smile appeared just thinking about his Mother's home cooked meals and her famous *Sweet Potato Pie*.

"Anyway, because my father kept such a close eye on me in school, my grades were very good. In fact I was always on the honor roll, which was a requirement in our house. My father always believed that we were smart kids and he would not accept any excuses for low grades. He said that being a good student was the least we could do since we weren't working or paying any bills. He would always tell us that getting good grades was our job and keeping a roof over our heads and food on the table was his job. Our father had such strict standards for me and my siblings that we all were able to get full college scholarships to the best colleges in the country. That was something our parents never had an opportunity to experience." Now Jay was sad. La Vonne was glued to his every word as he continued.

"After my brother and sisters and I finished college and started making a little money, we pitched in and bought our parents a big house. They never owned their own house. They always rented. We took care of them financially and made sure they never paid the rent or mortgage on another house for the rest of their life. Convincing our Father to retire from his job and let us pay the mortgage was very difficult. He was a very proud man and did not want to accept our offer. Finally he accepted and justified it as our way for paying them back for raising us to be great kids. Like I said, he did agree to retire from the school district, only to start his own cleaning business. Our Father worked until the day he died of pneumonia. That was the saddest day of our lives. Both of our parents were loving Christians who cared about everybody. Our parents were very happy together. I hope to someday find that kind of love in a relationship."

La Vonne smiled feeling hopeful as he continued, "The way they brought us up taught us to never take things for granted and always give thanks to God for our blessings. They taught us that nothing is guaranteed in this world and everything can be taken away from a person with a blink of an eye. That is why I help people whenever I can. I want to pay back a society that helped get me to where I am today. That is why I took on your case pro-bono. I take on a free case once a year. I don't ever want to get too big or too rich that I can't help someone who's unable to help themselves. I also volunteer my legal services two nights a week at the legal clinic by my office. This way I give back regularly and stay connected to the real world."

La Vonne was really impressed. She looked deep into Jay's big brown eyes and asked, "Are you seeing anyone, because I'm very attracted to you. I have dreamt about you being my man."

Jay was shocked by her admission and boldness. He quickly regained his composure and responded, "Well, yes I am seeing someone right now." La Vonne's expression suddenly fell with disappointment as he continued, "We've been seeing each other for over five years, but things aren't going so well right now. We've been going through a few challenges and I'm not sure if we'll get through them this time."

Suddenly La Vonne got excited, "This time? Has there been many bad times throughout your relationship?"

"Well kinda, the problem is we're both very busy. Our jobs keep us apart. She's a business executive and you know I'm a lawyer. Our time spent together is very limited and it causes problems. We thought we could work things out, but it seems that things are just getting worse as our relationship continues and we're drifting further apart. I don't know if it will last much longer." He was looking sad while La Vonne was secretly grinning.

"Oh, so things are that bad? Do you think you'll get through this roadblock?" She was hoping for the worst.

"I don't know if we can get through it this time. But right now I really can't see myself getting involved with anyone else, I'm sorry." He took a long drink of his apple cider and wiped away the sweat from his forehead.

"Oh, no problem, I understand," she said as she mentally wiped the egg off her face, trying to not let on that her feelings were hurt. Suddenly the food came and her face lit up. "Everything looks so good!" She was trying to forget what he just said. She knew that things were too good to be true for her to be with Jay. She also knew that being with him was only a fantasy. So she sucked in her pride and enjoyed her date with a smile. As they quietly ate dinner, they watched the sun go down behind the mountains and enjoyed the moment while engaging in pleasant conversation.

After they finished dinner, they ate a rich chocolate mousse

Mind Games

for dessert that was accompanied by flaming vanilla ice cream. When La Vonne saw the ice cream burning at her table she panicked and yelled, "Get the water." Jay and the waiter laughed. Soon the waiter assured her that the flames were normal. She laughed with them and enjoyed her dessert. After eating her dessert, La Vonne was so full that she could hardly get out of her seat. "The meal was fabulous! Thank you very much. I'll never forget tonight." She was trying very hard to forget what Jay said earlier about not wanting to date, but the words lay deep within her mind.

"You're very welcome. I'm glad you enjoyed yourself. It was my pleasure. We better get you back home so you won't be tired for your first day of work." Jay knew La Vonne was disappointed by what he said earlier, but he thought it was better to be truthful with her and not offer any false hopes. "So, are you ready to go?" he asked as he stood up from the table.

"Yes I am." La Vonne stood up while Jay helped her put on her jacket. As he paid the bill, La Vonne took one last look out the window to admire the water that shadowed the moonlit sky and froze. At that very moment a dark figure was spotted in the distance, shadowing the water. It was a tall man standing on the dimly lit boardwalk. From her vantage point, of about eight feet away, the man looked African-American. He was wearing a fedora brim styled hat and a knee length trench coat that resembled the same outfit she thought she saw at the grave site of her unborn twins. The man also favored Jonathan. After straining her eyes to get a better look at the darkened figure, she suddenly turned the opposite direction. A move that would hopefully make the figure disappear. She gathered enough courage and slowly turned in the direction of the figure again, but this time he was gone. She took a harder look searching the entire area. However, there was nothing in the darkness but the water, the moon and the dimly lit boardwalk that was now empty.

Jay looked at La Vonne and noticed her frightened expression and asked, "Are you alright?"

She quickly pulled herself together and responded, "Yeah, I'm fine. Why?" She picked up her purse and jacket and turned toward the exit door. She didn't want him to think she was losing her mind so she kept her image to herself.

"You had a strange look on your face, but if you say you're alright, I believe you."

"I'm fine. So, are you ready?" she asked while taking one last look at the empty boardwalk.

"After you," Jay said as he put his arm up for La Vonne to hold on to.

As Jay drove La Vonne home with the cool nighttime breeze blowing through the opened sunroof top, she sat in silence. She was trying to act like the words Jay spoke about his relationship didn't affect her, or the possibility of seeing Jonathan again didn't frighten her. However, deep inside her heart she knew that both experiences affected her badly. Nevertheless, she could not jeopardize her pride again, allow Jay to think she was losing her mind, or appear desperate to gain his love. She also didn't want to show him the hurt she felt inside. Especially after knowing that she would never have him as her man. La Vonne remained quiet all the way home, explaining to Jay that she was only tired.

After the twenty minute ride they finally reached La Vonne's house. Jay didn't want the night to end on a sour note, so before La Vonne got out the car, he tried to soften things up with her, "I know what I said earlier upset you, and I know it took a lot for you to say what you said to me, but you have to understand that I never meant to hurt you nor lead you on."

La Vonne sat in her seat and carefully listened as he continued, "Over the years I've gotten to know you very well. You've taught me one very important thing, true love. The love I see between you, your children and your mother is great. It reminds me of how my family was when I was growing up. However, now things are much different. It seems that since I decided to become a lawyer my time is very limited with everyone, including myself. I don't seem to have time for friends or family, and maintaining a relationship has been nothing short of a miracle. However, after watching your strong family bond, I realize that I need more than just a career. I need a real relationship that is genuine, which is something my girlfriend can't give me because she's too deep in her career. After thinking about what I told you earlier, and, I mean..., welllll..., what I'm trying to say is maybe with time things can change between us. Maybe there can be an 'us,' because I like you a lot."

Hearing the words that were coming from his mouth was music to La Vonne's ears. She was stunned by what he just said and she wanted to pinch herself to make sure what she heard was real. This was the best news she could have ever imagined. "Okay, I can understand. Everything takes time and I guess time will tell what will happen in our future." La Vonne's mind was racing a mile a minute. Her body was racing even faster with ideas and ways that she could make him happy in bed. Of course her smile was very noticeable, displaying hope of them being together as a couple.

"That's right, time will definitely tell." By her look, Jay knew that he had made La Vonne very happy.

"But tell me this, if things did change for us, would you have a hard time having a relationship with a murderer?" she asked with a serious look.

"I don't look at you as a murderer. I look at you as a desperate woman who went through more than she needed to go through in order to protect herself and her children. Your situation is different. I believe that your situation was really self defense and not murder."

La Vonne felt relieved by his response. "That's right, it was self defense. It's just hard to believe that someone other than my family sees it that way. Most people see me as a murderer and will always see me as such, no matter what I do to convince them differently."

"That may be true, but what's important is what you believe about yourself. As long as you know the truth about yourself, it doesn't matter what other people believe or think about you."

"That's so true, I tell my children that all the time."

"Good, so you better get some sleep so you're not tired for your first day at work tomorrow. I don't want to be responsible for you falling asleep on the job," he laughed.

"I'm going." La Vonne blushed and began to open the car door. Surprisingly, Jay gently grabbed her arm and pulled her toward him. As she turned in his direction to see what he wanted, he placed his lips on hers and kissed her. Things were happening so fast that she thought she was dreaming, but she quickly pinched herself and knew it was the real thing. La Vonne put her arm around the back of his neck and enjoyed the feelings of his smooth soft lips touching hers.

Suddenly the porch light came on and Gloria was standing in the front door, "La Vonne? La Vonne is that you? Are you still in that car?" she yelled while walking onto the porch wearing her

Mind Games

favorite pajamas and fluffy blue robe. She couldn't see into the car because the windows were darkly tinted. She continued looking, putting her hand on top of her eyes to block the glare from the porch light in order to get a better view.

Jay and La Vonne stopped kissing immediately and laughed as he slowly cracked open the window. "Yes Momma, it's me." La Vonne responded.

"Well come on in now, it's late. You need to get to bed. You've got to go to work in the morning and you don't want to be too tired. Goodnight Jay," Gloria said as she stood on the front porch waiting for La Vonne to get out of the car.

Jay and La Vonne knew that Gloria wasn't going back into the house until La Vonne was out of the car and in the house with the door closed behind her. She opened the car door, got out, and stood outside leaning over the car door while saying goodbye, "Thank you for a beautiful evening and the wonderful company."

"You're very welcome. I'm glad you enjoyed yourself. Have a good day at work tomorrow. Call me and let me know how your first day went."

"I will," she said and blew him a kiss. She walked toward the front door, blushing from ear to ear.

"Goodbye Jay. Thanks for taking La Vonne out to celebrate. I'm sure she enjoyed herself." Gloria said as she hugged La Vonne and walked through the front door, closing it shut behind them and quickly turning off the porch light. Jay couldn't even say one final goodnight because Gloria left him in the dark. He turned on his car, laughed at her actions and drove off.

Stacy was still awake. She came out of her bedroom smiling, waiting to hear the juicy details of her mother's date. Jr. was already asleep.

La Vonne was on cloud nine. "Hi baby," she said as she kissed Stacy on the forehead. "Thank you for the clothes. Jay really liked the way I looked." La Vonne looked at Gloria who was now sitting in her favorite rocking chair next to the couch. "Momma, why did you have to come outside? Me and Jay were discussing something very important," she smiled while knowing the truth about their so-called discussion.

"I'm sure that it was important, but it wasn't important enough to keep you out so late." Gloria lectured as Stacy stayed glued to every detail.

"But it's only ten o'clock. It's not that late," La Vonne replied.

"La Vonne, you need your rest child. You must remember that you've been on a totally different schedule. You have to allow your body to get on a new schedule now that you're home. So, tell me all about your date. How was it? What did you eat? And did you bring me a doggie bag?" Gloria was now ready to hear all the details of La Vonne's date, even though just moments ago she insisted that she end her date because she needed her rest.

Stacy was glued to every word, adding to her grandmother's request, "Yeah Momma, what happened? Did you have fun? Where did you go?" She flopped down on the couch next to her mother.

La Vonne laughed at their enthusiasm. "My date was very nice! I haven't had such a good time in a long time. I was treated very special tonight, just like a princess. Jonathan used to treat me very special when we first got together, but things later changed. Anyway, tonight will definitely be a wonderful night to remember." She finished filling them in on all the details of the night. However, La Vonne left out the details of when she told Jay she wanted him to be her man,

Mind Games

along with the goodnight kiss he surprised her with. She knew that if she mentioned those juicy details, Gloria would only make her feel bad and imply Jay's intentions as being simple and nice and not serious.

She also knew that Stacy would make a bigger deal out of the situation. She didn't want that to happen and be disappointed. So she felt she should just leave well enough alone and keep those details to herself. "Okay you two, that's all that happened. Now, I better go to bed so I won't be tired in the morning. Wake me at eight-thirty since I don't have to be at work until ten. I want to have plenty of time to get myself together. Goodnight Momma." La Vonne kissed her mom on the forehead and turned to Stacy, "Good night baby." She said as she kissed her on the cheek and walked to her bedroom.

Before she could leave the room, Gloria stopped her in her tracks, "Not so fast. La Vonne, you didn't tell me what you and Jay were doing in the car before I came outside?" Stacy was more glued to every word while quietly listening and waiting for all the added details.

La Vonne looked at her mother, then at her daughter, smiled and responded, "We were just talking, that's all. Now, don't try to make things more than what they are. Isn't that what you keep telling me to do?" She continued walking to her room smiling.

"La Vonne, do you want some warm milk before you go to bed?" Gloria asked, looking at her strangely, not sure if she was actually telling her the total truth.
"No thank you Momma, goodnight."

"Okay baby, goodnight. I'm glad you had a nice evening. Sleep tight and don't let the bed bugs bite. Stacy, you go to bed, too." Gloria smiled, sat in her rocking chair and began reading her Bible.

"Goodnight Grandma, goodnight Momma." Stacy said as she

walked back to her room.

La Vonne laughed as she closed the bedroom door and thought, "Yeah, I could have had an even better evening if you wouldn't have come to the front door. But that's my Momma and I love her dearly." As she took off her clothes, she still couldn't believe her date or his kiss. She felt as if she'd hit the lottery and became a millionaire overnight. Her mind wandered a mile a minute while she relived their kiss. "Boy oh boy what a night! I saw stars after he kissed me. Boy was that unexpected."

She turned off the light, got on her knees and said her prayer, "Lord, thank you for a wonderful evening with Jay, he's so special. I thank you again for bringing him into my life. Lord, thank you for freeing me and bringing me home to my mother and my children. Thank you for giving me a job so I can make some money to help support my family. Help me to be strong and do well in life. I need your help and strength Lord God. Please protect me and my family as we go through each and every day. I ask all these blessings in your holy name, Amen."

She rolled over and got comfortable in her big soft bed, submerging her head in a fluffy pillow. As she laid in the darkness on her back looking at the ceiling, her thoughts were totally focused on Jay until she fell asleep. While asleep, she began dreaming, "Jay, thank you so much for a great evening. I wish we could be together like this everyday."

"Would that make you happy if we were together everyday? Because I want to do whatever it takes to make you happy," Jay's voice responded to her thoughts.

"Yes, it would. Being with you everyday is exactly what I want."

"Well, let's be together, La Vonne, marry me! Marry me right now! Let's not waste one precious moment. Be my wife now. Let's elope tonight!"

"Tonight?"

"Yeah tonight. Is that too soon for you?"

"Oh no, it's not too soon at all. Nothing's too soon when it comes to being with you. I'd love to be your wife." La Vonne rolled over and cuddled up to her pillow to keep her warm as she continued to dream. The more comfortable she became, the closer she felt to Jay. Eventually, her thoughts went deeper, and the warmth of her pillow felt like Jay in her arms. "Ummmm, Ahhhh!" Were the moans she made. "Oh Jay, you feel so good to me. I'm so lucky to be your wife. Oh Jay, ohhhhhhhh Jay!" she continued as she made love in her sleep.

"Oh La Vonne, you feel so good to me! I'm so lucky to have you. You make me feel complete. I never knew good lovin' until I got with you."

During La Vonne's dream, she was working Jay over with good lovin'. She was making up for all the years of not being intimate with a man. She had energy that had been stored up for over a decade. Since La Vonne had not experienced the tender touches of a loving man in so long, her hormones and thoughts were working overtime. She did not know how good it felt to be gently held by a man while enjoying the sensual touches of his loving and warm body next to hers.

As La Vonne laid alone in her bed, emerged in feelings of Jay, she touched herself in ways that made her feel good. Throughout the night, her smile expressed her contentment of being in his arms, close to his body, submerged in his love. The warmth from the pillows assured her that she wasn't alone, but in his arms. These feelings were oh so real, yet totally make believe. The affection of a man's tender touches next to her body were feelings she longed to experience again for many years, even though the feelings she was enjoying were coming from a warm pillow. However, as she continued to sleep in peace, she wished those thoughts would someday come true.

****

After Jay arrived home, his phone began to ring. He dropped his keys on the table and ran to answer, "Hello."
"Where have you been?" a female's voice demanded with sarcasm.
"Hi Jerri. I was working late," Jay responded to his girlfriend of five years.
"Working late? I thought you were going to call me tonight. I had the night off and told you that I had some extra time to spend with you. So why didn't you call? I've been waiting for hours."
"Well I didn't have tonight off, and I told you that I would call if I got off early." Jay was disappointed by Jerri's possessive tone, but he was used to it. It seemed that every time she had a free night he was suppose to drop whatever he was doing to be there, ready and willing to take care of her every need. She didn't care if he had something to do, as long as it was what she wanted him to do. She was very demanding, which was why she was so successful as an executive vice president of a mortgage company. But her demanding ways were causing her relationship with Jay to become unsuccessful.
"You know, I'm really tired of your demanding attitude. I don't appreciate you questioning my every move, nor do I appreciate you telling me what to do just because you had the night off. Jerri, this relationship isn't going to work anymore, it's over!" Jay said with

anger as he undressed and threw his clothes on the floor.

Jerri was surprised by his response. Jay normally did whatever she wanted him to do. She was also surprised that he wanted to break up with her. She always believed that a woman should be the one to break up with a man, not the other way around. "It's over? What do you mean it's over? If anything's over, I'll be the one to say that it's over. So now, it's over!"

Jay knew that Jerri would try to turn things around. It was the way she was. This was something he put up with for years. "Whatever. You never think about anyone other than yourself anyway. So good, it's over! I can't handle this pressure from you another minute."

"Well fine. You weren't worth my time anyway," she said and slammed down the telephone.

Jay thought about what had just happened and felt good. He couldn't believe that the relationship between him and Jerri was finally over. In reality, the relationship had been over a long time ago. He just never had the nerve to admit it to her. However, after a wonderful evening with La Vonne, he gained the needed strength to think about his own feelings for once instead of Jerri's. As he got ready for bed, he thought about his day and his life. "My day went great while I was with La Vonne and my job gives me all the mental challenges I need to feel in control. The headache that came along with Jerri is not worth the hassle, nor my time."

His pleasant thoughts about his evening with La Vonne emerged deeper as he got into bed and fell fast asleep. "La Vonne, I had so much fun with you. Thoughts of you brighten my days. I look forward to being with you everyday of my life," he thought as his dream continued. "Your kind spirit is what I've missed for a long time. I want someone in my life who wants me for me and someone who enjoys me for who I am, and that is you. La Vonne, I want to be your man, day and night, night and day. You're the one I want. You're the one I need. Will you be my lady?" As Jay thought about La Vonne, a big smile pleasantly formed as he slept into the night.

CHAPTER SEVEN

"La Vonne, La Vonne, it's time to get up." Gloria said as she shook her. La Vonne was sleeping peacefully while wearing a big smile. La Vonne looked around the room and searched for the warmth of Jay. But instead she felt the warmth of her fluffy pillows snuggled tightly between her legs and next to her body. Realizing that she had been dreaming, her face dropped.

"What's the matter baby? Are you alright?" Gloria inquired curiously about her behavior.

"Yeah Momma, I'm fine. What time is it?" she asked as she got out of bed and began making it up.

"It's eight-thirty. Are you sure you're fine?"

"Yes, I'm fine."

"Well, take your shower and get dressed. I'll fix you something to eat. We'll leave at 9:30 so you can get to work on time."

"Okay, thank you for waking me up," La Vonne said. After making up the bed, La Vonne went to Stacy's room to find some comfortable clothes to wear, took her shower, got dressed, ate her breakfast and was ready to start her first day at work.

****

Stacy went to school on Thursday, after spending

Mind Games

Wednesday at home enjoying her Mother's freedom. Her first couple of classes went well. However, when she went to her gym class things changed. Everything seemed fine at first, until it was time for her to get dressed and go to her next class. Teddy, the most popular boy at school, and the star football player of her school's team, used to be Stacy's boyfriend. Teddy wanted revenge on her family. Teddy was still mad at Jr. for beating him up and leaving him on the ground bleeding for slapping Stacy in the face. In revenge, Teddy took the pleasure of getting back at their family by spreading their personal business to the biggest gossip and bully in the school, Danielle. Danielle was a large framed, unattractive brown-skinned girl who most students feared, while others backed up her every word. She had many friends because most people were to afraid to be her enemy. Everywhere she went she had at least four girls around her who had her back. They would fight for her if necessary.

"So Stacy, I heard that your momma just got out of prison for killing your daddy." Danielle said sarcastically while a locker room full of girls listened. Stacy was surprised by her comments because no one knew that her mother was in prison except for the few people who remained close to their family, or the neighbors who witnessed her return Tuesday. Embarrassed by the fact that her mother was in prison for killing her father, Stacy had originally told everyone that her parents were dead, and her grandmother was raising her and her brother. Stacy looked at Danielle and rolled her eyes, attempting to ignore her comment. She continued dressing, hoping she would leave well enough alone. Stacy was afraid of Danielle like everyone else. She knew that she was only trying to start trouble, which was an everyday thing for her to do. Stacy wanted no part of what Danielle was trying to start, so she continued ignoring her comments.

Another student, one of Danielle's girls, innocently asked, "Did your mother really kill your father?" Stacy looked at the girl and again rolled her eyes, continuing to remain quiet.

After Stacy's long silence, Danielle repeated her comment, but this time with more force and attitude, "Bitch, you heard me! Don't try to ignore me or I'll kick all up in your little light- skinned ass. I said that I heard yo' jailbird momma just got out of prison for killing yo' drug- addict daddy. So, is it true or what?" Stacy was scared to death. Sweat began running down her forehead and her hands began to shake as she listened to Danielle's threats. She didn't know what to do or what to say. Nor did she have anyone to back her up. She still felt that it was no one's business why her mother had been in prison. She continued getting dressed while cautiously ignoring Danielle's insults. "Bitch, don't try to ignore me!" Danielle said while getting closer in Stacy's face.

Suddenly Stacy gained great confidence and looked directly into Danielle's eye with fury, "None of your damn business what my mother did. If I'm not worrying about it, you don't need to worry about it either."

"Ohhhhhhhhh" was the sound that came from the girls in the locker room. Some started laughing, while others feared what would come next.

"Oh no, you didn't just front me," Danielle responded. "Who in the hell do you think you are, bitch? I guess you don't know who you talkin' to! Bitch, I'll kick your light-skinned, think you fine ass all the way back to the prison cell yo' momma just came from if you keep gettin' smart with me. Because nobody talks shit to me and lives to see another day." Danielle's head, full of attitude, rolled from left to right.

Mind Games

    Everyone in the locker room got quiet this time. Stacy turned toward her locker and tried again to ignore Danielle as she continued dressing. She carefully peeked behind her shoulders to make sure Danielle wasn't getting ready to sneak up on her. Stacy's silence had done her no good earlier, so Danielle continued, "You just think you're all that, you light-skinned bitch. Teddy told me how he fucked you with your virgin tight ass. He said he fucked you until you couldn't walk anymore, and you left his house crying and bleeding like a little bitch ass baby." Everyone in the gym really laughed after hearing Danielle's comments.

    Stacy was so embarrassed by what she had just heard. However, she now knew that Teddy was the one who gave Danielle the information about her mother getting out of prison. At that point Stacy couldn't just let that comment go unaddressed, so she got right up in Danielle's face and fired back, "Danielle, like I said earlier, you need to mind your own damn business. Maybe if you minded your own business as much as you mind everyone else's business, you'd have a man! At least I had Teddy. Your ugly ass would never be his type, or any other man's type, because you look like a damn man, and a man don't want a woman who looks like a man which is what you are." Stacy's hand was positioned on her hip demonstrating she meant business.

    "Ohhhhhhhhhh" the girls in the locker room said as Stacy continued, "And for your damn information, Teddy didn't fuck me until I couldn't walk. I was the best damn fuck he ever got! He'll never have anyone fuck him as good as I fucked him in his damn life. And since he felt that he had to tell you so much of my damn business, did he tell you that I'm the one who broke up with him, or did he tell you that my brother kicked his black ass and left him laying on the ground bleeding and crying like a little bitch?"

The entire room full of girls laughed and again said, "Ohhhhhhhhhhhhh." Danielle backed away from Stacy, along with her buddies. They looked at Stacy and didn't say a word. Danielle had finally met her match. Someone who stood up to her and didn't allow her words to put them down.

Stacy walked even closer to Danielle, so Danielle could feel her breath on her face, looked directly into her eyes as if she was ready to fight and said, "I didn't think so." Stacy grabbed her purse, closed her locker, and walked out of the gym to go to her next class. Danielle was left behind speechless, wearing a stupid look.

"Fuck you Stacy. If yo' momma's a jailbird, face it, she's a damn jailbird." Danielle finally responded after Stacy was out of the gym. But Stacy continued walking, never looking back to respond. Danielle added fuel to the fire, "Hey ya'll," she said to the girls in the locker room as they responded, "Yeah?" she asked, "What kind of bird don't fly?" Everyone looked around, shrugging their shoulders with no answer. Danielle responded, "A jailbird! So, Stacy's momma's a jailbird." Everyone laughed at her answer. "Repeat after me, Yo' momma's a jailbird, yo' momma's a jailbird!" Several of the girls joined in with Danielle as she continued insulting Stacy, "Yo' momma's a jail bird. Yo' momma's a jail bird!"

Stacy knew she couldn't beat all of them up at one time. She wasn't even sure if she could beat up Danielle. So she continued walking, ignoring their insults while thinking, "Damn, I wish they would just shut the fuck up and leave me alone!" Stacy kept walking, ignoring their insults. The group of girls finally disappeared and went their separate ways.

Mind Games

****

"Hi La Vonne," Sandra said when she walked through the door of her shop.

"Hi, Ms. Sandra." she said as she hugged her new boss. "I'd like for you to meet my Mother, Ms. Gloria Johnson."

"Good morning Ms. Johnson." Sandra gave Gloria a warm welcome which included a hug.

"Call me Gloria." she cheerfully responded. La Vonne was surprised by her Mother's response because she never allowed anyone, except her deceased husband and immediate family members to call her by her first name, it was a respect thing.
"And call me Sandra," they laughed and hugged again.

"I wanted to come in and meet you. I want to thank you for giving my daughter a job. Your kindness means a lot to our family. This job will help La Vonne get back on her feet and go on with her life in a positive way," Gloria explained.

"No problem, I'm happy I was able to help. I'm sure she'll work out just fine, Jay told me she would." Sandra held La Vonne's hand, smiled and gave her a shake.

"Jay's a sweetheart. He helped my baby through some very trying times. We'll always be grateful for what he's done for our family." Gloria said.
"That's so true," La Vonne echoed.

"Well, we better get busy. I have a lot of things I need La Vonne to do. Can you pick her up at five? I'm sure she'll be tired and hungry by the time she's done," Sandra said.

"Okay, don't let me hold you up. I'll be back at five honey." Gloria kissed La Vonne and walked out the door. "Nice meeting you

Sandra."

"Nice meeting you too Gloria. Have a good day."

"I will, thanks."

"Thanks for bringing me Momma, I'll see you at five," La Vonne said as Gloria waved and got into her car.

Sandra looked around the store and instructed La Vonne on her duties. "Now, first you can sweep the store. The broom is in the back storage room. When you're done sweeping, I'll have you touch up some of these walls with a little white paint. Within the next few months the store will be swarming with women. During the summer months, everyone's getting ready for their big day at the altar. I want the store to look nice when the customers come. I want the women to be proud and feel comfortable while doing business in 'Sandra's Wedding Boutique.' That was something Frank always stressed about, and since he's been gone, I haven't been in the mood to take care of the store like it should be taken care of. I'm glad you're here to help me." Sandra told La Vonne as they walked to the storage room to get the broom.

"Okay, Ms. Sandra. Thank you again for giving me this job. I really appreciate your kindness."

"You're very welcome child. But don't thank me yet. You need to make sure that this is the kind of work you want to do before you get too happy."

"Don't worry about that, after what I've been doing for the last ten years, I welcome this job. I'd do it for free if I didn't need the money. So thank you again Ms. Sandra. I really appreciate all that you're doing to help me." La Vonne began sweeping the floor.

"You're welcome child." Sandra smiled and went to do other work in the store.

Mind Games

****

When school was out, Stacy quickly walked home to avoid any trouble from Danielle or her bully friends. Once at home, she slammed the front door tight and dropped her backpack on the living room floor. She quickly went to her room. Gloria was in the restroom and thought she heard someone come in the house, but no one announced their arrival. When Gloria came out the restroom, she looked around the house, but didn't notice anyone. She called out, "Stacy, Jr., is that you?" No one answered. Then she noticed Stacy's backpack on the floor and called out louder, "Stacy, where are you child?"

Stacy suddenly came out of her bedroom with tears in her eyes and ran to her grandmother for comfort. Gloria became worried and hugged her granddaughter. "What's the matter baby? Are you alright?" Gloria's words made Stacy cry even more. "Stacy, tell me what's the matter baby? Grandma can't help you if you don't talk to me."

Stacy tried to dry up her tears long enough to tell her grandmother why she was crying. With a mumbled tone she explained, "Teddy told one of the girls in my gym class that my mom was in jail and the other girls started teasing me." She started crying again.

"Don't cry. Everything'll be alright. Things will blow over soon, you'll see. So stop crying." Gloria was hoping that her words added comfort to her situation.

"Thank you Grandma. Why did they have to call my mom a jailbird? She didn't do anything to them?"

"Baby, you must remember that people are not always nice. There are some very mean and hurtful people in this world. We have to learn how to avoid them, or get along with them. Like I said earlier, don't worry. Everything'll be alright. Those girls will forget about what happened very soon and things will be back to normal, you'll see. Forget about today, wash your face, and help me finish dinner. I'll have to leave soon to pick up your mother from work. I want everything to be ready so we can eat when we get back home."

"Grandma, can you please keep this conversation between us? I don't want momma to get her feelings hurt by knowing what they were saying about her."

"I sure will. It'll be our little secret. Don't worry about anything and remember, they'll only tease you if you let them think they're hurting your feelings. If you're strong and don't let them know they're hurting your feelings they'll stop teasing. Now, go wash your face and put your backpack in your room and help me in the kitchen."

"Okay Grandma. I'll be right back. I love you! Thanks for understanding." Stacy kissed her grandmother on the cheek and went to wash her face.

Just as Stacy left the room Jr. walked into the house and went directly to the kitchen where Gloria was cooking. "Hey Grandma," he said and kissed her on the cheek. He began searching through the cabinets for something quick to eat. "When's dinner gonna be ready?" he asked while eating a few chocolate chip cookies.

"Jr. don't eat too many of those cookies. I don't want you to spoil your appetite before dinner."

"I won't Grandma, but I'm hungry. What are we having?" He started looking under the tops of the pots that were on the stove. Stacy walked in the room and started helping Gloria.

"Jr. you need to get out my kitchen. You haven't even washed your hands yet." Gloria hit him on the back of his hand with the wooden spoon she was holding.

Mind Games

"Ouch," he yelled and laughed while massaging his stinging hand. Stacy laughed. "I'm going, I'm going," he said, while walking out the kitchen. "But you never told me what we're having for dinner?" he asked again.

"Fried chicken, black-eyed peas, white rice, collard greens, green salad, corn on the cob with lots of butter and cornbread," Gloria smiled while watching Jr. lick his lips after hearing her menu. "How does that sound?" she asked.

"That sounds good to me. How soon can we eat?" he asked smiling, while rubbing his hands together in anticipation.

"Dinner'll be ready shortly, but you're gonna have to wait for me to go get your mother from work before we can eat. I want us to all sit down at the table and enjoy a nice meal as a family," Gloria said. "How long will that be Grandma? I'm hungry now," he whined.

"Well I'm sorry you're so hungry Jr. Around here we're a family and we're gonna eat like a family. Go do your homework until I get your mom, then we'll eat."

"Okaaayyy," he moaned. "So what time will that be?" as he looked at the clock on the wall above the stove that read 3:40pm.

"She gets off work at 5:00, so we should be able to eat by 5:30." While Gloria's back was turned away from his facial view, Jr. frowned, but remained quiet. "Go on and get your homework out the way." Gloria stirred her food on the stove and finished cooking with Stacy's help. As the food was kept warm on the stove, Gloria went to pick up La Vonne from work.

****

"I'm home." La Vonne said as she walked through the front

door. She smiled as the words "I'm home" came from her mouth, knowing how good they sounded.

"Hi Momma." Stacy said.

"Welcome home Mom," Jr. added, looked at his grandmother and asked, "Now, can we eat?"

Everyone laughed at his comment. "Jr. can you at least let us get in the house good before you ask about eating?" Gloria said as she walked to the kitchen.

"Well I'm hungry, and you said we could eat after momma came home, and now she's home, sooooo..."

La Vonne laughed at her growing son who towered over everyone in the house. "I'm with Jr., Momma. I'm ready to eat, too, especially after walking in the house with everything smelling so good."

"Alright, alright! All you hungry people wash your hands and come to the table," Gloria began putting the hot food on the dinning room table. After everyone sat down, she prayed, "Dear Heavenly Father, thank you for this meal we're about to eat and bless each bite we take. Lord, thank you again for bringing La Vonne home to us. Thank you for once again making us one big happy family. Lord we ask that you watch over each and every one of us and protect us as we go out in the world." Jr. cracked open his eye, wondering when his grandmother would finish blessing their food as she continued, "Lord, please watch over my grandchildren and protect them while they're at school. And watch over La Vonne as she tries to get her life back together. Lord, thank you for allowing Ms. Sandra to bless La Vonne with that job. Help her to keep it for a long time. Lord, we ask all these blessings in your holy name, Amen!"

"Amen!" everyone said as they opened their eyes and began putting food on their plates. Jr. piled his plate so high that he needed a

Mind Games

second plate just for his salad and hot cornbread muffins. Gloria smiled. She was used to his pile-up's.

La Vonne couldn't believe his heaping portions. "Jr., are you going to eat all that?"

Buried in his food, Jr. looked up and answered while sucking his fingers, "Yes ma'am!" His mouth was greasy from the fried chicken. He put his head down and continued eating.

La Vonne laughed and ate her food while feeling blessed about everything that was happening in her life.

While everyone ate, Gloria started some conversation. "So, how was your first day at work?" she asked La Vonne.

"It was really nice. I did a little sweeping and cleaning up around the store. Everything was really easy. I'm so glad I have a job. Ms. Sandra is really nice and easy to work with. Jay has been a God send. Everything seems to be happening so fast and smoothly. I didn't expect to be working so quickly, especially after being locked away for so long. I didn't think anyone would trust me this fast. But thank God for all these wonderful blessings. God is definitely a good God." La Vonne put on a big smile of thankfulness as she thought about her blessings and her first kiss with Jay.

"Good, I'm so glad everything is going well for you baby, you deserve some peace and happiness." Gloria said and then changed the subject, "La Vonne, I'm so glad that you and the kids were spared from Jonathan. I don't know what I would have done if he took any of you away from me." Gloria said sadly.

La Vonne's happy expression sunk after hearing Jonathan's name, when suddenly a plastic red rose in a clear glass vase sitting on top of the fireplace mantel fell onto the brick covered floor. Everyone in the room jumped from the sound of the scattered glass. "Oh my

God! Oh my God" La Vonne screamed after literary jumping out of her seat.

"Lord Jesus, what was that?" Gloria followed.

Jr. and Stacy laughed at their reaction. "It was just the vase on the mantel that fell, so why are you guys so scared?" Jr. asked and got up from the kitchen table to pick up the broken glass.

"It scared us, that's why we jumped." Gloria said and laughed. "Jr., be careful, don't cut yourself." she told him as he picked up the small pieces. "I wonder what made that vase fall like that in the first place. I just put it up there today. I got it at the Thrift Store." Gloria told them, but no one answered. "I thought it would look nice up there. Oh well, so much for that." Gloria said out loud, talking to herself. Then she continued eating.

La Vonne had other reasons why the vase suddenly fell after Jonathan's name was mentioned, but she kept her theory to herself. "Momma, please don't mention his name anymore. He's a part of my life I'd like to forget. Today is a new day. I want to move on with my future and forget about my past. Do you think you can do that for me?"

"Sure I can baby. I'm sorry for mentioning his name. I was just making conversation." Gloria felt sad after seeing how upset La Vonne got by hearing Jonathan's name. La Vonne's comment caused everyone to get quiet at the table.

After picking up the broken vase, Jr. came back to the table and got his empty plate off the table and put it in the sink. "Boy that was good Grandma." he said rubbing his stomach. He was so full that he sat back down in a relaxed position to let the food go down.

"Thank you honey. Did you get enough to eat?"

"Yes I did. I can't eat anything else, that is unless you made

Mind Games

some peach cobbler."

Everyone laughed and Gloria responded, "No, I'm afraid I didn't make any peach cobbler today. Maybe I'll make some over the weekend, how's that?"

"That sounds good," he answered.

"That sounds good to me too, Momma," La Vonne added, while looking at the mantel in hopes of discovering a simple reason why the vase suddenly fell.

La Vonne changed the subject while still eating, "Okay, so, now that you all heard about my day, I want to hear what you guys did in school today," La Vonne asked as she looked at Jr. and Stacy.

Suddenly Stacy's appearance went sour as she thought about her day in her gym class. She looked at Gloria, who kept her head down avoiding Stacy's reaction. "My day was fine." Stacy responded, keeping the ugly details between herself and her grandmother.

"Yeah, my day was fine too." Jr. added. "Stacy, I heard that some girls were teasing you at the gym. What happened?" Jr. asked, unaware of the details.

La Vonne looked at Stacy and responded, "Honey, what happened? Why were some girls teasing you in the gym? Did your period start or something? Did you have a spot in the back of your pants?"

"It was nothing Momma, don't worry. I took care of it."

"Nothing? This guy at school came up to me and told me that a lot of girls in your gym class gave you a real hard time. He ran to catch his bus before I could find out what he meant. So, what happened? Do I need to help you take care of a problem?" Jr. asked, ready to defend his sister.

"No, you don't need to help me with anything. Your help is

what caused me to get teased in the first place." She got up from the table and ran to her room. Everyone looked surprised by her response except Gloria.

"There she goes again acting like a big baby. She's always whining about something. She's so dramatic with everything she does. I give up." Jr said, got up from the table, walked to the living room, and turned on the television set.

"Leave the girl alone. She'll be alright. She just had a hard day at school, that's all. It's nothing she can't handle," Gloria said.

"But Momma, I'm her mother. I want to help if something's bothering her," La Vonne responded, "How can you expect me to just leave her alone when I know something's bothering her? I'm gonna get to the bottom of this." La Vonne got up and went to Stacy's room but couldn't get in because the door was locked. La Vonne knocked, "Stacy, can I come in?" Stacy didn't answer so La Vonne knocked again, "Stacy, it's me Mom, can I come in please? I want to talk to you." Stacy still didn't answer.

Gloria could see that Stacy's behavior was upsetting La Vonne. "La Vonne leave her alone. She'll come out in a few minutes. She just needs a little time to herself. She'll come out and talk to you. Come back to the table and finish eating."

"Okay," La Vonne said as she slowly walked back to the dinner table. Jr. remained in the living room, minding his own business, ignoring Stacy's behavior.

While La Vonne continued to eat her dinner, she constantly looked toward the back room hoping that Stacy would come out. After finishing, she realized that Stacy wasn't coming out. So she put her plate in the kitchen sink and looked at her mother with sadness in her eyes and in her voice, "Can I help you in the kitchen Momma?"

Mind Games

"No, thank you. You go sit down and relax. You've been working hard all day long. Jr and Stacy can help me." Gloria told her. Jr. acted like he didn't hear Gloria and continued watching televison. Gloria ignored his actions for now. La Vonne walked to the living room while constantly looking toward the back room waiting for Stacy to come out. Gloria said, "Stacy's been in her room long enough, let me go get her." So she yelled, "Stacy come out of that room right now and help me with these dishes!" Gloria said with a firm tone.

La Vonne again looked toward the door, but nothing happened. There was total silence. Suddenly, Stacy's door opened and she walked to the kitchen and stood by the sink next to Gloria.
"Stacy are you alright?" La Vonne asked while still sitting on the couch.

"Yes," Stacy casually said as she grabbed a washrag and began helping with the dishes.

"Grandma, do you need my help?" Jr. asked, knowing that he would be in trouble for not offering.

"No thank you, me and Stacy can handle it tonight." Gloria decided against Jr.'s help so she could talk to Stacy in confidence. "But you can take out the garbage," she replied. Jr. looked at his grandmother, smiled and got up to take the garbage outside.

Gloria motioned to La Vonne that she would talk to Stacy. La Vonne agreed and quietly sat on the couch, while looking for something to watch on television. She was hopeful that Stacy would eventually open up to her, but knew it would take time. She understood that Stacy didn't feel as comfortable talking to her as she felt talking to her grandmother. La Vonne kept quiet and allowed her mother to get through to her daughter and convince her that she could confide in her.

As Stacy helped Gloria clean the kitchen, she kept quiet

and busy. Gloria also remained quiet for awhile, then whispered to Stacy, "Baby, I think you should tell your mother the entire story." Stacy looked surprised by her grandmother's comment, but continued to stay quiet and busy. "Did you hear what I said?" Stacy remained quiet. "Stacy, I said did you hear what I said?" Gloria said with a firm tone and looked at her granddaughter for a response. Eventually Stacy's sad eyes looked up at her grandmother and nodded yes. However, she continued to keep quiet as she cleaned.

"Baby, I think you should tell your mother exactly what happened today. Now is not the time to be keeping secrets from each other. She wants to help you and I'm sure she'll understand the situation, and even if she doesn't, she still needs to know how her situation is effecting you and your brother. So go on over there and talk to her. Do it for me, Okay?" Gloria hugged her granddaughter and hoped she would take her advice.

Suddenly Stacy put down her dishrag and walked toward La Vonne and sat next to her on the couch. "Momma, the reason I was upset today is because some girls at the gym were teasing me. They were saying that you're a jailbird. Teddy told this girl, Danielle, who has the biggest mouth in school, that you just got out of jail. She started spreading our business to everyone in the locker room." Jr. walked into the room while Stacy was explaining.

"Oh hell no!" he said with anger. "Wait until I see him tomorrow. I'll kick his black ass again. Excuse me for cussing, but he ain't getting away with talking about my family and spreading stories like that." Jr. was ready to beat Teddy down worse than he beat him after seeing him slap Stacy in the face because she chose to spend time with her family instead of going over his house for sex.

"Jr., you can't just go around beating up everybody who says

Mind Games

things about me that's true. I'm sure this won't be the last time somebody says something to try to hurt one of us. We'll get through it, don't worry. I'm sure we will because we're a strong family that sticks together no matter what we're up against. My situation is a testimony to that. It's also a testimony that we can solve anything we put our minds to. So, don't worry about it, everything'll work itself out in time," La Vonne said, remembering how her father always taught her that what goes around, comes back to kick you in the butt. She hugged Stacy and said, "I'm so sorry baby. I hate that you have to go through that kind of pressure at school because of me." They both started crying. Gloria smiled at the reunion and shed a few tears of her own.

"If they were my true friends, they wouldn't say all those mean things. Why are they being so mean anyway? I didn't do anything to them. Neither did you." Stacy said, still crying.

"Baby, some people are just mean. They don't think about the things they say to people. You're right, if they were your friends they wouldn't say things that would hurt your feelings, or try to hurt your family. So I guess if you learned anything from all of this is that everyone who smiles or talks to you isn't your friend."

"Well, I told off the girl who started it all. Her name is Danielle. She's a big bully and definitely not my friend," Stacy said.
"You told off Danielle?" Jr. asked, knowing Danielle's reputation.
"I sure did." Stacy admitted with confidence.

"Don't worry about what they said. So what, I was in jail. I'm not anymore. Their words don't hurt me and they shouldn't hurt you either. You see, if people know that their words can make you feel bad they'll continue teasing you. What I want you to do for me is be strong and hold your head up high. Yes I made a mistake, but I also paid for my mistake. Now it's time for us to get on with our lives and put the past behind. If they tease you again just ignore them. Once they see that their words won't upset you, they'll stop teasing you. But I'm really sorry you had to go through all of that. I knew it was coming, I just didn't think it would happen so soon. As for you Jr., I don't want you fighting anyone over this either, or fighting over anything else someone may say. You also have to ignore what people say. Like I said, people can sometimes be cruel. But we have to be bigger than them by ignoring what they say. Trust me, it'll all go away soon. The sooner both of you ignore what people are saying about me, the sooner it'll all go away. Can you both ignore what people are saying? Can you both do that for me?" La Vonne looked right into Stacy's eyes, wiped her tears, and waited for her answer.

"Yes, I can." she said.

She looked at Jr., who had revenge written all over his face. "I didn't hear anything from you young man. Do you think you can be the bigger person and ignore them as well?"

"I guess I can," he hesitantly said.

La Vonne stood up, hugged him and smiled, "Good. Now Stacy, quit crying and let's get some ice cream."

After hearing about eating ice cream, Jr.'s entire attitude changed and he smiled, "I want vanilla." Everyone walked into the kitchen where Gloria took out the ice cream and served everyone a bowl. They ate their dessert and watched television until it was time to go to sleep.

Mind Games

CHAPTER EIGHT

It was a beautiful Thursday morning. The sun was shining and the temperature was warm. Stacy was making her routine stop to pick up her best-friend Kathy so they could walk to school. Kathy lived three blocks from Stacy. They've been friends since elementary school. Kathy knew how Teddy treated Stacy and felt sorry for her. Knowing what Stacy went through with Teddy, Kathy vowed to never let anyone abuse her. Kathy's boyfriend, Doug, was Teddy's best-friend. When it came to women, Doug and Teddy had different opinions and how they should be treated. Doug was raised in a family where men respected women and never hit them. Doug's calm behavior allowed his and Kathy's year long relationship to stay strong.

However, Teddy grew up in a family where abusing and disrespecting women was something that was an everyday thing. Teddy's father justified his abusive behavior toward his wife as those needed in order to keep his woman in line. Teddy followed the ways of his father. Since Teddy was a popular jock on campus, had a cool and smooth demeanor and was one of the most good looking boys at school. Most of his girlfriends put up with his abusive behavior, except Stacy.

While walking to and from school, Stacy and Kathy often talked about controversial issues but respected each others opinion while never jeopardizing their friendship. "Stacy, did you tell your mother what happened at school yesterday?" Kathy asked.

"Yeah, I told her and she was pretty upset. She said she understood. But girl you should have heard Jr. He was ready to kick Teddy's ass again. My mother had to calm him down and make him promise to leave Teddy alone."

"I don't blame him. I'd be mad too. When I told Doug what Teddy did he had the nerve to take up for that ass-hole. Now I know they're best-friends, but wrong is wrong and what Teddy did to your family was wrong. He didn't have to tell Danielle all your business so that she could go around and spread it to everyone." Kathy felt badly for Stacy and wanted to offer any words of encouragement she could.

"I agree, he should have just kept his mouth closed. And if he wouldn't have hit me, Jr. wouldn't have kicked his ass the way he did. But what can I say? It's over now. At least I hope it's over now that the gossip has been spread."

"Yeah, I hope it's over too. Girl, you have to ignore them bitches if they say anything about your mother today. They sure ain't worth fighting over or getting suspended from school."

"Yeah you're right. That's why I'm gonna try to ignore them. But if I have to handle my business, than I'm gonna handle my business," Stacy said with confidence.

"I heard that," Kathy agreed as they arrived at school giving each other a high five.
"Well, I'll see you after school."

"Okay, see you then," Kathy said as she went to her class and Stacy went to hers.

****

Throughout the day a few girls passed Stacy and mumbled, "Yo' Momma's a jailbird!" and laughed. Stacy ignored their comments and went on with her day.

When she walked into the gym, she came face to face with Danielle and a few of her bully friends. "Look what just flew in,

Mind Games

the jailbird's daughter," Danielle said as her friends laughed.

Stacy ignored her comments and kept walking to her locker. One of the teachers, Ms. Benson, a small, dark-skinned, aggressive woman who had been raised in the hood as a sista' girl with an attitude, passed by as Danielle and her friends stared at Stacy, waiting to start more trouble. "Girls, keep moving. I heard what happened yesterday and if there's going to be any more problems or comments about Stacy's mother, you'll all be expelled. So get dressed and keep your comments to yourself." Ms. Benson said with a firm and threatening voice, standing with her hands on her hips, looking dead into Danielle's eyes, daring a negative response.

Danielle rolled her eyes at Ms. Benson and her friends followed in her footsteps, ignoring her comment.

"Excuse me, is there a problem?" Ms. Benson asked with an attitude.

Danielle and her friends quickly straightened up and responded with respect, "No, there's no problem here, Ms. Benson."
"Good, now, get ready for your class before you're late."

The girls went to their lockers while Ms. Benson watched them disperse. The powerful threats aimed at Danielle and her friends from Ms. Benson allowed the rest of Stacy's day to go well.

****

After school, Stacy met up with Kathy, who was talking with Doug as they got ready to head home. "Hey Girl," Kathy said, as Stacy joined them in their walk home.

"Hey," Stacy responded unenthusiastic. She wasn't comfortable around Doug because he was Teddy's best friend.

"Hello Stacy," Doug said.

"Hey Doug," Stacy responded with little interest as she kept walking, leaving any additional conversation to herself.

Kathy began talking to Doug about what Teddy did yesterday. Stacy listened, kept walking, while remaining quiet.

Just as their talk heated up, Teddy joined them. "Hey Man, what's up?" Teddy spoke only to Doug, ignoring Stacy and Kathy. They also ignored him and kept walking.

Stacy couldn't put up with the sight of Teddy. Every moment he remained around her made her sick to her stomach. "I gotta go. I'll talk to you later," she told Kathy. The guys looked at each other and sarcastically smiled.

Kathy understood her friend's feelings and knew what prompted her decision. "Okay, I'll talk to you later." Kathy continued walking with Doug while Teddy followed. After Stacy was gone, Kathy knew it was time for her to defend her friend. She could not hold back the anger. She looked at Teddy with rage and addressed him, "Why did you dog my girl like that?"

Teddy was not surprised by her comment. He knew it was eventually coming and he was ready for the attack. "What you mean, 'Why did I dog your friend?' Hell, I didn't do anything I wasn't supposed to do. It ain't my fault that her damn momma was stuck in prison for killing her daddy. Oh, I see how it is, since I said something that everybody would eventually find out about, I'm wrong. Hell no, I'm not wrong and don't tell me I am. Man, you better put your woman in place before I do it for you." Teddy began to get mad and started pacing in circles as they walked, hitting his fist in his hand to scare Kathy.

"What you mean you're gonna put me in my place?" Kathy

stopped walking and got directly into Teddy's face, challenging his response.

Doug was trying to calm things down and make light of the situation, "Hey, hold on, it ain't that serious," he told Kathy. "It's true, Teddy didn't say anything that wasn't gonna get out eventually. So why you tripping?" Doug kept walking, leaving Kathy behind while Teddy followed him.

"Yeah, why you tripping? You need to listen to your man and stay out of other peoples business," Teddy said sarcastically as Kathy caught up with them.

His sarcastic remarks made her anger grow stronger, especially after realizing that Doug would not take her side. "I'm not tripping, and Doug you need to be man enough to take my side and not let your boy talk to me like that. I ain't his woman and I'm not gonna let him talk to me or treat me the way he treats his women. So you need to handle your friend," she said to Doug as she looked at Teddy, who was laughing.

"Man, you gonna let her talk to you like that? I wouldn't put up with that shit from a woman, oh hell no!" Teddy instigated.

"Fuck! I'm tired of this shit. Kathy just shut the fuck up! I don't want to hear anything else from you about this shit. Everything that was gonna be said has been said. It's done, it's over, so leave it the fuck alone!" Doug said as he was getting angry, but Kathy wouldn't let up.

"Oh hell no! I'm not gonna just leave it alone. Stacy's my best friend and your friend dogged her and her family. The least he could do is apologize. But his damn ego won't let him do something so simple. Hell no am I gonna just leave it alone. He needs to be a man and apologize, that's all I'm saying." Kathy had her hands on her hips, her neck was doing the sista' girl roll, and she wasn't backing down to anyone. During this time, they were making a scene for everyone that passed.

"Man I'm telling you, you better shut your woman up before I do it for you," Teddy warned, still hitting the palm of his hand with his fist.

"Man, just calm down. She's cool. She's just a little mad," Doug defended Kathy to Teddy.

"Teddy, you ain't gonna do shit! And you better watch who you're talking to because I ain't one of your stupid bitches. So don't tell me what to do."

"Bitch, shut the fuck up!" Teddy hit Kathy right in her face, causing her to fall to the ground, making her nose bleed.

Doug helped her get off the cement sidewalk and addressed his friend, "Hey Man, don't hit her like that. I told you she's just tripping. Just ignore her. She'll get over it," Doug said still protecting his friend.

"Bastard! I can't believe you just hit me." Kathy said as she got up swinging in Teddy's direction attempting to give him a piece of what he had just given her. "Oh hell no mutha' fucka', hell no!" She screamed, as Doug blocked her swings and tightly held on to her until she calmed down.

"Man, I told her to shut the fuck up, but she just wouldn't leave things alone." Teddy explained to Doug. He looked at Kathy, "And you better shut the fuck up before I hit you again," he warned.

"Calm down," Doug told Kathy, "You women are always starting shit and when someone handles their business you get mad."

Kathy was surprised by his comments and lack of action. She wiped the dirt off her clothes and the blood that ran from her nose and shock her head in disbelief. She looked at her so-called boyfriend, ready to hit him for not defending her and gave him a piece of her mind. "You're just gonna let him hit me like that and not kick his ass? What kind of man are you? Both of you bitch ass, mutha fucka's can kiss my black ass. And Doug, as for you, we're through! I don't need a punk ass whimp like you who won't take up for me, but will take up for his boy! So kiss the crack of my black ass. Teddy, I'll get Jr. to kick your ass. He did it once, he'll do it again. You'll see how it feels." She stormed off, leaving Teddy and Doug standing together shaking their heads, smiling.

As Kathy walked away, Teddy yelled, "Yeah, and if that punk-ass mutha-fucka' touches me, his black ass is going to jail where his momma was since now they have an extra bed. Keep that bit of news in your head when you tell him to come kick my ass, because this time I'll press charges." Teddy and Doug laughed. Kathy kept walking, ignoring his every word.

Kathy became so upset with Teddy and Doug that she ran straight home. Once at home, she went to her room and cried like a baby. No one was at home, leaving her a big empty house to wallow in her misery. After hours of crying alone, she thought about Stacy and knew she would say the right words to cheer her up. She put on some dark sunglasses to cover her swollen face and walked the few blocks to her house.

Stacy had just finished eating dinner when the doorbell rang. "I'll get it," she yelled as she quickly got up from the table and ran to the door.

"Hi Stacy." Kathy said with a sad look that was covered by her dark shades.

Stacy was surprised to see Kathy at the door. Normally they

talked on the telephone to catch up on gossip, but tonight Kathy wanted to talk in person. "Hey girl, what's up? Come in," Stacy told her.

"Can we talk outside? I don't want anyone to hear what I have to say." Kathy whispered.

Stacy was surprised by Kathy's request, but interested in hearing what was so important. "Hold on. Let me get my jacket." While Kathy waited outside on the dark porch, Stacy got her jacket and told everyone she was going outside to talk to Kathy. Stacy came outside where Kathy was sitting alone. "Okay, what's up? Are you alright? And why do you have on those dark glasses? It's nighttime." Stacy was worried about her best friend as they sat on the porch in the dark.

As soon as Stacy asked the question, Kathy started crying. Surprised, Stacy took her friend in her arms. "What's the matter?" "Teddy hit me," Kathy told her through her tears.

Stacy pushed Kathy away from her and looked into her watery eyes through the dark sunglasses. She was surprised and blown away by her comments, "He did what?"

Kathy lowered the oversized glasses, revealing her swollen eyes and bruised nose. "Look at your face. That Bastard!" Stacy said as she put Kathy's head back on her shoulder while Kathy continued to cry.
"He hit me!" she repeated.

"That mutha' fucka', what did he hit you for and where was Doug when all this happened?"
"Doug was right there. He saw the whole thing and didn't do shit!"

"He didn't do anything?" Stacy couldn't believe what she was hearing. "So how did it happen?"

Kathy told Stacy the entire story while crying through her

sentences. Stacy was amazed to hear what had happened and upset that she wasn't there to help. "That black ass nigga'. Who does he think he is hitting you like that? It's bad enough that he hits his girlfriends, but you ain't his girlfriend. He's just a bully, that's all. A damn bully. We need to have Jr. kick his ass again. I guess Teddy forgot about the ass whuppin' he gave him after he hit me. I guess we need for Jr. to remind him to keep his hands off of girls."

"No, leave Jr. out of it. I don't want him fighting because of me. Don't worry, I'll find some way to take care of Teddy. He'll get his. Besides, if Jr. gets involved Teddy will have him arrested. So please leave him out of this." Kathy told her.

"Are you sure? Because Jr. won't have a problem kicking his ass. He already warned him about touching me again and you're like my sister, so the same thing goes for you, too." Stacy was trying to convince Kathy to let Jr. teach Teddy another lesson, but she refused the offer.

"No, no, no! Thank you for offering, but he'll get his. I believe in what goes around comes back to kick you in the ass." They laughed, although Kathy still displayed tears.

Just as they were laughing, Teddy walked by. "So, how's your face feeling?" he joked with Kathy. "I guess the next time I tell you to shut the fuck up you will." he teased again.

Stacy stood up and gave Teddy a piece of her mind. "Fuck you, and get your ass away from my house before I have Jr. come out here and kick your ass again. You're a bitch ass nigga who only hits on girls that aren't as strong as you. Why don't you hit on somebody your own size? Are you afraid to fight someone who has the same strength you have, you sissy mutha' fucka?" Stacy said.

"Just ignore him," Kathy told her, "Act like we don't even

hear him. He isn't worth our time."

"Hell no! I'm tired of his shit, and we don't have to put up with listening to it either, especially in my own front yard." Stacy told Kathy, then continued warning Teddy. "Get away from here now!"

However, Teddy wasn't listening, nor was he acting afraid of the fact that Stacy was going to call her brother. "Yeah Stacy, listen to your friend and stay out of it." He directed his sarcasm to Kathy, "Hey Kathy, I know you heard me bitch, I said how's your face feeling? Is it swollen and sore yet?" Teddy laughed while ignoring Stacy's comment, directing his comments only to Kathy. Again, Kathy didn't respond.

"Well that's alright. By tomorrow it should be feeling pretty big," He joked and kept walking.

"That bastard! Who does he think he is coming in my front yard doggin' you like that? Hell no, I'm not having it, and I wouldn't have had it if I was with you today. That damn Doug, some boyfriend he is. I'm glad you broke up with his punk ass." Stacy was mad as they watched Teddy walk down the dark street and turn the corner into the alley. After he was out of sight, Stacy was about to walk Kathy home. Before they could leave, Jr. came outside. "What are you two up too?" he asked, looking suspicious.

Kathy hurried and put on her shades while her and Stacy looked at each other with blank looks. They knew that if Jr. found out that Teddy was just at their house harassing Kathy, he would have ran around the corner and jumped him. So they answered, "Nothing." Stacy said, "We were just talking."

"Talking about what?" Jr. asked. "Normally I can't get you two off the telephone, and why do you have on those dark glasses?" he said while trying to look through Kathy's glasses.

Mind Games

"I just wanted to wear my shades because I don't have on any makeup, that's all." Kathy quickly responded.

Jr. was surprised by her answer, but kept quiet. However, Stacy and Kathy knew he wouldn't keep quiet for long. They also knew that they couldn't tell him the truth. "I was just telling Kathy how Teddy hurt my feelings when he hit me that day." Stacy hesitantly said.

"That Stupid Ass fool! All Teddy does is pick on young ladies. I didn't see his Black ass holding his own when I kicked his ass. The big man on campus couldn't even hang. That's why he hit ladies. He's a Stupid-Ass Fool! He needs his black ass kicked real good again! He's always picking on ladies. I need to kick his ass againin case he thinks about hitting another lady." Jr. joked. He looked around the empty street in search of Teddy. Kathy and Stacy became afraid knowing that if Jr. knew the truth and looked closely at Kathy's face, he would go after Teddy. They didn't want to tell Jr. the truth of their conversation because Teddy had already threatened to press charges on Jr. if he attacked him again.

With a sad look on her face, Kathy knew that Teddy hadn't learned his lesson. "Well, I'm gonna go home now. It's getting late and I still need to do my homework."

"Okay, let's go. I'll walk you halfway down the street," Stacy told Kathy.
"See you Jr," she told Jr. who was still on the porch.

As they were leaving, Jr. asked, "Where do you guys think you're going in the dark?"
"I'm gonna walk Kathy halfway home," Stacy responded.
"No you're not," he said.

Surprised by his comment, they both looked at him, then at

each other. Stacy said, "What do you mean I'm not? I can't let her walk home by herself." Stacy and Kathy knew the real reason why Kathy couldn't walk alone.

Jr., being the protective brother he was insisted, "I'll walk her home."

They looked at him wondering what he was up too. Stacy responded, "I'll walk her."

"You don't need to be walking her home, it's too dark," Jr. told his little sister.

"I'm not afraid of the dark," she said as her and Kathy laughed.

"I know you're not afraid of the dark, but you're not gonna walk her home this late. I said I'll walk her home. Besides, Grandma wants you to wash the dishes. So go in the house and bust those suds."

Kathy looked at Jr. and said, "Whatever, I just need to get home."

Stacy gave in as she hugged her friend goodbye, "Alright, I'll see you tomorrow."

Kathy turned to Stacy and whispered, "And don't be tripping with Teddy, he'll get his."

Stacy whispered back, "Yeah, but if I help out I'll know for sure that he got his," she laughed. Kathy turned to walk home while Stacy went into the house, "See you tomorrow," Stacy went in the house while Kathy and Jr. walked down the sidewalk.

"Lock the door behind you," Jr. added.

"Yeah, yeah, yeah! I know what to do," Stacy teased her overly protective brother.

As Jr. walked Kathy home they began talking, "So, how are you really doing?" he asked in a serious tone.

Mind Games

"I'm fine," she responded, trying to keep the truth to herself. Kathy had known Jr. and Stacy for so long, they were like family.

"Are you sure?" By knowing Kathy for so long, Jr. knew that something wasn't quite right about her conversation with Stacy, so he pressed harder for answers. He wasn't convinced that she was telling him the entire truth. He felt that she was only giving him the answers he wanted to hear. He stopped her dead in her tracks as they stood under the glow of a streetlight and asked again, "Are you sure you're alright? Because if you're not, I can take care of things for you. Kathy, you're like my little sister. I'll do what I need to do to protect you and Stacy."

Suddenly Kathy began to cry while keeping her oversized dark glasses on to protect her bruise. She could no longer hold a straight face to his comforting words. As she cried like a baby Jr. took her in his arms and held her tight. "Me and Doug broke up today. I hate him. I just hate him!" She still didn't want to tell Jr. the truth. Her trembling words were so low that he could barely hear her. The only reason he could understand what she was saying was because of their closeness.

"Doug's a stupid ass fool anyway, just like his punk-ass friend Teddy!" he told her. "I need to kick his ass too. I still can't see what you saw in him from the beginning. You're too much of a lady to be messing around with a fool like Doug. It's good that you finally saw the light and let him go. Besides, you need a real man." Jr. was a warm and sensitive young man. He had several girls who were interested in him, but he was very choosy with whom he chose to have in his company. Kathy was someone he had always admired from afar.

After growing up in a family that was troubled with domestic violence, Jr. vowed to take a stand of never hurting a lady the way his father hurt his mother. The scars that laid deep within his memory were too painful to relive. When he saw the tears coming from her eyes, it allowed the sensitive side in him to be released, causing him to express long overdue feelings hidden deep inside.

    Jr's feelings began to soften even more as he wiped away her tears. He looked deep into her weary eyes and quietly told her, "You need a real man like me!" Then he took her chin and directed it toward his face. He bent down, gently held her tight and kissed her soft lips while caressing her warm body next to his. Kathy was taken by surprise from his actions. However, she was enjoying the warmth of his body and kiss while his moist tongue caressed hers. She found herself fully embracing him back with feelings that were also hidden deep inside, while avoiding the pain and minor swelling she felt from the hit Teddy gave her.

    This was the first time their connection grew this intense, causing their brotherly, sisterly feelings to fade away. The kiss seemed to last forever, when in fact it was only for a few short minutes. Within those precious minutes, Kathy felt safe, like she was floating on air and saw stars shooting in the sky. She never felt so close to any guy in her life as she was feeling at that particular moment.

    Jr. also felt the attraction. He had always kept a close eye on Kathy, but tonight his feelings opened wide, allowing them to grow deeper than ever. After their kiss was over they laughed. "What just happened?" Kathy asked.

    "What should have happened a long time ago," he responded with a smile.

"Is that right?" she blushed.

    "Yeah, that's right." He bent back down and kissed her again while she held on as tight as she could, not wanting the night or the kiss to end.

Eventually, they came up for air feeling happy and satisfied. "Well, I better get you home before your mother comes looking for you," Jr told her. They were only a few houses away from hers.

"Okay," she said. At that moment anything he said was good enough for her. She felt so good that she didn't want the moment to end. She also felt so good that her problems had suddenly disappeared. She thought about what he said, "Do I have to go now?" hoping the magical moments could last forever.

"Yeah, you better. But we can pick back up tomorrow where we left off tonight, I promise," he grinned while assuring her that their kiss was not a mistake.

"I'd like that," she whispered softly. He continued walking her home, but now they were walking hand-in-hand, feeling emotions of love. After reaching the front of her house, Jr. gave her one last kiss. After he was done, he told her, "That should last you for the rest of the night."

Kathy wanted more of his tenderness and wasn't afraid to ask, "Are you sure? Because I'm not so sure about it lasting that long." She blushed.

While smiling, he held her tight in his arms again and gave her another kiss, but this time it lasted a whole lot longer.

With her eyes still closed and a big smile on her face, she savored the moment and said, "Now, that one will last me through the rest of the night."

"Good. Well, goodnight! I'll see you tomorrow," he said as he watched her walk to the front door, go into the house, and close the door. As he walked away, she watched him from her living room window as he slowly went back home. The thought of Kathy made

Jr.'s walk very pleasant.

CHAPTER NINE

The next day Stacy stopped by Kathy's house so they could walk to school. "Hey girl," she said as Kathy joined her.

For Kathy, it was more than just another day, it was a new and exciting day! "Hey," she responded with a silly smile on her face, still wearing the dark sunglasses.

"What's the matter with you?" Stacy asked after noticing the silly grin.
"Nothing."

"Yeah right it's nothing!" she said as Kathy kept quiet, still wearing that same silly grin. Stacy stopped dead in her tracks, "OH HELL NO! Don't tell me that you and Doug got back together! Please don't tell me that." Stacy was upset at the thought, but she was waiting to see exactly what was going on with Kathy and why she seemed so happy.
"No, OH HELLLLL NO!" Kathy quickly responded.

"Well why do you keep smiling like that?" Stacy wasn't letting Kathy get away with not telling her the real reason she was so happy. She wanted answers and she wanted them now! "Welllll, I'm waiting!" she said with suspense.

"Okay, okay! I'll tell you. But don't tell anybody else," Kathy warned her best friend.

"Tell anybody what?" Stacy was getting antsy and confused by her delay. She couldn't understand why Kathy had to keep the reason of her happiness to herself. Although, she knew that if she didn't agree to keep the secret, Kathy wouldn't tell her the truth. "Okay dammit! Tell me! Just tell me what's going on!" Stacy demanded and they both laughed at her desperation.

Kathy was enjoying Stacy's enthusiasm. She also knew that she was about to bust if she didn't tell someone her secret. So she finally spilled the beans and put Stacy out of her misery. "Welllll, when Jr. walked me home last night he was so sweet and concerned about my feelings."

"Yeah, yeah, yeah! So what's that have to do with your silly grin? And don't tell me a lie."
"Well, if you quit talking so much I could finish." Kathy told her.
"Okayyyyyy, just hurry up and tell me!"

"Me and Jr. kissed!" Kathy was so excited as she waited for Stacy's reaction. However, to Kathy's surprise, Stacy didn't react the way she thought she would.

"Well, what about it? Jr. always kisses you on the forehead. What's the big deal?"

Kathy knew that she was going to have to give her best friend the full details in order for her to understand what was really going on. "The kiss wasn't on my forehead, it was on my lips and his tongue was deep inside of my mouth. And it happened more than once! So now, does that explain my silly grin?"

Suddenly Stacy got it! "Damnnnnnnnnnnnnn!" she smiled. "Seeeeeeeeeeee, I told you a long time ago to hook up with my brother. He's one of the good guys." Stacy bragged.

Kathy laughed, then blushed at her comment, "Yeah, he is one of the good guys."

Now Stacy wanted all the details, "So what happens now?" she asked. "Are you guys a couple or what?"

"I don't know. We didn't discuss anything like that, our mouths were occupied." Kathy joked.

"What do you mean you don't know? Didn't you say you guys kissed more than once?"

"Yeah, but that doesn't mean we're a couple."

Stacy had now become the protective sibling and got serious, "Let me tell you something, first of all my brother doesn't just go around kissing on girls that he doesn't like. Hell, as long as you've been knowing him you should know that! And he sure don't be hoein' around. So, from what you just told me, you guys are a couple." Stacy started smiling and chanting, "Kathy's gonna be my sister-in-law, Kathy's gonna be my sister-in-law."

Kathy stopped her by putting her hand over her mouth. "Shhhhhhh, I told you to keep this information to yourself. You're already marrying us and I don't even know if we're a couple yet, so be quiet! When we're ready for everyone to know, we'll make sure they know. But for now, just hold tight!" They laughed as Stacy put her hand over her mouth to keep from saying another word. Shortly after, they finally reached the school campus.

"I'm gonna be watching you guys," Stacy told Kathy while they were still laughing, giving each other a high five hand shake.

"Yeah, yeah, yeah! We don't need you to watch us. We're old enough to handle our own business. We handled it pretty well last night," Kathy teased.

"I'll see you after school, Ms. Love Thang." Stacy was so happy with the news that she hugged her friend for good luck.

"Okay. See you later," Kathy said while grinning.

Before Kathy and Stacy walked away to go to class, Doug walked up to them enraged. "Who did you guys get to jump Teddy?" They looked at each other wondering what he was talking about. He repeated himself, "I said who did you guys get to jump Teddy? He's in the hospital with a broken arm, leg and nose, and he has bruises all over his body. His mouth is so swollen that he can barely talk, he's damn near in a coma. He may never play football again if his leg and arm don't heal right. So, who did it because they're going to jail?" Kathy and Stacy continued looking at each other in amazement and confusion. Doug was looking directly into their eyes with anger, waiting for them to reveal the truth as he continued, "Stacy was it Jr.? Did you have your brother jump Teddy in the alley last night?"

Stacy and Kathy still didn't know what Doug was talking about, but they were very interested in hearing more of the details, even though they were going to be late for their first period class.
"Hell no, my brother didn't jump on your bitch-ass friend," Stacy responded with anger.
"He sure didn't," Kathy responded with confidence.

"And how do you know so much?" Doug asked with a suspicious look.

"Because Jr. wasss....," she immediately stopped her sentence, catching herself from spilling the beans about her and Jr.'s whereabouts last night, and what they shared. Stacy quietly laughed at the slip.
"Why are you laughing?" he asked.
"I was laughing at Kathy, not at what you said." she grinned.

"So Jr. was where?" Doug asked, trying to get the truth out of Kathy that would nail Jr. as the attacker.

"He just wasn't there, that's all you need to know," Kathy stated, trying to put a stop to Doug's questions before he caught on to what her and Jr. were really up to.

Stacy caught on to Kathy's cover and detoured the

conversation, "Slow down, why do you want to know where Jr. was last night anyway? For your information, he was at home last night. So why are you saying he jumped Teddy? What are you talking about? Jr. didn't jump anybody, but if Teddy did get jumped he had it coming. Jr. would have loved to have been the one to jump him if I would have told him what Teddy did to Kathy, which is why I didn't tell him. So what are you talking about?" Stacy asked while Kathy carefully listened in silence, still pissed off at Doug for not defending her, but happy that Teddy got what he deserved.

Doug began explaining what he heard, "Well, I got a call late last night from Teddy's mother saying that someone jumped him in the alley. She said that he was on his way home and somebody approached him and said, 'You punk ass mutha' fucka', I'm gonna kick your black ass for messing with my daughter.' She said that some guy who wore a long trench coat with one of those detective kind of hats, beat Teddy's ass in the alley and left him there for dead. She also said that the guy told him that if he ever messed with his daughter again he would be back to finish him up."

"Who stopped the guy from killing Teddy?" Stacy asked.

"There was a guy in the alley making out with his girl, they heard the entire thing. They didn't try to stop anything because they thought it was just some guys handling their business, so they kept doing what they were doing. They didn't think it was any serious shit going on until they heard Teddy yelling and screaming while being thrown around like a puppet. After hearing the loud screams, the guy got himself together and ran over to where Teddy was getting his ass kicked. He started making a lot of noise and scared the guy away. But by the time he scared the guy away, Teddy was messed up pretty bad. But still, it's a good thing that they guy heard Teddy

Mind Games

scream, because the stranger was getting ready to kill him. Teddy's mother told me that after the police came and investigated, they found a red rose laying in the alley, close to where Teddy was laying all bloody. They don't know if the rose was already there, or if the stranger left it as a sign. Teddy's parents are saying that the police are now calling this mystery man the red rose bandit or something like that."

The red rose bandit fits the same description of the mystery man La Vonne assumed she saw on several occasions who resembled Jonathan. On the night that Teddy came past Stacy's house when she was talking to Kathy, this mystery man was standing very close in the darkness and overheard their conversation about Teddy. However, no one knew that he was lurking in the darkness. While watching, he heard Teddy cussing at them and decided to take his revenge. Kathy and Stacy were both unaware of the meaning behind the red rose or the conversation that was directed toward staying away from his daughter, especially since Stacy's dad was assumed to be dead and Kathy's dad died several years ago as well.

Kathy and Stacy laughed while Doug explained Teddy's unfortunate situation. "I told you he would get his. Didn't I tell you?" Kathy joked with excitement to Stacy.

"You sure did," she responded and they continued laughing.

"Oh, so it's funny?" Doug said sarcastically. "Why you guys gonna trip on my boy like that? He's half dead and you guys are standing here laughing."

"Have you forgotten how he tripped on me yesterday?" Kathy asked as she lowered her shades to show the black and blue colored bruise on the side of her face, and folded her arms as she raised her eyebrows, while leaning on her hip.

"Yeahhhh, and did you forget how he tripped on me before

we broke up?" Stacy added.

"He didn't mean any harm from what he did to either of you. He was just trying to scare you guys, that's all. He wouldn't really hurt any girls." Doug was again taking up for his no good friend.

"Whatever!" they said, putting their hand up high in his face. "Talk to the hand." they said.

"So you guys really don't know who jumped him? Or what the guy meant when he said to leave his daughter alone? Because both of your fathers are dead so he couldn't have been talking about you guys." Doug was searching for answers.

"No, we don't know anything about Teddy being jumped by some mystery man wearing a hat and long jacket. This is the first time hearing the story. Besides, that's what he gets. I guess he must have messed with someone else's daughter and they weren't taking his shit. Good for them! My only regret is that I wasn't there to see him get his ass beat!" Stacy said while she and Kathy continued laughing.

Doug turned and walked away. "Okay, I see how it's gonna be, later!" He went to class.

Hearing the news about Teddy made Stacy and Kathy happy. This news was the kind of news that would assure them that their day would be wonderful. They went to class giving each other high fives, knowing that this would be the last time Teddy would ever put his hands on another girl.

****

Everyone was eating at Gloria's house when Stacy brought up the subject about Teddy. "Did you hear what happened to Teddy?" she asked Jr.

Mind Games

"Yeah, I heard something about him getting jumped in the alley last night. That's what that nigga' gets." Jr. laughed.

"Jr. watch your mouth," Gloria scolded after smacking his hand.

"Sorry, Grandma," he laughed as he pulled his hand away from her, "But he had it coming. I also heard he hit Kathy." Jr. said with raised eyebrows. He knew that Stacy and Kathy purposely held back that bit of information from him. He continued, "He never fights guys, only girls. I guess somebody's father took care of him real good this time. Now he's in the hospital and I'm sure he's hoping and praying that he'll be able to start when football season begins," shaking his head, still laughing.

"Yeah and he's probably hoping that his face heals up too, because without football and that pretty face, he ain't got nothing going for him. All the girls are starting to stay away from him because they've heard how he treats them," Stacy added while also laughing.

Jr. looked at Stacy and warned, "Well, all I have to say is that the next time that fool, or any guy, hits you or Kathy, you better make sure I know about it, because I'll teach them a lesson and make them pay!"

La Vonne was eating while listening to the conversation. "So what happened?" she asked.

Stacy preceded to tell the rest of the story. "Teddy got jumped in the alley last night by somebody's father. No one knows who jumped him. All we know is that the man who jumped him told Teddy to leave his daughter alone and if he didn't, he'd be back to finish him off. From what I heard, he's hurt pretty bad, almost in a coma."

La Vonne continued listening while eating, "Oh, that's too bad," she said, knowing that she was also happy Teddy got what was coming to him.

Stacy continued, "Teddy's parents told Doug that the police came and investigated everything. It happened right in the alley around the corner from our house. I'm surprised that me and Kathy didn't hear anything. He was at our house talking mess right before he went into the alley. Doug said that Teddy's mother told him that the guy who jumped him left a red rose on the ground. So now they're calling this guy the red rose bandit." Stacy and Jr. laughed at the thought.

La Vonne immediately choked on her soda, spitting it all over her food and the table.

"You alright, Momma?" Stacy asked, while helping La Vonne wipe her mouth and hands that were covered in soda. Gloria got up from the table and began patting La Vonne on the back so she could regain her breath. Jr. was stunned as he watched in amazement.

While barely being able to speak she said, "You can stop Momma, I'm alright." La Vonne wiped the tears from her face. "I guess my soda just went down wrong."

"Are you sure you're alright, Momma?" Stacy asked again.

"Yes, I'm fine. Thank you for asking." La Vonne said and got up from the table and took her plate to the sink, while cleaning the rest of the mess that was still on the table.

"Well, anyway," Stacy continued, "That's what Teddy gets for putting his hands where they don't belong. I bet that'll be the last time he messes with a girl." Everyone continued eating while La Vonne fixed herself a new plate and sat back down.

Mind Games

CHAPTER TEN

It had now been over three months since La Vonne had been released from prison and working with Sandra. Sandra grew to trust La Vonne so much that she gave her the keys to the shop to open and close. Sandra also gave La Vonne more duties and responsibilities to handle. On this particular spring day, it was raining and lightening. The storm was raging throughout the darkened sky like it was winter. La Vonne was all alone in the store. Due to the storm and off-peak season, no one was visiting the store, keeping work to a bare minimum. La Vonne took a bridal magazine and began glancing through the pages. While looking at all the beautiful wedding gowns, she smiled and thought good thoughts. Eventually, after a long day at work, staying up late the night before, and listening to the crashing sounds of the fierce wind blowing throughout the sky, she laid her head down on the counter and nodded off to sleep. Soon her happy thoughts took her back to a happy day, her wedding day, when her and Jonathan said "I do." This was the very day they vowed to be with each other through sickness and good health, and until death parted them both.

Her thoughts allowed her to see the five maids of honor standing in the front of the church. They were wearing beautiful silk fitting sky blue dresses. She also saw the five groomsmen. They were standing in front of the church wearing handsome black on black tuxedos with silk sky blue shirts, which match the bridesmaid's dresses. La Vonne saw the beautiful flower girl all dressed in white ruffles walking down the isle. The ring bearer, with his black tuxedo, was walking with the ring on a fluffy white pillow. She also saw herself walk into the crowded church on her uncle's arm, who escorted her down the aisle in her deceased father's absence. She wore one of the most beautiful gleaming white fitted wedding gowns she ever saw. It was filled with layers of lace and had a long train that trailed behind.

Then she saw Jonathan standing next to his five groomsmen. He looked more handsome than she had ever seen. She looked through the pews while walking down the aisle and saw bright smiles on everyone's face. She saw her mother who was very happy with a few happy tears that flowed down her cheeks, as she blew her a kiss. This was the happiest day of La Vonne's life.

Abruptly, her happy thoughts turned painful as her mind took her back to a beating Jonathan gave her, slapping her in the face, socking her in the chest and pushing her down to the floor. Her small children were watching with fear in their eyes wanting to help. But they were not able to defend the forces of their father's strong and powerful hands. La Vonne became terrified by his actions and began to shake uncontrollably. However, his actions were very familiar and painful to her petite body. She was in love and believed that his abuse was due to his strong love for her. She believed that he often hit her because it was his duty as a man. She also believed that he hit her because she did something wrong, and had not been the best wife and mother she could be. She learned to believe that love had to hurt in order for it to be real.

All of these beliefs came from Jonathan's mouth. He was the one who constantly told La Vonne that he treated her badly because she deserved it. He also assured her that this is what a man had to do in order to keep his family together and in line. She saw all of this before. La Vonne's mother went through it, her aunts went through it, and several of her friends had also gone through abusive relationships. They all grew up thinking that domestic violence was something that was supposed to happen. So no one complained, nor do they tell. They

Mind Games

just accepted it as a part of their lives.

As La Vonne continued her dream, she heard the cries and screams coming from the mouths of her children getting louder as they watched the horror. Their screams frightened her, causing her to cry even more while Jonathan beat her. Jonathan hollered at everyone while throwing things onto the floor, breaking lamps, tables and chairs. Suddenly, La Vonne was awakened by the loud sounds of what she thought were her children's screams, but in reality the sounds were the lightening and thunder roaring through the night sky. Its fury knocked out the electricity in the shop, causing her to scream out loud, "Ahhhhhh!"

She reached to the back of the counter and got a candle and lit it. The flicker of the light seemed to blow with every blow of the wind. She stayed put so she wouldn't miss her mother's honking of the car. While still sitting behind the counter, La Vonne continued to duck and dodge each lightening bolt while she searched for her mom through the shaded window.

Her heart fell as she noticed a tall dark shadow quickly walk past the door. The shadowy figure was wearing the same brimmed hat and long coat that she saw earlier. "Could it be?" she thought. Due to her dream, her worst fears came alive, thinking that Jonathan had come back to get her. But this time his arrival was to finish her off for good. Suddenly, her thoughts shifted to good, "Nooooooo, this isn't real, neither is Jonathan." Still unsure of what she saw or where her thoughts took her, she clung to the back of the counter shaking, waiting for her ride as each lightening bolt streaked through the sky.

While waiting alone in the candle-lit darkness, the reality of her thoughts took her back to her dream. Soon her body calmed down and her concerns changed, "No! That was not supposed to happen, nor will it ever happen to me again! I won't let it, never!" her thoughts raged out loud. "If I would have stopped the violence sooner I wouldn't have gone to prison, nor would Jonathan have died. Women need to know that love doesn't have to hurt! They also need to know that they have the power to stop abuse!" Then La Vonne heard a horn blow outside. Gloria had finally arrived to pick her up. La Vonne gathered her things, blew out the candle and locked the door, feeling reassured that Jonathan would never be able to hurt her again.

Once out the door she stepped on something that was laying on the wet ground. She looked down and saw a red rose. The sight of the rose frightened her, causing her to quickly jump into the car and tightly shut the door. As she sat in the car with the rain pouring down, the water blocked a clear view out the window. However, she could still see that there was a rose laying in front of the doorway. She studied it from the short distance, wondering how it got there.

"What's the matter baby?" Gloria asked, noticing La Vonne's empty reaction.

"Nothing," she immediately responded as they drove away. "I'm just ready to go home. I've been sitting in the dark for the last twenty minutes and the storm is scaring me, that's all." She didn't want her mother to think she was losing her mind. However, she was beginning to wonder if her mind was, in fact, playing games on her, or if Jonathan had really come back from the dead.

CHAPTER ELEVEN

It's a normal day at the Hallsworth County Prison. Sherri was doing her daily chore of mopping the floor when a prison guard with a firm tone approached her. "Hey, put your mop in the closet, you

Mind Games

have a visitor."

Sherri looked around the empty dinning room in case the guard was talking to another prisoner, but she was the only person in the room. "Who me?" she asked with surprise. After the guard nodded yes, Sherri gladly put up her mop, allowed the guard to put hand and leg chains on her, and was escorted to the visitors room.

After reaching the visitor's station, Sherri walked into the small room and received a big surprise. "Hi Sherri. It's been a long time," smiled Sonny Waters, her ex-boyfriend and father of her eleven year old daughter, Denise.

The sight of Sonny sitting in front of her in his wheelchair left her speechless, which was something very unusual for Sherri. She hadn't seen or spoken to Sonny since the night she found him in her bed having sex with her best friend. This was the same night she tried to shoot off his dick for the betrayal. It was also the night that changed her life forever by making Hallsworth Prison her new home.

After spending over ten years of her life in prison, away from her daughter, made it hard to look into the eyes of the man who ruined her existence. The sight of Sonny immediately threw her into a rage, causing her to go wayyyy back to her ghetto days. "What' the fuck you doin' here, you bitch ass nigga?" she demanded as she put her hands on her hips and rolled her head from left to right as only a sista' girl would do. "After all these years don't tell me that you came to see how I was doing." Her attitude changed to panic and she asked frantically, "Is Denise and Momma okay?" Sherri loved and missed her daughter and mother dearly. Her mother was raising her daughter and would bring Denise to see her on rare occasions. Sherri and her mother had both agreed that the prison was not a good or healthy environment for Denise to visit on a regular basis. So the visits are very far a part, and due to the large phone bills, they have also been limited.

Since Sherri's incarceration and after Sonny's gunshot recovery, Sonny had been a model father to his only daughter. He visited Denise and sent money for her expenses every week. "They're doing just fine?" he reassured her.

"Well, if they're alright, why are you here?" she asked.

"Sherri, it's been a long time since we've crossed paths. It's also been a long time since I accepted God as my Savior and became a minister. However, during that time I have never personally forgiven you for putting me in this wheelchair. After we helped La Vonne, I felt that it was time for me to face you personally and tell you that I forgive you for shooting me. It's also the time to tell you that I was wrong for sleeping with Suzy and I want to ask for your forgiveness."

"Damn right you were wrong! And hell no, do I forgive you! If you wouldn't have fucked my best-friend in the first place neither of us would be in these situations. And now that you're sitting in that damn wheelchair and can't fuck anybody, I'm sure that everyday you think about how wrong you really were. So tell me, can you still stick your crippled ass half-dick in anybody's pussy now?" Sherri laughed at the thought of Sonny not being able to have sex anymore, especially after knowing how much he enjoyed sex while they were together. She remembered it being a must have for him on a daily basis.

Sonny couldn't believe what he was hearing, but remained quiet looking at her with a shocked expression. "I didn't think so, you bitch ass nigga," she said angrily. While Sonny remained quiet she added, "I guess you had to learn the hard way of not fuckin' with a sista' when I tried to shoot your dick off. Is that the real reason you couldn't face me sooner? You knew that your dick would hurt just by looking at me, wouldn't it? You also know that I shouldn't have gotten locked up. This whole thing is all your fault! All your damn fault!" Sherri was now crying as she thought about the day she saw Sonny and Suzy in her bed together and shot him. "Because of you, I can't even take care of my own child. She was just a baby when I got locked up. You took away my opportunity of raising my only child. Now the only person she identifies as a mother is my mother. The only thing she knows about me is that I gave her life."

Sherri was fuming at the thought of him wanting her forgiveness. Each day she had spent in prison only reminded her of the pain she has suffered due to Sonny. After ten years, forgiveness is still something she wasn't ready to give, causing her heart to remain very cold toward him and his apology. "Well, at least I see that you've come a long way from being a drug pushing bastard! Now you're just a holier-than-thou, paralyzed, wheelchair pushing Bastard!" she laughed again to keep from crying.

Sonny refused to give in to Sherri's insults. Nevertheless, his silence didn't stop her from continuing, "Tell me this, asshole, since you were always a hoe when I was with you and now that you only have half a dick, are you letting a man fuck you in your ass now?" She laughed at the thought of how her once macho boyfriend was now helplessly bound to a wheelchair, stripped of all of his sexual pleasures.

Sherri's comment shocked Sonny, causing him to shake his head in disbelief. In his defense, he shot back and went to his old ways, before he was a minister. "Well, a brotha's gotta do what a brotha's gotta do! Hey, I gotta get mine some kind of way, and telling you the truth ain't no big deal to me anyway, because no one would ever believe you. First of all, I'm a man of the cloth and everyone knows I've changed my old ways. Secondly, everyone knows how much you hate me, so they wouldn't believe what you said about me even if you did tell someone what I do to satisfy my needs. So yeah, I get mine, and it feels damn good! In fact, it feels better than you ever felt! So swallow those apples and juice them." Sonny was giving Sherri a piece of her own payback pie.

She was blown away by his confession and began giving him some more of her ghetto attitude. "I knew your black ass was a mutha' fuckin' faggot, you bitch ass nigga. As much as you always liked to fuck and suck, I knew you couldn't go too long without a little satisfaction. In fact, I could tell by the way you smiled when I said that you had a dick up your ass that you were a faggot. And I assume that sucking dick is also something you've grown accustom to. I heard that the bullet I tried to shoot your dick off with missed your spine and cut your dick in half, you no walking mutha' fucka.' So I guess bending over and opening wide are your only acrobatic talents. Which means that your ass is getting fucked, and you're swallowing a hell of a lot of cum these days. So, what Catholic priest took you out?" Sherri laughed as she enjoyed every chance she could get to make him feel bad. It was the only satisfaction she was able to get from him and enjoy since she'd been locked up.

Sonny smiled at her bold comments and realized that she still wasn't ready to accept his apology or forgiveness. She was determined to make things as hard as she could for him and his visit. He knew that God needed to deal with her soul a whole lot more before he could return or before she would accept his apology. "Sherri, I didn't come here to argue with you, or to hear all your negative and hurtful comments. I only came in peace and to tell you that I forgive you. I also want you to forgive me. Now that I'm living for the Lord I don't want anything to block my blessings." Sonny was trying to be sincere, but Sherri wasn't having any part of what he was serving.

She couldn't let Sonny get to the soft side of her by using psychology, so she lashed out again. "See, there it goes. It's always about you. That's always been the problem. Everything has always been about you and nobody else. You only came here because your guilty conscience told you to come, not God. And since I shot you, your conscience probably bothers you everyday because you don't have a dick anymore."

"We all make mistakes and I made mine. None of us are perfect." he responded to her powerful blow to his ego.

Sherri still felt that her words were not hurting enough, so she decided to give him a powerful blow that was sure to damage his ego. "Well, Mr. Smart-Ass, while you were fuckin' my best friend, I was fuckin' yours, Jonathan." Sonny looked up at Sherri, surprised by her confession as she continued, "Yeah, that's right, I said it! I was fuckin' Jonathan and he fucked me so good that when I fucked you, it felt like I was riding a tricycle, compared to riding a powerful motorcycle in full gear with him. And while I'm at it, Denise ain't your daughter, she's Jonathan's." Sonny looked at Sherri with total disbelief as she ranted on, "That's right, I said it, she's not yours! So close your big ass mouth, because shock doesn't wear well on you."

Sonny was furious, "Ain't that a bitch! You were fuckin' my best friend all along while acting innocent when you found out I was fuckin' your girl. And now you're gonna try to say that Denise isn't my baby. You're a mutha' fuckin' liar! As soon as I leave this place I'm gonna get her tested. And so much for the innocent role you played on La Vonne. It all makes sense to me now, you knew the information all along that she needed to set her free, but you held out on the girl because of revenge of not being able to be with Jonathan.

Some friend you are." Sonny knew that Sherri was devious, but he never thought she would do something so hurtful to La Vonne, who was an innocent party in the entire situation.

"I never said that I was that Bitch's friend in the first damn place, you guys said all that shit! I only told her the information she needed after I figured she served enough time, and when I realized that my confession may get me out of here sooner. I did it for my sake, not her's. That's what the Bitch gets for killing my man! Hell, if she didn't sweat him so much we could have handled our business regularly, with either of you never knowing a thing. But between you and her sweating us so bad about what we were doing, and who we were doing it with, we had to handle our business when we could." Sherri laughed while enjoying Sonny's bizarre look.

"Sherri, you're a Bitch! A mutha' fuckin' Bitch is what you are." He lashed out. "I hope you rot in this damn place, because after today, you'll never get any sympathy from me."

"Good, because sympathy is something I can do without, especially from you!" she answered.

Sonny knew that talking to her was hopeless. "I'm leaving now since I see you're still very bitter. I've done what the Lord told me to do. The rest is up to you. I guess its goodbye." He began rolling his wheels in motion to exit the room.

As he got to the door, Sherri became filled with more rage, but Sonny never turned to face her. "Just get the hell out of here and stay out of my life! If it weren't for you fuckin' around in the first place I wouldn't be in here! I wish I would have killed you when I had the chance, especially after knowing that I had to come to prison anyway. At least if I killed you, I wouldn't have to ever see your sorry face again. So, you best ta' roll your sorry ass outta here if you know what's best for you, and get your cripple ass out of my life and don't ever come back! Get out of here now and stay away from my daughter because you ain't her daddy, her daddy's dead. And hell no do I accept your forgiveness. So get out of my face before I do something that'll make me stay in this hell hole even longer. Guarddddd! Take me out of here now!" she demanded with fury. Sherri's outburst caused the guard to immediately open the door and escort her out of the small visitor's room.

After she left the room, Sonny looked over his shoulder and shook his head in disappointment. After all the years he'd known Sherri, she never acted this bitter. He was ashamed that her behavior had elevated to such heights. However, he could understand her pain and inability to forgive, leaving him speechless.

While the guard escorted Sherri back to her mopping duty, she fumed from the thought of Sonny's presence. Although, her anger quickly turned to laughter as she thought about what she said. "Asshole! I'm sure he'll have Denise tested to see if she's his daughter. That'll just make him spend hundreds of dollars that he doesn't have to spend. I know that Denise is his child. The dumb ass should know that Jonathan wasn't even around when I got pregnant. He should also know that his drawls were the only ones I was smelling when Denise was conceived. But if he's dumb enough to believe what I said, then let him spend the money it takes to get the DNA test done. Then let him sweat while he waits for the answer. Now, watching him sweat is something I'd really like to see." Sherri laughed at the thought of Sonny being inconvenienced while wondering about the truth behind their daughter's paternity. "Besides, that's what he gets for fuckin' with me. That'll teach him not to fuck with a sista' no mo'."

Once Sherri and the guard arrived at her work area, he

uncuffed her. She asked for permission to use the telephone. "Can I make a call please?"

The guard wasn't allowing any extra privileges, "No! You know it's not time for phone calls. Wait like everybody else. Besides, why do you think you should have special treatment? Get back to work," the guard instructed as Sherri got her mop and continued doing her chores, waiting for the phone lines to be opened.

****

When it was time for Sherri to use her phone privileges, she made a collect call to La Vonne.

After accepting the call, La Vonne welcomed the conversation with pleasure. "Hey girl. How you doing?" La Vonne asked. She was happy to hear from Sherri. This was the first time La Vonne had heard from her friend since she'd been released over six months ago.

Sherri was feeling pretty happy when she called La Vonne. "Girl, it's a trip in here, but I'm cool. Hey, when are you gonna have your cute lawyer friend come here and handle my case?" she asked. "Let me see what he's doing, maybe he can come tomorrow."

"Okay, that'll be cool because I need to gather some information that'll get me out of here quick and in a hurry. I have some business to handle on the outside world."

"Do you need me to do anything for you?" La Vonne innocently asked.

Sherri quietly mimicked La Vonne's whinny and helpful voice, "Do you need me to do anything for you?" before speaking out loud. "Did you say something?" La Vonne asked.

"No." Sherri quietly laughed and continued, "This is some

thing I need to handle myself. Talk to your friend and tell him I need his help now. Tell him that he owes me for helping you."

"Okay, call me tomorrow and I'll tell you what he said."

"Okay, I gotta go now and don't let me down. Remember, you guys owe me," Sherri reminded her.

"We sure do. Talk to you tomorrow."

"See ya!" Sherri hung up the phone before La Vonne could say goodbye.

Sherri didn't like La Vonne. She was only trying to be her friend long enough to gain her freedom. La Vonne was unaware of Sherri's motives or her past association with Jonathan.

****

The next day came and Sherri was preforming her mopping duty when a guard came to her, "Hey you. You have a visitor." Sherri was again surprised by the summons because she wasn't expecting anyone. She put away the mop and the guard cuffed her and escorted her to the visitor's room.

After reaching the visitor's room the guard opened the door and led her inside as he stood outside the closed door. Once inside, Sherri was pleasantly surprised by who she saw. "Hey there you good looking thang!" she said with a big smile. Jay received La Vonne's call to help Sherri. So he rearranged his schedule so he could talk to her about building a case to free her from prison.

"Hello, my name is Attorney Bethel "Jay" Mitchell. You can call me Jay. La Vonne told me that you called yesterday and want me to help you get out of prison." He said as he held out his hand.

Sherri held out her hand, but instead pulled Jay close to her body. She was trying to come on to him and immediately let him know her intentions. While he was close to her, the clinging noise of the arm and leg chains rang loudly in the background.

Jay quickly backed away, "Excuse me, but if I'm going to help you, you can't come on to me." He was surprised by her actions and didn't want to appear unprofessional in any way.

"Come on to you?" Sherri tried to act like she didn't know what he was talking about and continued to walk around the room casually.

Jay was embarrassed by her comments, thinking that maybe he took things the wrong way and that her gesture was just a misunderstanding. "Okay, let's get to work. Tell me all about your case." He sat down at the small wooden table and pulled out his yellow legal pad. He was ready to take notes while Sherri paced the room, gleaming at his every move.

Sherri was a large women with a lot of muscle who wore her short nappy hair in a bandana. Weight training was a regular thing for her. So, taking on Jay's medium build was an easy challenge. As he attempted to do his job, she couldn't stop smiling at him. She walked around the table, pulled his chair away from the table, slid it on the waxed floor and sat on his lap. Her big butt flattened his legs, as she placed the biggest tongue kiss she could offer right into his mouth.

"Heyyyyyyyy!" Jay said as he used his strength to push her off of his legs and stand up, while trying to move as far away from her as he could. "What are you doing? I thought you wanted someone to help you get out of here, not screw em'," he declared with a ghetto tone of anger. Jay began wiping the moisture from her kiss off his mouth as he looked at her with disgust.

"Well, the way I feel and as long I've been locked up in

here, a good screw would do me pretty damn good right about now." She said as she quickly walked toward Jay in an attempt to catch him and passionately make him hers, if only for a few minutes.

"Sherri, if I'm going to work with you it has to be on a professional basis only! Nothing else." He threatened while quickly walking around the table, trying to stay as far away from her as possible.

Sherri was ready to give him her entire body right then and there. She felt that he would be like any other red-blooded man and give in to her gesture of having sex with her right in the visitor's room. "Jay, the least you could do is represent me, especially after I gave you the information you needed to free La Vonne. But now I want to be rewarded, and my reward is you baby!"

Out of desperation, Sherri unsnapped her jumpsuit, lifted up her bra and exposed her double E chest to Jay and smiled, "Now I know you want some of these! Come on over here and give momma some of that good stuff!" She said as she chased him around the table.

"Guard! Guard!" he yelled because Sherri wouldn't stop coming after him. "Come get this woman. I can't work with her. She's out of control."

Sherri quickly snapped up her shirt so the guard would not see her chest. He quickly came into the room and held on to Sherri. "Is there a problem, Sir?" he asked.

"Yes, can you please take this prisoner back to her cell immediately! I won't be representing her," Jay told the guard. Jay looked at Sherri, who was now frowning and said, "Find yourself another lawyer because I won't be back!" He gathered his belongings and quickly left the room.

Sherri was enraged by his comment, but laughed off her

anger. The guard took her out the room while she yelled, "You'll be sorry you didn't take my case, you'll be sorry!" After being too far for Jay to hear any of her comments, she vowed to make La Vonne pay for his actions. "Now she's gonna really pay," she promised herself.

****

Once it was time for the nightly telephone privileges Sherri called La Vonne. "A collect call for La Vonne Brown?" the operator said to the person who picked up the phone.
"Hold on, let me get her," Stacy said before getting her mother.
When La Vonne came to the phone the operator had already hung up and Sherri was on the line. "Hello?"
"La Vonne?" Sherri asked.
"Sherri?"
"Yeah, it's me."
"What's up girl? Did Jay come by to see you today? He said he would try to come by."
"Yeah the nigga came by."
La Vonne was surprised by her tone. "Why'd you call him a nigga? He came to help you."
"He is a black ass nigga and the nigga wouldn't give me any. How the hell is a fine ass nigga like Jay gonna come up in here knowing that a sista' has needs and not take care of them?" Sherri's ghetto personality was in rare form.
La Vonne couldn't believe what she was hearing. Sherri's comment caused her to get a little sista' girl attitude of her own while responding, "What do you mean not take care of your needs? He was only supposed to help you with your legal matters, not your sexual

Mind Games

needs."

"Damn my legal matters!" Sherri lashed back. "Hell, I know I ain't getting out of here anytime soon, so I wanted to get fucked! All I wanted from him was a good fuck! Besides, after hearing how fine his ass was from you, I wanted to see for myself. I wanted him to take care of my needs while he was here. But noooooo, the nigga ran out of here like a lil' ass Bitch!" Sherri was mad at Jay, so she took her anger out on La Vonne since she felt she owed her a big favor for securing her freedom.

"Well, I can't make the man fuck you. That's out of my hands." La Vonne snapped back with a toned down sista' girl attitude.

"Out of your hands, Bitch, you better talk to the brotha' and tell him to come up in here and handle a sista's needs, that's what I'm talking about." Sherri was rolling her neck and head from right to left, with that sista' girl got an attitude motion.

La Vonne also started rolling her neck back and forth and put her hand on her hip, to keep in the accompanying mood. She was in a very defensive mode since Sherri called her a Bitch. "Don't call me a Bitch! You Bitch! It takes a Bitch to know a Bitch," she hollered. After hearing her mother's loud response, Stacy, who was sitting on the couch watching television, turned away from the TV and began focusing on her Mother's conversation, which was obviously more exciting than the program she was watching. As Stacy listened, she was tripping off her Mother's stern and sassy tone while laughing under her breath. Jr. and Gloria had gone to the store for ice cream.

"La Vonne, you ain't nothing but a Bitch! Bitch!" Sherri responded. "Hell, for your damn information, I could have given you the information you needed about Jonathan when you first got here, but I was too pissed off at you for killing my man. Yo' nigga had been fuckin' me during that time, and he was fuckin' me damn good! Hell, me and him had a good thang going on for a long time until you messed everything up by killing him. So don't call me a Bitch, you yellow-ass skinny bitch!"

La Vonne's eyes began to water hearing Sherri's confession. She became enraged and began pacing the floor of the kitchen as she responded, "I don't believe you were fuckin' Jonathan. Me and him were happy until your sorry ass boyfriend came into his life with those damn drugs. He was taking care of us and being a damn good husband and father. So don't tell me no shit about you and him fuckin', you're a lying ass Bitch!"

"Yeah, you probably were happy once upon a time. But once he tapped into my good ass pussy, that was all he wrote." Sherri laughed at the thought of making La Vonne mad but she continued the torment, "That nigga was begging for me like a dog begs for doggie treats. Hell, he was eating me up better than a dog eats his treats, and I was also giving him everything he wanted and more. You better believe he was lovin' every bit of me and my good ass pussy!" Sherri was doing all she could to make La Vonne as angry as possible because she knew that she couldn't do anything about it. She also knew that La Vonne would have to deal with her confession forever.

Sherri was also taking her anger out on La Vonne because she was still angry at Sonny and needed someone to feel her pain. "And while I'm at it, my daughter Denise is Jonathan's daughter, not Sonny's, so take that little bit of information to the bank."

"Denise isn't Jonathan's daughter you lying Bitch! She's not!" La Vonne blasted back.

But Sherri wasn't finished, "Keep thinking that, Bitch! And another goddamn thing, the next time I ask you to do a mutha' fuckin'

Mind Games

favor for me, your skinny yellow ass better run, and run fast!" Sherri slammed down the telephone, leaving La Vonne helplessly crying like a baby.

"I can't believe her! I can't believe what she just said. I thought she was my friend when all along she was out to get me. What did I do to her? I didn't even know her until I got locked up. I never did anything to upset her, so why is she saying all those things to me?" La Vonne cried out loud.

Stacy quickly got off the couch and ran to her mother's side. "Momma, don't cry. I'm sure that lady is just saying those things to make you upset. Don't cry." Stacy held her mother tight in her arms while trying to console her and convince her that Sherri wasn't telling the truth.

"But why did she have to say that her daughter is really your father's daughter? She didn't have to say that." La Vonne painfully wondered.

"She said that?" Stacy was shocked herself by the news. She didn't know how to respond to that kind of information. But after watching her mother cry like a baby, she knew that she had to try. "Isn't there some way you can check to see if she's lying or not? What about that DNA stuff we always hear about on the news. They're always saying how you can tell a lot about a person from those tests. Can't you get one of those tests done to see if that lady's baby is really daddy's baby?"

La Vonne looked at Stacy through her tears and began feeling better. "Yeah, that's right, maybe I can call Sonny and have him test their daughter. He could find out for me. Thank you baby." She told Stacy as she hugged her back and immediately picked up the telephone and called Jay to get Sonny's number.

"Hello." Jay responded.

"Hi Jay, it's me La Vonne. Is this a good time to talk?" she asked.

"Sure, what's going on?" Jay was happy to hear from La Vonne and thought the call was a social one.

La Vonne told Jay the entire story and asked for Sonny's phone number.

After hearing the details, Jay suggested something different. "Let me call Sonny. I have a good relationship with him and I think he'll respond better to me with that kind of information than you."

"Okay, if you say so."

"I say so, so don't worry about it let me handle it. When I find some information I'll get back to you. So don't worry, I'll talk to you soon."

"Okay, I'll be waiting." La Vonne responded. They hung up their phones and La Vonne went to sleep wishing her conversation with Sherri was a dream while knowing that it wasn't. She hoped for the best with any news Jay could come up with.

CHAPTER TWELVE

La Vonne had now been working at the dress shop for about seven and a half months. Things were going very well. It was during the month of June, one of the busiest months of the year for a bride and her bridesmaids. Everyone seemed to want to get married during these summer months. During this busy season, Sandra kept the store open until eight o'clock at night in order to make sure she could accommodate her customers. She welcomes the crowd with open arms. It's also during those summer months that keep her business financially in the black for the entire year.

Mind Games

However, on June 10th it's unusually busy. Customers were coming in the shop all day long. Sandra and La Vonne assisted the soon-to-be brides and bridesmaids with fittings, hemlines, measurements and the ordering of wedding dresses. The cash register was running over with lots of money. Sandra smiled every time she heard the bell ring as the door to the cash registrar opened to deposit money. La Vonne was also assisting with the cash registrar. The day grew long and tiring, but La Vonne and Sandra continued working until the last person left the shop.

As the day came to an end, Sandra could barely walk because her feet hurt so bad. "La Vonne, can you straighten up the store so I can go home early? My feet are hurting so bad that I can hardly walk, and I'm too beat to take another step. Besides, I need to get some rest or I won't be able to handle tomorrow's crowd."

"Sure Ms. Sandra, you go on home. There's not much to do around here. I tried to pick up as we were working so there wouldn't be a big mess to clean up this evening. All I need to do is a little straightening up and empty the trash. So it won't be a problem. Besides, we don't want the shop to look a mess when customers come in the morning. Go on home, I'll be fine."

"Are you sure? Because this neighborhood isn't the best after dark and it's already dark now."

"Don't worry, I'll be just fine. There isn't much that can scare me after what I went through in prison, also the door will be locked to protect me. Go on home, I'll be alright by myself. Besides, my mother called earlier and said she'd be running a little late. She has to pick Stacy up from a track meet that's running overtime. She'll be here to get me later. I'll just finish cleaning the shop while I wait for her. So, go on home and get you some rest. I'll see you in the morning." La Vonne got the broom and began sweeping while Sandra got her keys to leave.

"La Vonne, I already locked up the money in the safe, even though I hate to leave that kind of money in the store after hours. But I'll take it to the bank the morning. Right now the only thing I want to do is get off my feet and lay down."

"Do you want me to drop it off for you? We have to pass the bank on our way home."

"No, that's fine. It's insured, so if someone's stupid enough to break in, let em'. I'll come in early tomorrow and take it in."

"Okay. Goodnight Ms. Sandra," La Vonne said as she continued sweeping.

"Goodnight." Sandra replied as she pulled down the shades, locked the door and went home.

The store was finally quiet after a long noisy day. La Vonne was enjoying the peace and quiet. It was a sound she learned to enjoy, especially after hearing the constant sounds of cell bars opening and closing, hand and leg chains dragging as prisoners walked throughout the prison facility, and voices crying out for freedom. After she finished sweeping, she gathered up all the trash she could fine so she could take it outside. She didn't want to take a chance of missing the trash pick up the next day. She gathered as much as she could and stuffed six oversized trash bags. She took them to the back of the store to empty in the bins located directly outside.

After getting all six bags outside by the trash bin, two at a time, coming in and out of the store, La Vonne lifted the top and put the first two in the bin. She stopped to admire the full moon in the sky. Suddenly her pleasant thoughts were halted and she froze in her tracks. She heard an unfamiliar sound and quickly looked around. "Who's there?" she asked, hoping no one would respond, although, the noise sounded like someone was walking in her direction wearing squeaky shoes. However, when she looked, she didn't see anyone. She gained her confidence and stuffed two more bags in the trash bin. "Maybe I'm just tripping," she thought, "Sandra said that the neighborhood is bad around here after dark, and it's very dark, except for the full moon. Normally I'm gone by now, so maybe I'm just tripping since I'm out here alone." La Vonne was trying to convince herself that she hadn't heard anything.

Suddenly, the sound was there again, but this time it was closer. She quickly turned again. Except no one was there the second time around as well. She quickly threw the last two bags in the bin and got ready to close the top and make a run into the store. However, before she lowered the top, she noticed a freshly cut red rose laying on the ground next to where the bags were laying. After seeing the red rose, La Vonne panicked and began losing her breath. She quickly dropped the lid of the trash bin and made her way back to the rear door of the store.

Once at the door, she turned back and took another look. She noticed a set of shoe prints that lead away from the store where a puddle of water had gathered. When she looked toward the direction of the shoe prints, she saw the shadow of someone quickly walking away wearing a long trench coat with a brim hat. After seeing the shadow, her heart started beating faster, causing her to sweat. She quickly went inside the door, closed it with all her strength, and locked all four deadbolts as fast as she possibly could.

"Oh my God, Oh my God!" she repeated as she laid against the back of the door, still breathing hard and hoping her extra weight would keep out any intruders. She was trying to catch her breath, but she couldn't because the beating of her heart wouldn't slow down. "Oh my God. Who was that out there? It looked like the same shadow I saw at the grave site AND at the restaurant. Who is that? Is someone trying to scare me or what?" While La Vonne's mind was going a mile a minute trying to figure out what she saw and heard, she heard another sound. It was light tapping noises coming from the front door. She yelled and ran to hide in the storage area, "Ahhhhhhhhhhhhhh!!"

After hiding for several minutes she came from behind the wall and ran to the front door to make sure it was locked. The front light of the store was broken which made it hard to see. While checking the locks and looking outside of the slightly opened mini blinds for any signs of her mother, a tall, dark figured man appeared. She found herself looking directly into the face of a six-foot tall man who was looking down, precisely into her eyes. He wore a black sombrero hat positioned so low that it was hard for her to get a good look of his face. "Ahhhhhhhhhhh!" She screamed again while running back to storage area to hide. "Oh my God, oh my God! It's him, it's him!" she repeated softly as her heart raced with fear. "He's come back to finish me off. Oh God, please help me! Please help me!" While shivering with fear, she was too afraid to move out of her safety zone, so she waited for any signs of security.

After hiding for what seemed to be an eternity, but was only twenty minutes, nothing was happening. Her sense of safety made it easy for her to be curious. Then she slowly stood up from her ducked position while her knees knocked together with fear and surveyed the store. "I can't see anything. Maybe he left," she thought as she tried to peek through the partly opened mini blinds while still standing behind the back wall. She was trying to be brave and convince herself that

Mind Games

everything was alright. But deep down inside she knew that was far from the truth.

Later, another tap on the window was heard, "Ahhhhhhhh." La Vonne screamed again. She screamed so loud that it frightened Gloria, who was there to pick her up from work. "La Vonne? La Vonnne? It's me, Momma. Are you alright?" Gloria said as she tried to peek through the blinds of the front door of the store. La Vonne's scream caused Gloria to worry, fearing that something bad had happened to her daughter. Gloria started beating on the windowed door and yelled louder, "La Vonne it's me Momma! Open up the door. Are you alright in there? Open the door baby. It's me, Momma." Gloria motioned for Stacy to get out of the car to help. Stacy didn't hear her mother's scream because she was listening to the music she had turned up louder after Gloria got out of the car. After motioning for her help again, Stacy turned down the music and rolled down the window and finally answered, "What is it, Grandma?"

"Something's terribly wrong with your mother. I heard her scream, but I don't see her. Come and see if you see her in there."

Stacy got out the car and walked to the window. She had become very concerned and tried to see if she could see her mother through the crack of the door. Suddenly La Vonne peeked out from behind the storage room and recognized her Mother and daughter standing at the door, so she came running out for their protection.

La Vonne's hands were shaking like a leaf in a windy tree as she tried to unlock the four deadbolts with the keys. She had tears in her eyes as she desperately tried to escape her bad experience. Gloria and Stacy felt helpless since they didn't have a key to help her and couldn't get in until La Vonne opened the door. They attempted to calm La Vonne down so she could concentrate on opening the door.

"Baby, calm down. It's alright. Take your time," Gloria said.

"Mom, we're right here. No one's gonna hurt you. Calm down so you can get out safely," Stacy added.

Finally, La Vonne calmed down long enough to unlock the door and open it. She fell into Gloria's arms crying. She was exhausted. "Are you alright baby? What happened in there? Why are you so scared?" Gloria put La Vonne in Stacy's arm and looked around the shop. After noticing that nothing was out of place Gloria walked La Vonne to the car that was parked right in front of the store.

Stacy took the keys out of her mother's hand and locked the front door as Gloria helped La Vonne get into the car. Then she got in the car and Gloria quickly drove off. "Momma, are you alright?" Stacy asked with concern while Gloria waited for her daughter's response. La Vonne's mouth was frozen, which caused her not to answer.

"Honey, are you alright?" Gloria asked again. La Vonne sat there frozen with only empty stares into space.

Stacy looked at her grandmother, "Grandma, what's the matter with her? Why won't she say anything?" she whispered.

"I don't know. But something must have really frightened her. Just leave her alone for now. Hopefully she'll be alright by the time we get home." Gloria drove home as fast as she could with La Vonne saying nothing during the entire ride.

Once at home, Stacy and Gloria helped La Vonne out of the car and sat her down on the couch. "What's the matter with her?" Jr. asked.

"We don't know. She won't say anything," Gloria said and added, "All I know is that I heard her scream after I tapped on the window to let her know I was there to pick her up and I haven't heard a word from her since."

"Mom, are you alright?" Jr. was very concerned while trying to see if he could help.

After quietly sitting and looking into space for over thirty-five minutes, La Vonne finally came to, and realized she was safe at home. "What happened?" She looked around the room. "How did I get home?"

"Don't you remember baby? I picked you up at the store and drove you home." Gloria responded.

"No, I don't remember anything. The only thing I remember is taking out the trash and being here now. So what's for dinner? I'm hungry." La Vonne apparently blocked out her frightening experience. It was something her mind wouldn't allow her to revisit. Everyone looked at her, not knowing what to do or how to help.

"Dinner will be ready in a minute honey. You wait right there. I'll warm you up a plate," Gloria said and went to the back room to call Jay. However, Jay wasn't home nor at his office, and his cell phone only took messages. Gloria didn't want to leave a message so she hung up the phone, promising herself to call tomorrow. She went into the kitchen to warm up the food for everyone to eat dinner.

****

After a very long and exhausting day, La Vonne was finally ready to call it a night. She worked so hard all day long that as soon as her head hit the pillow she fell fast asleep. For some strange reason she couldn't get Jonathan out of her mind. The guilt of killing him would not allow her to let go. She often found herself holding onto every good thought about him in order to make up for the bad ones. However, the bad thoughts often outweighed the good ones. After she was asleep, she began dreaming pleasant thoughts about him.

Her initial thoughts emerged after seeing a happy couple in the boutique earlier that day. They were making a payment on the bride's wedding gown. The love they displayed made La Vonne reminisce on how it was when she was in love with Jonathan. She began reliving the very first time they made love and how deeply in love they were. She remembered how being with him was the best love making experience she had ever had. These pleasant thoughts were very rare, because most of the thoughts surrounding Jonathan haunted her dreams, which was the reason she reacted with fear to his possible appearance.

The terrifying dreams began shortly after the night she killed him. These were also the same dreams she learned to live with because of the guilt. Since her release from prison, La Vonne's dreams increased. Especially after the thought of possibly seeing him standing at the grave site, along with the other strange sightings. This time the dream was pleasant. It was very unusual from her past dreams.

Gloria peeked in on La Vonne and noticed that she was smiling as she slept. Seeing a smile on her daughter's face made her happy, especially after knowing how she reacted earlier that evening. "Thank God she's getting a good nights rest. I'm really worried about her. I'll call Jay right after I take her to work in the morning and tell him how she acted tonight. I'm sure she'll open up to him." Gloria closed the bedroom door, went into the living room and began reading her bible while everyone slept.

"Umm, Ummmmm" were the moans coming from La Vonne's mouth as she slept. She was in a deep, deep sleep. Her thoughts were totally focused on Jonathan. They were centered on the first time they made love. The beginning of what they both thought would last forever. "Oh yessss! That feels soooooo good! Baby I've missed you so much. Where have you been?" She whispered as his luscious lips caressed hers and his soft tongue slowly tasted the sweet juices of her body.

"La Vonne, I've been close to you all along. I've been waiting for you to want me like you want me right now. Your body is so hot! It's calling my name."
"Jonathan, Jonathan....." she softly moaned.

"Baby, you've always been the woman I love and the woman I want in my life forever. I won't ever let another man get anywhere close to your good lovin'. No woman will ever make me feel the way you do." Jonathan's voice responded to the caressing touches he felt from her smooth and petite body. Her body massaged his better than it had ever done, focusing on secret areas only known to each other.

La Vonne knew that no man had ever made her feel as good as Jonathan had made her feel, he was her first love. The soft touches of his warm body next to hers made her feel soooo good inside. She wanted him to take his time, knowing that they had all night long to make sweet love. "Ummmmmm!" she moaned as she enjoyed his body softly caressing her's.

"Baby I'm feeling you. You feel so good to me. I love you!" he told her.

"Jonathan you're my first love and you'll be my last. I've missed you so much! Why did you leave me? Whyyyyyyy? I thought you were dead. I thought I killed you. I didn't mean to hurt you. But I didn't want you to hurt me or our kids. I'm so glad I didn't kill you."

"Baby I would never hurt you guys, never! I love you too

much to do anything like that. And no, I'm not dead. I'm right here, laying beside you. Don't you feel my hot body deep inside of your juicy body? Hold me tighter, feel me inside of your naked body. Rub your fingers around my body like I'm rubbing mine around yours. Touch me. Feel me. Feel my body all on top of yours. Baby I'm right here beside you, massaging every inch of your passionate body. I'm never gonna leave you again." were the promises La Vonne thought she heard from Jonathan.

"Ohhhhhh Jonathan, I love you so much! Ohhhhhhhh babyyyyy! Ohhhhhhhh!" She moaned as she smiled the night away.

****

"La Vonne, are you up yet?" Gloria yelled. "Get up baby, you're gonna be late for work."

La Vonne slowly woke up, yawned, stretched and looked around her room. She felt happy and refreshed. Her night was so peaceful that she felt like she had slept for three days. This was an unusual feeling because her dreams normally caused her to feel uptight when she woke up. But today was different. Today was starting off as a good day. "I'm up Momma, thanks for calling me. I didn't hear my alarm clock," she yelled to Gloria.

When La Vonne got ready to get out of bed she noticed that one of her pillows was centered directly between her legs while another was tightly positioned between her arms. Both pillows were damp. "Ummm," she wondered. "Why am I hugging my pillows so tight again? I guess I was sweating through the night and put them under me while I was asleep." She got out of bed and began to make it up. As she straightened the covers, she noticed an unevenness in the

Mind Games

bed. So she pulled back the blankets and froze dead in her tracks as she slipped into a trance.

"La Vonne, are you getting ready for work yet?" Gloria yelled out again from the kitchen as she prepared breakfast and helped Jr. and Stacy off to school. "La Vonne, wake up baby. You don't want to be late," she said a little louder to make sure she was heard.

After hearing Gloria's voice, La Vonne suddenly came out of her trance. "What'd you say Momma?" She became so frightened by what she saw under her blankets that she didn't hear what Gloria said.

"I said are you getting ready for work? I don't hear you moving around in there. Are you sure you're up?"

"Yeah I'm up," La Vonne spoke with hesitation in her voice as she took a closer look at the object on the bed. She couldn't believe her eyes but she gathered enough courage to slowly reach down and pick up a single red rose. As she touched the rose her entire body quivered. She was afraid, but trying to be strong. She needed an answer. "This red rose looks like the same one I saw at the grave site," she thought.

Her memory abruptly came back from last night at the dress shop, "Oh my God. Oh my God! It also looks like the same red rose I saw at the trash bin. What happened to me last night? Am I losing my mind or what? It seems like every time I see a red rose I'm freaking out. I gotta get a hold of myself before I totally lose my mind, or before my family thinks I'm losing my mind. After the way I acted last night I bet Momma and Stacy already think I'm losing it. I can't be freaking out every time I see a red rose and think that Jonathan left it somewhere just to scare me. He's dead and I killed him so why am I tripping so hard? I have to stop. I just have to stop tripping!" La Vonne declared as she trembled.

La Vonne picked up the rose and threw it in the small trash can in her bedroom. After getting rid of it, she looked around her room for an answer that would solve her problem, but no one or nothing was there but her. She went to the window to see if it was opened. She noticed that it was slightly cracked open, just enough to put a small finger through the opening. She closed it as tight as she could and stormed out of the room with a bad attitude. "Who left the window open in my room last night?" she asked in a demanding tone.

Gloria looked at La Vonne. Stacy and Jr. were already gone to school. "What are you talking about?" Gloria responded as she continued washing the dishes, ignoring La Vonne.

"Somebody left my window open last night. I want to know who did it?" she again fumed.

After hearing the anger in her voice again, Gloria knew that something was seriously wrong. "Calm down Baby, calm down. Nobody's been in your room except you. So, what are you talking about?"

"Momma, somebody's been in my room besides me because the window was left open and I didn't open it!" La Vonne continued to keep the secret of the mysterious roses to herself. She didn't want her mother to insist that she see Pastor George, or recommend she be locked up in a mental ward.

"Baby are you sure you didn't open it last night to get some fresh air? You know it's been rather stuffy in your room since you leave the door closed all day long. So maybe you opened it last night and forgot that you did." Gloria thought La Vonne was getting much too upset about a window being left open and didn't understand why. Nonetheless, by La Vonne's reaction Gloria didn't want her daughter to get any more upset than she already was, so she kept her cool.

Mind Games

"I didn't open the damn window!" La Vonne insisted.

Gloria looked at her daughter with raised eyebrows that peeked over her prescription glasses, and with her hand on her hip she said, "La Vonne, I'm not gonna have you cussing around this house. So, watch your mouth. Do you hear me?" Gloria was reminding her who was the boss in her house.

"Sorry, Momma, but it was too cold last night for my window to be open. Are you sure one of the kids didn't open it while I was asleep, because I don't remember it being opened when I came home from work?"

"Baby, I'm sure they didn't open your window because they went to bed before you did. So neither of them could have opened it and I sure didn't. Maybe it's been open for a few days and you're just now noticing it. Anyway, what's the big deal about the window being left opened in the first place? A little cool air will do you some good and help you sleep better. Besides, when I peeked in on you last night you looked like you were sleeping good. You looked like you did when you were a baby. So maybe the open window helped you sleep better. Now run along and get dressed before you're late for work." Gloria turned away from La Vonne and went back to cleaning the kitchen. When La Vonne wasn't looking Gloria carefully peeked at her from the corner of her eye in an effort to try and figure out her moody attitude.

When Gloria turned her back to La Vonne, La Vonne scratched her head and quietly went back to her room to get dressed for work. "I wonder who opened my window and how that rose got in my bed," she whispered.

When she went back to the room to finish making up her bed, La Vonne found a few light-colored spots on the sheets. She carefully rubbed her right hand on the strange spot and noticed that it was hard. The feel of the spot felt like hardened cum that validated a night of sex. La Vonne's first thoughts wondered if Stacy had sex in her bed when no one was home, especially since her room was the farthest from the front of the house, giving her privacy. So she immediately pulled her hand back and yelled to Gloria while grabbing the sheets from her bed and bundling them in her hands, "Momma, can you wash these sheets please, something very strange is on them." She threw the soiled sheets outside her bedroom door and went to the bathroom to take a shower and get dressed for work.

As she stood in the warm water she scrubbed her body well. Her mind began to wonder about the red rose she found and the spot on her sheet. "How did those things get in my bed? I don't remember anything in my bed like that before I went to sleep." Suddenly her mind took her back to a vision hidden deep within her dream. It was Jonathan making love to her all night long. The vision frightened her, causing her to almost fall on the wet and soapy surface.

The loud noise frightened Gloria. "Are you alright in there?" she yelled.

"I'm fine Momma. I just slipped." After she gained her composure she hurried and put on her clothes. She went to the kitchen table so she could eat.

"Here you go baby, oatmeal, toast and milk." Gloria said, as she placed the food in front of her and walked away. La Vonne's back was turned away from Gloria. Gloria walked over to the table where La Vonne drank her milk and placed a small white vase in front of her with a freshly cut red rose in it. The sight of the rose frightened La Vonne so much that it caused her to spit her milk out all over the table.

Mind Games

"La Vonne, what's the matter?" Gloria asked as she ran and got paper towels to clean the mess.

La Vonne jumped up from the table, spilling the bowl of oatmeal and toast on the floor, while dropping the glass of milk out of her hand. "Where'd you get that rose?" she demanded with anger. She was in a complete panic and began shaking tremendously.

"What's wrong baby? What's wrong with you?" Gloria asked as she cleaned up the mess in the kitchen.

"Where'd you get that rose? I have to know now!" she insisted and slammed her fist on the kitchen table.

Gloria screamed, "Ahhhhhhhhh!! You've lost your mind!" She wasn't used to seeing anyone act like La Vonne, and didn't know what she was capable of doing next since she'd been locked up for so long. She was ready to call the police for help. However, she attempted to calm her daughter down before she made any hasty decisions. "La Vonne calm down baby, it's all right, just calm down! What's the matter with you? It's just a rose." Gloria was crying.

"Where did this rose came from?" La Vonne backed away from the table as she waited for an answer while pacing in circles.

"I picked it out of my garden. It was the only rose fully bloomed on my vine. I thought you would enjoy the fresh smell of a rose with your breakfast. But I can take it outside if you don't like it. Just calm down." Gloria reached for the vase with the rose to get it out of La Vonne's sight.

La Vonne felt stupid after hearing Gloria's explanation and began crying. She held Gloria's hand in an effort to encourage her to leave the rose on the table. "I'm sorry Momma, I'm soooo sorry! I don't know what's happening to me, I just don't know." She sat down on the couch and continued to cry.

Gloria set the vase back on the table and slowly walked to the couch and sat next to her grown daughter. She hugged La Vonne like she was a little baby, rocking her back and forth in her arms where they cried together. "It's all right Baby. It's gonna be all right. Now, don't you worry, everything is gonna be all right."

After crying for about ten minutes, La Vonne wiped her eyes and looked up at the clock on the wall. "Oh no, we better hurry up. I'm gonna be late for work."

"Are you sure you want to go in today? You've had such a bad morning and last night didn't go so well for you either. Are you sure you want to go in today? Why don't you just call in and take the rest of the day off. You haven't missed a day since you started. I'm sure Sandra can do without you for one day."

"No, Momma, I can't stay home today. This is the busiest seasons of the year. I can't let Ms. Sandra down like that, I just can't. She's counting on me to be there. I'll be alright. Come on, let's just go."

"If you say so," Gloria said in uncertainty.

"I say so. Thanks for being concerned. I'm sorry if I scared you, I didn't mean to. I guess I'm just having a bad day and that red rose brought back a bad time in my life that's all. But I'm fine now, I promise. I'm sure the rest of the day will be better because I'll be too busy at work to think about anything else. I guess I'm just going through a few things right now that I have to work out on my own, that's all. So, let's hurry up before I'm late. But let me clean the mess on the table."

"I'll clean it up when I come back, let's go." Gloria told her and they grabbed their purses, while Gloria grabbed her keys and took off to the dress shop.

Mind Games

****

After Gloria came home from dropping La Vonne off at work she immediately called Jay at work.

"Hello, is Jay there?" she asked the office secretary, who answered the telephone.

"Who's calling please?" the secretary responded.

"Tell him Ms. Johnson's on the phone and it's an emergency."

"Hold on Ms. Johnson, let me see if Mr. Mitchell can take your call."

"He better take my call. Don't forget to tell him it's an emergency," she said with force.

With a surprised look, the secretary put Gloria on hold while she informed Jay of her call. After about one minute, he came to the phone. "Ms. Johnson, what's wrong? Is La Vonne all right?" he asked with worry and concern.

"No, she's not alright! I'm afraid she's losing her mind. She hasn't been doing well for the last few days. You have to come over here and see about her, you just have to!" she began to cry as she spoke.

"Calm down and tell me what's going on. And where's La Vonne now?"

"She's at work. I tried to get her to stay home but she didn't want to let Sandra down so she went in. But anyway...," Gloria started as she told Jay the entire story about La Vonne's two emotional episodes. She didn't know what to do to help. She desperately needed Jay to give her the answers to make everything alright.

"Calm down Ms. Johnson, calm down. Everything'll be alright." After listening to Gloria, Jay knew he needed to calm her down. He knew that he needed to give Gloria the answers she needed to solve La Vonne's troubles. He could tell that she was also losing control. "Ms. Johnson, why don't I come over tonight and take La Vonne out for some ice cream after dinner and talk to her. Maybe if we're alone I can get her to talk to me and help her."

"That sounds fine. What time do you think you can get over here?"

"I can be there by seven, is that alright?"

"Sure, seven'll be fine. I'll make sure she's ready for you." Gloria was happy to hear that La Vonne was getting ready to get some help.

"Good. Don't worry about anything. I'm sure it isn't anything serious."

"I hope not. I've seen her in action and I know something's going on with her that isn't right."

"Well, I'll see what I can do to help, how's that?"

"That sounds just fine," Gloria responded, "Okay, I'll see you tonight at seven."

"Okay, goodbye."

"Goodbye, and thank you Jay. I thank God for you! I don't know what I would do without you. You are truly a God sent."

"Thank you. I'll see you tonight, goodbye." he smiled and hung up the phone.

Shortly after hanging up the telephone from Jay, Gloria called one of her dear church friends, Thelma. When Gloria needed help, Thelma, Mary and Daisy, considered as the gossipers of the church, were the only ones who stuck by Gloria's side. Everyone else abandoned her. After this occurred, Gloria acknowledged that friendship comes in many strange ways. She learned to value friendship and never put her nose down to anyone again. "Is Thelma there?" Gloria asked.

"This is Thelma. Gloria, is that you?" From the tone in Gloria's voice, Thelma could tell something was wrong with her friend.

"Hi Thelma, yes it's me. I'm okay, just a little worried about La Vonne."

"What's wrong? Is she in any trouble?"

"No, not really. She's just been acting strange and I don't know what to make of it." Gloria told her.

"What's she doing? Is she still having those nightmares you told me about?"

"No, she's just acting strange. She came into the room this morning with a bad attitude, accusing the kids of leaving her window open last night. I don't know what to think. She scared me by the way she was acting."

"Do you think she's got the devil in her or some kind of curse? Maybe she needs an exorcism preformed on her. Maybe one of those devils running around in that prison came out, jumped inside of her and took over her body. She sounds like she needs Jesus. Have you spoken to Pastor George yet? Maybe he can help you." Thelma was filled with suggestions. She was good at making a molehill into a mountain. Her negative thoughts didn't help Gloria one bit, causing her to worry even more.

"Do you think that's it? Oh my God help me. I can't deal with anything like that in this house. This is God's house. I've blessed this house and Pastor George has blessed this house. There can't be any devils running around in here. I have to protect my grandchildren." Gloria was afraid of the thought that what Thelma was saying was true.

"Well, you did say she was acting crazy. Has she ever acted that way before?" Thelma was trying to be helpful, but wasn't doing a very good job.

"No, she's never acted like this before. I don't know what to think."

"It sounds like you better get Pastor George to come back over and bless your house again. It also sounds like something done got up in there without you knowing it. Well, I gotta go now, Harry is waiting for me to take him to work. Call me if you need anything."

"Okay, bye." Gloria said as Thelma got ready to hang up the phone. Gloria stopped her, "Thelma, are you still there?"

"Yes, I'm here. What else you need?"

"Do you think you and the other ladies can come by this evening and talk to La Vonne?"

Thelma wasn't sure if she could help her friend this time, especially after knowing that the devil might be in her house. "Wellllll, I'm not sure if I'll be able to come tonight or not. Let me call you when I get back from taking Harry to work. I'll also see what the others are doing."

"Okay, bye.

"Bye and don't worry about her. She'll be alright. Throughout the years you've prayed enough for all of us to have strength." Thelma told Gloria. "Now it's time for the Lord to shine down on you."

"Thank you. Well, alright. Call me later."

"Okay, bye."

"Bye."

****

Later that afternoon, after Thelma told the church ladies about Gloria's situation and how worried she sounded, they made up their minds to surprise her by meeting at her house.

Mind Games

"Lord have mercy! Thank you Jesus," Gloria said with a surprised tone in her voice, after answering her doorbell and seeing her three faithful best friends standing there ready to help. "Come in, come in and have a seat. I'm so glad you came." Gloria directed them to the couch. "I just don't know what to do about La Vonne," she whispered. La Vonne was in her bathroom and Gloria didn't want to let on that she had called on her friends for help.

Shortly after they sat down, La Vonne walked into the living room. She was surprised to see the ladies sitting on the couch. "Hi, La Vonne," they responded. After Thelma spoke to Gloria this morning, she called the ladies and told them her concerns. After hearing Gloria's concern's, they felt that they needed to see La Vonne themselves in order to evaluate her strange and inappropriate behavior. Realistically, they wanted to be nosy like they were known to be.

La Vonne was a little surprised by their sudden appearance. However, she figured that her mother had called them to see about her since she acted so strange this morning. Except, she acted like nothing had happened and remained courteous. "Hi, Ladies, good to see you," she said and made an about-face to go back to her room to change out of her work clothes.

"You doing alright La Vonne?" Thelma asked.

"Yeah, you feeling alright?" Mary followed.

Daisy was the analyst among the group and remained quiet while watching La Vonne's actions carefully.

"I'm fine, and you Ladies?" La Vonne responded.

They looked at each other and said' "Yes, we're fine." La Vonne continued to her room.

After La Vonne was out of sight the ladies gathered close together and began gossiping quietly. "Gloria, she looks and sounds fine to me." Mary said.
"She looks fine to me too." Daisy followed.

"I can't believe that she was acting so strange this morning. She seems perfectly fine now." Gloria said. "Even in the car she was fine. She seemed to be tired, but fine. I don't know what got into her this morning." Gloria was puzzled about La Vonne's sudden attitude change and felt embarrassed in front of her friends.

"Do you think the devil got into her?" Thelma asked. The other ladies froze in their tracks. They slowly and carefully looked around the room for any signs of the devil.
"I don't think so." Gloria responded.

"Well, I still say you should get Pastor George to bless your house again. Your house can never get enough blessings." Thelma told Gloria. The other ladies nodded their heads in agreement. At that moment La Vonne began humming a sweet song as she walked to the bathroom to wash her hands for dinner. The ladies froze again.

"Gloria, are you sure La Vonne was acting weird this morning? She seems to be perfectly fine." Mary said.

"Yeah, are you sure you weren't just making things more than they were?" Daisy added.

Gloria looked at them, "No, absolutely not! I tell you just as I'm sitting here talking to you, La Vonne was losing her mind. I don't know what happened but she was extremely upset." Gloria wasn't sure what to think about La Vonne's behavior. She was confused about her about-face attitude and didn't know what she was looking for, or why she felt she needed help.

"Well, she seems to be doing fine now." Daisy said while

Mind Games

looking around the room with her glasses resting low on her nose. "Are you fine Gloria? Maybe you're imagining things."

Gloria was shocked by Daisy's insinuation, stood up, put her hands on her hips and raised her voice, "What do you mean am I alright? Or am I imagining things? Are you saying that I'm crazy?" Gloria demanded answers as she became upset. The other ladies were silent, but holding on to every word being said while looking at Gloria and Daisy to see what was next.

"Heavens no was I trying to say that you're crazy. Gloria you know better than that. I was just making sure that you weren't imagining things. You know things have been hard for you since La Vonne got locked up and I know they're still hard for you since you're adjusting to her being back home. Honey, I know you're a little stressed right now. But I didn't mean anything bad about what I said. All I'm saying is maybe you're making more out of what you saw than what actually happened, that's all." Daisy was trying to clear the air before things got out of hand.

La Vonne walked into the room and broke up their intense assembly. "Are you ladies going to have dinner with us?" She asked with a sarcastic smile.

"Oh no, we gotta go now," they said and gathered their purses.
"I gotta get dinner ready for Harry," Thelma said.
"I gotta finish my dinner too," Daisy and Mary responded.

"Okay ladies, thanks for stopping by," Gloria said as they walked out the door.
"Bye La Vonne, take care," Mary said.

"I will, thanks," La Vonne laughed at their reaction and went into the kitchen to get some dinner. Gloria went to the porch to say her goodbyes.

Before they left, Daisy said, "Well Sister Gloria, La Vonne seems fine to me. But if she starts acting funny again call me and I'll come over and bring Pastor George. And please forgive me if I sounded out of line earlier, I was just thinking about your well-being. I didn't mean any harm in what I was saying. You know I love you like the Lord loves you." Daisy hugged Gloria.

"I know, and forgive me for thinking the worst, things have been stressful around here. I'm sorry for taking my stress out on you," Gloria responded to Daisy. She hugged the ladies and they went to their cars.

Before the ladies got into their cars they stopped to talk amongst themselves, while smiling and waving goodbye to Gloria, who went back into the house. "Can you believe her?" Daisy asked. "She was actually getting mad at what I said. I was only saying it like I see it." The other ladies shook their heads in agreement as she continued, "She asked us to come over here and give her some advice on what we saw, and when we tell her the truth she gets all upset. The nerve of her! Well, that'll be the last time I come to her rescue." The other ladies agreed again.

Thelma stopped shaking her head in agreement and added her own two cents, "Well, we have to remember that Gloria's just under a lot of stress right now. We have to forgive her like the Lord forgives us and try to understand. I'm sure she didn't mean any harm by what she said."

"Well, there's only so much understanding a person can give and we've giving her a lot over the years. How dare her think that I was calling her crazy. If she is crazy she brought it on herself, and I can't help that. Anyway, I have to go. I have to get my dinner fixed before I hear it from my grouchy husband." The other ladies shook

Mind Games

their heads but kept their comments to themselves. Daisy hugged them and they got into their cars and drove home.

****

Later that evening the doorbell rang. "I'll get it," Stacy yelled as she ran to the front door.
"Hello, Stacy," Jay said.
Stacy was surprised by his presence, "Hi Jay."
"Is your mother home?"
"Sure, I'll get her for you. Mommmmm!" she yelled.
"Yes?" La Vonne yelled back.

"You have a visitor," Stacy responded as she invited Jay into the house.

Jay took a seat on the couch and waited for La Vonne to come to the living room. "Hi," he said smiling as she walked into the room.

"What are you doing here?" she asked with suspicion and looked at her mother for answers, wondering if she summoned Jay.

Gloria acted innocent. "Hi Jay, what brings you here tonight?" she said, knowing that she was the only person who suspected Jay's visit. However, she didn't want to let in on her knowledge.

He didn't want anyone else to know the real reason for his visit so he made up an excuse. "I had a light day at work and thought I'd drop by to see how everyone was doing." Throughout the last seven and a half months that La Vonne had been home, her and Jay saw each other on rare occasions, when he came by to see her, or called to see how she was doing. However, nothing serious had happened between them since their memorable kiss. Jay thought about La Vonne and their kiss often, but did not want to lead her on with a relationship that he wasn't ready to take further, especially after recently getting out of a long relationship.

"Well that was nice of you to drop by like this," Gloria said innocently.

La Vonne was still unsure if Jay's arrival was planned or by chance. Even though Jay stopped by on occasions to visit, the timing of this particular visit was suspicious. "So, how's work?" La Vonne was only making light conversation since Gloria and Stacy's eyes were glued on Jay. Jr. was in his room with the door closed.
"Work's fine. How's work at Sandra's?" He innocently asked.
"Busy, but fine."

"Jay would you like anything to eat? I can warm you up a plate. We have plenty of leftovers." Gloria asked.

"No thank you. I ate already." Jay looked at La Vonne, "Would you like to go out and get some ice cream? The night is beautiful."

"Sure, that would be nice. Let me get my sweater because it's a little chilly out there." La Vonne went to the closet and got her sweater. Gloria looked at Jay and smiled, giving him a nod of thanks and approval. "Okay, I'm ready," La Vonne came out, ready to go.
"We'll be back shortly," Jay said as he opened the door for La Vonne as she smiled.

"Take your time." Gloria responded. They walked to his car and drove away.

****

After ordering their ice cream they sat at an outside table to enjoy the evening.

Mind Games

"So, how are things really going with you? And you know you can tell me anything." Jay assured La Vonne that she could confide in him, which really made her suspicious about his visit.

"Everything's fine." She casually said and decided to stop the games, "Did my mom put you up to this visit of yours? And don't lie to me." She looked him dead in his eyes to see if she would catch him in a lie.

Jay couldn't lie to La Vonne. They had become so close over the years that lying just wasn't his nature, especially when it came to her. He revealed the truth hoping it wouldn't put a barrier between them. "Well, yes she did. But she only did it because she's concerned about you."

La Vonne shook her head and smiled. "It figures. She thinks she's slick."
"You're not mad?"

"No I'm not. I guess the way I've been acting lately I would have called someone on me too. I'm just glad she didn't call the cops."

"So tell me the truth and you know you can trust me. What's really going on with you?"

La Vonne wasn't sure if Jay would believe her explanation about sleeping with her dead husband so she made up a story. "I just had another dream about Jonathan and it really got to me this time, that's all. But I'm fine now."

"What was the dream about?" Jay knew that La Vonne had many dreams about Jonathan, but never heard of one that made her react totally out-of-control the way Gloria explained earlier.

"It was just a dream. I'm so tired of dreaming about him. I wish I could just go on with my life and forget I ever met him. But it seems that it's more difficult to do than I expected." La Vonne continued eating her ice cream to avoid it from melting.

"Are you sure that's all it is? Because you know you can tell me the truth and I'll try to help you."

"That's all it is. I guess it'll just take some time getting over what I did. I guess you can't just kill somebody and think everything's gonna be okay, that is if you have a guilty conscience."

"Well, you shouldn't feel guilty. You did what you had to do, paid your price and now its time to get on with your life. So trust me, everything will be okay. And if things aren't okay, you tell me and I'll come to the rescue."

As Jay hoped his words would offer encouragement, La Vonne laughed at his comment, thinking they were cute.

"Good, I like to see you laugh. You have such a beautiful smile, why waste it? Laughing is a good thing, helps to make you strong." They continued eating their ice cream and laughed while La Vonne blushed with hope of something developing more serious with Jay.

After they finished eating their ice cream, they got in the car and drove around town. Their destination was headed to nowhere in particular while riding with the sunroof top opened as the wind blew through their hair. "So, where do you want to go?" Jay asked. "The night is still young."

La Vonne decided that she would be bold with her response and shock him, "Let's go to your place. I've never seen your place and I'd like to see how you live."

Jay was very surprised with her answer. He was also unsure if he wanted to take her to where he lived, then changed his mind, "Alright. I don't live too far from here. To my house is where we'll go." They took off to his house, which was about ten minutes from where they were driving.

After reaching the driveway of his luxury condo, La Vonne's eyes grew large with excitement as she looked at every inch her eyes would take her. "This is nice! I'm very impressed. But I should have known you'd live life large."

"You should have known what?" Jay laughed as he parked his car in the underground parking structure.

"I should have known that you would live large in a fancy place like this."

After parking, he took her up to his condo and she looked around, again sizing up every inch of his place that she could. "This is nice! Very nice!" La Vonne couldn't help but make herself at home when she plopped down on his oversized plush-black leather couch. "Boy this is nice." She rubbed her hands on the leather and enjoyed the feel.

"I see you like my place."

"Like it? I love it!" Jay's condo had the best furniture money could buy. He was also a fine art collector, which included rare and expensive artwork and paintings that hung on his walls and throughout his condo. His hard wood floors sparkled like diamonds and his large picturesque windows gave a clear view of the entire town from the twentieth floor.

"And look at how clean it is in here without even knowing you were having company."

"I'll tell my maid she's doing a good job." he laughed.

"A maid? You mean you don't clean your own house?" La Vonne was surprised by his answer.

"I don't have time to clean my house. After working as hard

as I do, coming home and cleaning around here isn't what I call fun."

"Well, if you can afford to hire a maid, go on with your bad self. I wish I could afford one. So the next time you're hiring maid's, hire an extra one and send it to our house." They laughed. La Vonne got off the couch and walked to the windows to view the night, "This is so nice. You're definitely living large," she said as she continued making herself at home, viewing every inch of his condo. As she went to his bedroom her eyes grew with amazement, "Man, look at this bed. It's large enough for six people to sleep in it."

Jay laughed at her response. "Well, it can hold quite a few people comfortably." He didn't want La Vonne to get any ideas while admiring his bedroom so he quickly guided her out and back to the windows in the living room. "Did you see the pool?"

"Where? Where's the pool?" La Vonne ran out the bedroom to view the pool. "That's nice. Can we go down there so I can get my feet wet?"

"Sure, come on." Jay took her downstairs to the Olympic sized swimming pool that had a Jacuzzi large enough to hold twenty people.

"I can't remember when I've seen a pool as nice as this one. In fact, I don't think I've ever seen a pool like this." It was big enough to hold hundreds of people at a time. La Vonne went to the pool, took off her shoes and put her feet in the warm water. "Ohhh," she said. "This water's nice and warm." They were the only ones at the dimly lit pool.

"The manager keeps it warm so it's comfortable to swim whenever we want." Jay smiled as he watched La Vonne enjoy the water. Her reaction was like a kid playing at the playground for the very first time, as she gently splashed the water in circles with her hands. She was truly enjoying the things Jay took for granted. Her reactions made him realize just how blessed he actually was. "So, do you want to get in? They keep extra swim suits in the dressing room."

"They do? Now, that's really something. They're prepared for everything around here. That's alright, I better not get in because I won't want to get out." La Vonne sat down on the side of the pool, pulled up the legs of her pants, immersed her feet in the warm water and enjoyed the relaxing feeling.

Jay came over and sat next to her, but didn't get his feet wet. "How would you like to live in a place like this?" he asked.
La Vonne was surprised by his question. "What do you mean?"

"Well, with hard work and determination you can live like this yourself. How do you think I made it here? I worked hard and believed in myself. My family didn't grow up with silver spoons in our mouths. We worked very hard for everything we have. Now my brothers and sisters live very well, and together we make sure that our mother also lives well."

"I remember what you told me about your upbringing."

"So, always remember that if you work hard and strive for the better things in life you can have all of them."

La Vonne was happy for the accomplishments of Jay's family, except she was hoping that his question was leading to something that included him and her living together. However, since it didn't, she didn't want to ruin her pleasant time. She kept the mood positive and away from the possibility of them being anything other than friends. "I believe you because six months ago I would have never believed I'd be out of prison sitting here talking to you. So yes, hard work, prayer, and miracles definitely pay off and come true." La Vonne enjoyed the warm water on her legs and hands as she lightly splashed it around in circles.

"So, are you ready to go back home now?" Jay asked.

"No. Are you ready to take me home now?" La Vonne wanted to spend eternity with him. Going home was something she totally avoided.

"No, I'm cool. We can sit out here a little longer, but remember you do have to go to work tomorrow. You don't want to get home too late."

"I'll be alright. Don't worry about me," she responded as she splashed the water around more, eventually wetting Jay. After getting wet, he jumped up and ran farther down the side of the pool, where he began splashing water back at her. "Ahhh!" she lightly screamed as the water wet her clothes. "Okay, I see how's it's gonna be," she got out of the water and ran over to where he was and pushed him in the water with all his clothes on. However, as she pushed him he held on to her hand and she followed him into the water, also fully dressed.

"Seeeeeeeee, you can't start something and think you're gonna get away with it," Jay said as they laughed. He was having so much fun with La Vonne. The excitement they shared was something he never experienced with his prissy ex-girlfriend.

"Oh well, at least the water feels good. Now tell me, does that storage room have dry clothes for me to go home in, too?" La Vonne asked.

"No, I'm afraid you're on your own with the dry clothes. You'll have to go up to my condo and I'll dry them in my dryer."

After floating in the warm water, La Vonne and Jay drifted closer together. She hugged him and he hugged her back with them again kissing. This time their kiss had no interruptions. After kissing for about ten minutes they came up for air. "Boy that felt good,"

Mind Games

La Vonne responded, feeling like she was floating in heaven.
"It sure did," Jay responded while still holding onto her waist.
"Listen," said La Vonne.

Jay looked around to see what she heard, "What? I didn't hear anything."

"Exactly. We didn't hear Momma interrupting us this time." They both laughed.

"So, are you ready to get out now," Jay asked while still holding her in his arms. They had been floating in the water for about twenty minutes.

"Yeah, we better get out since now I need to wait for my clothes to dry."

"Okay, after you my lady." As La Vonne made her way to the pool, Jay's eyes closely followed her every move. He was pleasantly checking out her behind that revealed every curve she had through the skintight wet clothes she wore. On their way upstairs, they grabbed towels that were in the changing room and quickly walked back to his condo, shaking from the cold air. As La Vonne was shaking, Jay put his arm around her to keep her warm.

Once in his condo he went to his bedroom and gave her his robe. "Here, you can take your wet clothes off in the bathroom and put on my robe when you're done. I'll throw them in the dryer and after they're dry, I'll take you home." Jay handed La Vonne his robe and closed the door. While she changed, he changed in his bedroom.

When she was done, she came out and gave him her wet clothes. "Here you go," she said as he took the clothes and put them in the dryer.

When he came out of the laundry room, he noticed that she was still shaking, "Are you still cold?"

"Yeah, that night air is something fierce tonight," she responded.

"Let me turn on the fireplace, it'll warm you right up."
He walked to the gas fireplace and turned it on. He turned off the other lights throughout his condo and allowed the fire to burn brightly in his living room, which set a mood of romance.

The fireplace was lit. So La Vonne sat on the floor, where an oversized white bear rug laid in front of the fireplace to keep her warm. When she sat down, her robe raised, exposing the full length of her leg, almost revealing a treasured area. "I love your place," she said while admiring her surroundings and pulling the robe closed.

The sight of La Vonne's bare leg caused Jay's body temperature to suddenly become heated. His mind began exploring an area that would lead to her private garden. However, he played it off like he didn't see a thing, "Would you like some hot chocolate while we wait for your clothes to dry?"

"Yes, that'll be great."

Jay walked into the kitchen and put the pot on to boil some water for the hot chocolate. After the water was heating, he turned on the CD player where the soft sounds of *Marvin Gaye's* "*I Want You,*" serenaded the room. Then he went to the bear rug, sat next to La Vonne, and together they quietly watched the fire burn while grooving to Marvin.

Shortly after, the music changed to Marvin's "*Let's Get It On.*" While grooving to the words, all La Vonne could think of doing was getting it on with Jay. Her body was beginning to truly realize what it had missed while being locked up. These feelings were causing her womanhood to become wet, while also feeling comfortable and sexy. "The music sounds good. I can't remember the last time I heard Marvin's voice. Everything is so nice around here. Being

Mind Games

here will definitely make me forget about Jonathan."

To her surprise Jay put his arm around her. "Well, I have something else that'll make you forget about him." He kissed her, with her admiring every bit of his passion. The more they kissed, the more she wanted to undress his body that sported some long pants and a tee shirt. The more she desired his body the more he also admired hers. Soon La Vonne's robe was on the rug and Jay's clothes also disappeared, leaving them naked, as they enjoyed each others desires. The tender touches of his lips made her body hotter. Soon, she reached down and caressed his excited manhood. The touches of his manhood, held firmly in her hand felt ohhh so good, as his juices melted down his chocolate wand! Just to feel the strength of his inner-most valued asset was heavenly.

To satisfy her long awaited passion, she gently tasted the juices that flowed onto his warm body. It was a taste she hadn't sampled in years. It was also a taste she was quickly drawn too, every inch of its flow. While in her ecstasy, she took her time, while together they enjoyed every minute of their pleasure. While La Vonne enjoyed the juices that flowed from his manhood, he tasted and enjoyed the passion that flowed from her garden of paradise. Together, they became one! And just when she didn't think things could get any better, they did!

"Ohhhhhh, ahhhhhh!" Were the sounds coming from her mouth as she moaned from the softness of his naked body inside of hers.

"Ohhhhhhh, you feel so good. I've been wanting to make love to you for a long time," Jay responded to the passionate touches he felt from her as she stroked his body with hers.

"I've been wanting you even more," She seductively

responded, wanting to make sure that this moment happened before fate put a stop to it.

The more they stroked each others bodies with great passion and strength, the more they wanted each other. The more he kissed every inch of her neck and naked breast, caused their bodies to become hotter with passion. This feeling caused his manhood to rise to higher levels then it had ever reached, while her womanhood got hot and wet like a steamy sauna on a hot summer day. Just as they were getting ready to emerge deep within each other's soul, a continuous piercing sound was heard. "Beeppppppp!"

La Vonne's sensuous mood was instantly broken as she jumped up and looked around the room. "What was that?"

Jay jumped up laughing and ran to the kitchen. "It's the pot. The water for our hot chocolate is ready."

La Vonne laughed, "I don't need any hot chocolate now that I have you! You're all the heat I need!"

After her comment, Jay returned and continued where they left off, making love like it was the first time for both of them.

La Vonne's body was so hot. This was the first time she actually made love to a real man in over ten years. Jonathan was the only man she had previously spent passionate moments with, he was her first love. She felt so good in Jay's arms as his manhood gently rocked the inside of her garden of paradise that it caused her to scream, "Glory Hallelujah! Oh thank you, you feel so good!!!" she yelled with passion. He made sure to be gentle, because her virgin-like body revealed that it had been awhile. The feeling she felt in his arms while his manhood softly caressed the inside of her body made her feel real good. She had not felt like this in so long that she could hardly remember how good making love could actually be. This time, the physical caressing she was feeling from his warm body was so much better than how she felt when she made love to him in her dreams.

Jay was also happy about their passionate experience. Since the break up of his longtime girlfriend and the infrequent times they spent together romantically, along with the many lonely nights he spent alone, sharing his feelings with La Vonne was a welcoming feeling. In his opinion, being with La Vonne was the closest thing toward making love and satisfying his overly deprived needs. While they were enjoying the moment, little talk was going on, just actions of satisfying each others needs. It had been a long time since either of them had made love. So pleasing each other's passionate needs ranked most important. La Vonne had not made love in so long that she welcomed any sex she could get, especially with Jay. From what she had remembered while being with Jonathan, the only man she truly loved, she knew that Jay's true feelings of love for her didn't compare. She hoped that she would turn him on good enough that he would beg for more, so that this wouldn't be the last time they were together. But she enjoyed the feelings that were inside and tried to block out any others that came her way.

During this wonderful experience, La Vonne's mind was making love to Jay, yet her body was only having sex, as they went through the motions of passion of only satisfying each other's needs. She knew he didn't love her, so making love was not what they were doing, but she didn't care. The only thing she cared about was being in his arms and feeling his aroused manhood inside of her body. However, what her mind was feeling did not faze her body in the least. In her opinion, the hour long session of stroking and pleasing was definitely worth the wait of true desire and satisfaction. This was a night she would treasure forever! After their passion cooled down she laid in his arms with both of them smiling. "Boy that was good. I've been wanting to make love with you since the first day I laid eyes on you," she told him.

"I've been wanting to make love to you, too. I just didn't want you to get the wrong impression."

La Vonne looked at Jay, wondering what he was talking about. "What do you mean the wrong impression?"

"I didn't want you to think that I just wanted to have sex with you and that was it. I wanted to make love to you."
La Vonne smiled, "Well, you did an excellent job!"

Jay knew that he wasn't actually making love, but only having sex to satisfy his needs and desires. But he didn't want to spoil the mood, so he continued getting everything out of their experience that he could. "You didn't do so bad yourself," he joked. They began kissing again when suddenly the buzzer from the dryer sounded and interrupted them. "Well, I think I need to take you back home now. It's eleven o'clock. Your mother's gonna be calling here soon if I don't get you back home."

La Vonne laughed, "Yeah, you're right. I have a long day at work tomorrow. It's the busiest time of the season. But at least while I'm busy working I'll have something good to think about, which is you."

"I hope so." He gave her a quick kiss, got up, went to the dryer and gave La Vonne her warm clothes. She put her clothes on and he put on his. He took her back home, sealing the night away with a passionate kiss. "Good night," He said as they finished sealing their newfound love.

"My night will be very good thinking about you." She got out of the car and floated into the house while thinking about Jay.

Mind Games

CHAPTER THIRTEEN

The next day La Vonne went to work walking very slow, but smiling every aching inch of the way. Today, would be a good day, no matter what happened!

****

After a long, exhausting, and painful day at work, La Vonne was more than ready to go home. Gloria was in the car waiting so they could go home to eat, where Stacy and Jr. waited to dig into the food. La Vonne was tired, but happy. Gloria figured that her daughter's good mood was because of the time she spent with Jay last night.

"La Vonne, I didn't get a chance to ask you this morning about your night with Jay. I was so tired last night that I fell asleep before you got home. What time did you get back?" Gloria looked at La Vonne, who was smiling from ear to ear.

"I don't know what time I came home. I didn't look at the clock, but I had a very good evening." La Vonne didn't want to go into any details. She wanted to avoid any negative comments her mother was ready to give.

"So that's all? You just had a good evening, not a great evening? Girl, you're smiling much too much for it to have just been a good evening. Now tell me what really happened." Gloria continued driving, waiting for La Vonne to share more details.

"Momma that's all. I was just happy to be able to spend a little time with Jay talking. He was really nice and helpful. Since our talk, I don't think I'll be thinking about Jonathan anytime soon," she smiled as she thought about last night and why she had such a hard time walking all day long.

Toi Moore

****

After everyone finished eating dinner and was sitting at the kitchen table talking, the telephone rang. Stacy quickly got up and ran to answer the phone, "I'll get it," she yelled while trying to beat Jr. to the receiver.

"Is La Vonne home?" the male caller said.

"Hold on," Stacy said while getting her mom. "Mom, it's for you. It's a man," she teased and gave La Vonne the phone.

La Vonne smiled and took the phone, "Hello," she said with excitement after recognizing Jay's voice.

"Did you have a good day today?" he asked.

La Vonne had taken the cordless telephone to her room and closed the door for privacy. "Yeah, it was real good because I was thinking about you." She caressed her hand between her legs.

"Well, mine was equally good because I was thinking about you. In fact, I was thinking about you so much that I couldn't get any work done. My mind was not on work, it was focused totally on you!" He gleamed as he spoke to her while massaging his manhood and reminiscing about last night.

"Now that's music to my ears," she told him. As La Vonne listened to his conversation she became excited. She hoped that his comments meant they would be together again. She also hoped he wasn't calling to say goodbye, or that last night was a mistake.

"Are you glad to hear that I couldn't get any work done, or that I was thinking about you all day long?" he joked.

"What do you think silly? I guess that's why I looov...." La Vonne stopped dead in her tracks and continued by changing the subject, "You need to work so you can pay the mortgage on your

Mind Games

fancy condo and your fancy car. However, I am glad that I was on your mind. Believe me, you were also on my mind in more than ways than you can imagine. You were literally on my mind every step of the day because I was still feeling you inside of me as I took each step throughout the day." she laughed.

"I'm sorry. Are you alright? I was trying to be gentle." he felt bad.

"Yes, I'm alright, and yes you were gentle, so and please don't be sorry. That is a good kind of pain, especially when I enjoyed how the pain came. So, when can I come back and get some more of that kind of pain?" she blushed. La Vonne was waiting to hear Jay's response while hoping for the best.

"Well, we'll have to just see about that, won't we?"

Grinning from ear to ear, "We sure will. So when?" She boldly asked.

"Soon," he responded. "But first, I think you better recover from last night before soon comes around."

"Don't worry about me. I'll be alright." La Vonne was willing and ready to make love to Jay again. She didn't need to wait for anything, she wanted him now! She was ready and willing to accept him anyway she could have him, pain and all!

"Well, being the gentleman that I am, I say we wait, no matter how good you said you felt last night, I don't want you walking around in pain at work. Now, I don't mind the thought that you're thinking about me all day long, but I don't want you thinking about me while being in pain. Don't worry, our time will come soon enough, maybe sooner than you think. Because making love to you last night blew me away. I haven't experienced love-making like that from anyone! So coming back for more is definitely a must have in my books!" he told her with confidence.

"Well damn! When you say it like that, a must have is

definitely something I want to add to my books as well!" La Vonne and Jay laughed while enjoying their conversation into the late night hours as everyone slept.

CHAPTER FOURTEEN

It's been over a month since La Vonne has seen or heard from Jay. After thinking about La Vonne during the day at work, Jay decided to call her when he got home. "Is La Vonne there?" he asked Stacy who answered the telephone.

"Yes she is. Let me get her for you," she responded and put down the phone, "Mommm, telephone," she yelled and went back into her room.

"Do you have to yell so loud?" La Vonne asked before coming out of her room to pick up the phone. But Stacy was already in her room with the door closed. "Hello?"
"Hi La Vonne, this is Jay."

Suddenly she beamed with joy at the sound of his voice. "Hi, how are you doing?"
"I'm fine and you?"

"I'm fine, too. Where have you been hiding? I can't catch you on the phone. Every time I call your office your secretary tells me that you're busy or out of the office. What's going on?" La Vonne was becoming concerned about not hearing from Jay, fearing that a serious relationship between them was not going to happen.

"I haven't been hiding if that's what you're thinking, just working. There's a lot of people who need my help these days. I've just been busy. Besides, it hasn't been that long since I've spoken to you, it's only been a few weeks," Jay responded to La Vonne's comment.

Mind Games

After the first time they made love, they made it a point to see each other at least once a week to satisfy their needs. The weekly visits lasted about two weeks. Then every other week, eventually becoming once a month when they were able to spend quality time together.

As time went on, Jay's schedule didn't allow them to see each other as much as La Vonne wanted, which resulted in them not seeing or talking to each other in the last month. During the times spent together, they became very good friends in an intimate way. However, during those months no serious commitments were ever made.

"A few weeks, try over a month since I haven't heard anything from you."

"A month?" Jay asked with confusion. Time had passed by so fast that he didn't even realize the distance.

"Yes over a month. In fact, it's been 35 days since we've last seen or spoken to each other, and that's too long! Jay I need to see you more. It seems like we're seeing each other less and less. I'm starting to feel that you don't want to spend any time with me."

"I want to see you more, but I can't. You know that my time won't allow that to happen." He was trying to get her to see his point.

La Vonne frowned. She didn't want him to know that she was upset or desperate. "So, why did you call today?" she asked.

"I found the information you needed about Sonny and Sherri's daughter, Denise."

La Vonne's ears peeked with excitement. "What did you find out? Is she Jonathan's daughter?"

"No, Sherri was lying to you and Sonny. She told Sonny the same story she told you. She was just mad and wanted to get revenge."

"Why was she mad at me? I didn't do anything to her. I thought I was her friend." La Vonne's feelings were very hurt because of what Jay told her.

"She was mad at me for not wanting to get with her, so she took her anger out on you, that's all."

"Well thank God that's all. I've been a nervous wreck ever since she told me that story. Now that I know the truth I can get her out of my mind and get on with my life. I have too many other things to worry about besides worrying about her lies."

"That sounds like the best advice you could ever give yourself. So, how have things been going for you and Sandra? How's the store holding up?" he asked.

La Vonne knew that Jay was keeping the subject of them being together closed, so she went along with his plan. "Things have been going fine. It's a little slow right now since summer has passed. But that gives us a chance to catch up on other things and put some new touches on the store. It also gives us a chance to catch up on the latest fashion designs. Sandra is giving me more responsibilities now. She's leaving me in the store on my own quite a bit. Everything is working out very well. I'm very happy. Thanks again for getting me that job. It has really helped me and my family tremendously. It has also helped me get a new start on life and feel good about myself."

"That's good. I'm glad to hear that. Well, I gotta go now." Suddenly, his passionate concern turned into impatience and he didn't want to hear anything else she had to say.

"You gotta go already? You just called," La Vonne was shocked by his sudden mood swing.

"I know I just called, but I have a few cases I need to review

Mind Games

before I go to court tomorrow and I want to be prepared." You could hear the paper ruffle in the background while he was talking.

La Vonne was upset that he had to go so soon, but she had learned to understand and deal with the situation. Although his lack of spending quality time with her wasn't enough to satisfy her needs. She looked forward to the fun times they shared, especially the passionate moments when they made love. So she figured that she would approach him again about their meetings, since this would probably be the last time she would talk to him. "Okay, so when are we gonna get together again?"

"I'm not sure," he responded in a very insensitive way. "I'll call you when I get a chance," he told her while trying to hurry off the phone.

"Okay," she said in a sad and disappointed tone.

"Tell your Mom I said hi. I'll talk to you later, bye," he said. The phone went dead leaving La Vonne stunned while looking at the receiver in disbelief.

"Bye," she said to an empty phone line as she hung up. "I can't believe he just hung up on me. Damn him!" She walked to her room, closed the door, and cried in silence. As she laid in her dark room, she thought about what had just happened. "Jay doesn't want me. I need to just accept that. I should have accepted that a long time ago. All he wanted was to have sex with me, that's all. I was stupid for ever thinking that we could have a relationship. But now I know that it just isn't going to work." La Vonne had finally faced reality and was ready to go on with her life, without Jay.

As she laid on her bed feeling sorry for herself and Jay's lack of interest in her, she began thinking more about the cleaning man, Craig, who cleaned Sandra's store each week. In the beginning,

La Vonne kept her distance from Craig because he resembled Jonathan so much, but shorter. His strong resemblance made her also fear him and avoid his many advances and conversations. She often wondered if it was Craig whom she saw on those lonely dark nights and in those dark alleys. However, after being in his company several times over the months she felt more at ease and comfortable in his presence.

Craig was a nice man who stood about five feet nine inches tall. He wasn't the finest man alive, average looking and clean-cut. He had dark skin, a kinda chubby build, and short well-groomed black hair. He had two grown kids in their twenties who were raised with his ex-wife, whom he was still very close to. He lived alone in a small bachelor's apartment, which was a turnoff for most women he dated.

Craig was very attracted to La Vonne, giving her plenty of attention when she wouldn't shy away. Eventually she loved every bit of the attention he showed. However, she repeatedly resisted his advances because she felt that she had a real chance with Jay. Now she knew that things were not meant to be between her and Jay and that their relationship would never amount to the affection and attention she longed for, or the attention Craig was willing to give.

****

Stacy was at school eating her lunch alone when she was approached by a young man from school. "Hi, my name is Frank." Frank was the new kid on campus and stood over her with his lunch in his hands.

Stacy looked up at him and hesitantly responded, "Hi, I'm Stacy."

"I know," he said with confidence. "Can I sit next to you?"

Mind Games

he asked as he made his way next to her without waiting for her to respond.

"You know who I am? And how is that?" She was confused by his response and surprised by his forward approach.

"Yes. I've been watching you. You have P.E. during the same period that I have." Frank had been attracted to Stacy from the very first day he came on campus, but was too afraid to approach her. For some reason he got up enough nerve to speak to her today.

Stacy smiled at the handsome and polite young man with silky brown skin, brown eyes and curly brown hair. "Oh, so you've been watching me?"

He shook his head in agreement as he ate his lunch.

"So tell me Frank, that is your name, right?"

"Yes, it is," he smiled, wondering if she was just playing hard to get.

"So tell me, why have you been watching me, and what have you noticed while you've been watching?" she questioned his motives. She was used to Teddy's smooth personality and approach. She didn't want to fall prey to anyone else who was a smooth operator like Teddy.

"Well, I haven't noticed a lot about you, especially since I've only been at this school for two weeks. But I've noticed that you're a nice young lady."

"How have you figured all of that out in just two weeks? And why am I just now finding out about you?"

"Well, you're just now finding out about me because I've stayed in the distance. I'm actually shy, but I got up enough nerve to finally come and talk to you." She was flattered by his comments. "When I'm in gym I hear the guys talk about the girls in your class and when your name comes up, they always say nice things about you.

After hearing how nice you are and how your old boyfriend did a number on you, I started paying closer attention to you. I thought, 'She's too nice and pretty for a guy to treat you the way Teddy treated you.' I noticed how you mainly eat lunch alone, or sometimes with one of your friends. I also noticed how you don't seem to be a busy body like a lot of the other girls around here."

Stacy was blushing over his comments. "Ohhhhh I see, Mr. Shy Guy got up enough nerve to talk to a nice girl like me?" she joked. Stacy was enjoying her conversation with this handsome stranger. "Well tell me Frank, why do you think I stay to myself or just with my one friend?" She wanted him to spill the beans on what else he knew about her and what rumors were floating around campus. She wanted to see exactly where he was coming from and what his intentions were. Ever since she broke up with Teddy her guard had been up. She hadn't allowed any guy to get close enough to hurt her feelings again.

"I figured that your girlfriend has a boyfriend who she eats with and you end up eating alone. Am I right?" The friend Frank was talking about was Kathy. Since her breakup with Doug, Kathy and Jr. have made their relationship official and spent most of their lunches together. They'd become one of the hottest couples on campus and are doing very well. Kathy put Doug totally out of her life since her and Jr. became an item.

"I guess you're right. So tell me Frank, since you think you know me so well and you claim to be so shy, how did you get enough nerve to come over here and talk to me?"

"Like I said I've been watching you and I've also asked a few of the guys about you. But don't worry, they've only told me good things about you. Now when guys say good things about girls, the girl

Mind Games

has to be nice, and I'm looking for a nice girl like you."

Stacy's mouth fell to the ground. "You're what?" She was stunned by his blunt comment, but flattered.

"I said I'm looking for a nice girl and you seem to be the girl I'm looking for, that is unless you're already taken." Frank was hoping that Stacy wouldn't disappoint him. He was also hoping that today was his lucky day to make a love connection.

"What if I was," she teased.

"I'll wait because I think you're worth waiting for."

She thought, "Ummm, he's cute, he's a gentleman, he knows what he wants, and he isn't afraid to ask for it. This can't be for real." She addressed his comment, "For your information I'm not taken. I'm single and free and I'm enjoying every bit of my freedom."

"Well, if you don't mind I'd like to spend a little of your free time with you." He smiled, gleaming ear to ear, hoping for the best.

Stacy also gleamed. She was speechless after hearing his last line. She thought, "He didn't waste any time for someone who says they're shy."

"So, can I spend a little of your free time with you? Can we start with you being my date for the Homecoming Dance in two weeks?" Frank held up two tickets to the dance for Stacy to see.

"You already have the tickets?" She was surprised when she saw the tickets in his hand and knew that his offer was serious, but she didn't know how to answer him. She didn't have a date for the dance and wasn't sure if she wanted to be escorted by Frank. He was a total stranger, although she appreciated his offer.

"You see them in my hand so please don't make me waste them because I don't want to go with anyone else but you." Frank was really trying to make brownie points with her.

Stacy shook her head and laughed at his plea, "Let me think about it first. Everything is happening too fast. I can't just say yes, I just met you. You'll have to give me a few days to think about it."

"Can you tell me tomorrow? I don't want you to think about it too long and say no. Besides, we only have two weeks to get everything together."

"Get what together?"

"To get ourselves together so that everyone in the room envies us. You know, you may have to get a new dress and I know I need a new suit. So, what do you say? Can you tell me by tomorrow?" After talking to Stacy over lunch, Frank knew that she was definitely the girl he wanted to spend time with, so he pleaded with her to be his date.

"Okay, tomorrow then," she blushed.

"Good." The bell rang for class to start. "I'll meet you back here tomorrow for lunch and I'll be waiting for your answer and please don't let me down, unless you want to see a brother get on his knees and beg, and I will do that for you," he said with a smile of confidence.

Stacy smiled back, "Let you down? I don't even know you, and I definitely don't want you to beg in public." She gathered her belongings to go to class while Frank helped.

"Can I call you tonight?" he asked with hope. "That way we can get to know each other a little better before you give me your answer?"

"You don't waste any time do you?" she blushed, but loved his boldness.

"No, not when I have a pretty lady like you standing across from me who's as nice and sweet as everyone says." By the looks Stacy gave Frank, he was sure he was impressing her.

Mind Games

"Sure you can call me." Stacy took out a piece of paper, wrote down her telephone number, and happily gave it to him.

He looked at it and smiled. "Thanks. I'll call you around nine."

"Okay, I'll talk to you tonight. Bye."

"Bye," he said and they each walked away from the table smiling while going to their next class.

****

Later that evening the telephone rang. "Hello!" Stacy said with excitement, hoping it was Frank.

"Is Stacy there?" the masculine voice asked.

"Hi, this is me." Stacy's voice got soft as she blushed, knowing that the caller was Frank. Stacy took the cordless phone to her room where she could have some privacy.

"How are you doing?" he asked.

"I'm fine."

"Have you made up your mind about the dance yet?"

"No, it's not tomorrow yet." she laughed. "I told you that I would give you my answer tomorrow."

"Okay, I'll wait," he smiled while teasing her, knowing she wasn't going to answer that soon.

As the two talked, Stacy felt more comfortable with her new friend. She began feeling like they had known each other for years. She even felt comfortable talking about her mother to Frank, which was also something he learned from his classmates. After talking to him for over two hours, she gave him her answer, "Yes, I'll go to the dance with you." Stacy wasn't used to a guy being so polite. This was the type of treatment she never got from Teddy. Frank was different, which allowed her to possibly take another chance on love.

Frank was surprised by her sudden answer, especially since they weren't even talking about the dance when she told him her answer. "What did you say?" he asked.
"I said yes, I'll go to the dance with you," she blushed.

He smiled so hard that he exposed all his shiny white teeth. He was so happy that she accepted his invitation. "Good. I'm glad. So, tell me what color dress you'll wear and I'll make sure to match my shirt and tie to what you're wearing."

"Okay, that sounds good." Stacy was happy that Frank had her best interest in mind. At that moment she felt that this was the beginning of something special.

****

Two weeks had passed and Stacy and Frank became closer than ever. They talk on the telephone for hours every night and Frank has visited Stacy's house a few times to meet her family. It's the night of the Homecoming dance at their school. As they walked into the dance hall, they immediately drew attention. While making their entrance, everyone's mouth fell open. Over the last two weeks they've made it a point to keep their relationship a secret. They wanted to keep things to themselves to avoid any problems. They also wanted to see the expressions of everyone when they came to the dance as a couple.

Stacy learned within the last two weeks how it felt to be treated kindly by a man. She learned how a man could be a friend, while not being a lover in order to be classified as his lady. She also learned how to feel relaxed with a man in a way she was never able to do with her first love. Frank respected her and made sure that she always came first.

"Hey Sis', you look nice," Jr. said as he kissed Stacy's forehead as he and Kathy passed the couple in the dance hall. "Girl you do look good! In fact, you both look good," Kathy said. "Thanks," Stacy and Frank said.

Since Jr. left the house before Stacy was fully dressed, he was impressed with how nice and happy his sister looked. Stacy was wearing a long yellow silk dress with white lace around the neckline. She had white baby's breath in her hair which was pulled up in a bun on top of her head, with *Shirley Temple Curls* coming down on her forehead and on the back of her neck. Frank bought her a yellow corsage that she was wearing on her wrist.

Frank was wearing a black suit with a yellow shirt that highlighted Stacy's dress. His hair was freshly cut and he walked through the room like he was the luckiest man alive, with Stacy proudly secured to his arm. Together they looked like the perfect couple.

"Looks like you guys have all the eyes glued on you tonight," Jr. said. "I'm happy for you," he whispered in his little sister's ear, knowing how Teddy made her feel. Jr. shook Frank's hand and smiled, granting his approval. "Thanks man for lookin' out for my little sister, she seems to like you a lot."

Frank gave Jr. a brother's hand shake of thanks. "It's my pleasure. I like her, too," Frank responded with Stacy blushing and Kathy smiling.

"Well, we'll see you guys on the dance floor," Jr. smiled and gave Stacy another kiss on her forehead and took Kathy to dance. "Yeah, we'll see you guys on the dance floor." Kathy repeated.

Stacy and Frank soon joined them, ignoring all the watchful

eyes, including Teddy's, who was standing alone in a corner on crutches still recovering from his attack. He was trying to act unconcerned while Doug was by his side, alone as well, trying to act like he wasn't jealous of Kathy and Jr.

Stacy and Frank danced into the late night hours. Later, he delivered Stacy home where he walked her to her front door, gave her a sweet goodnight kiss and went home. He did not expect anything from her besides having a good time. She walked into the house feeling on cloud nine, happy that she gave love another try. Kathy was also happy that Jr. became her man, treating her the way a lady should be treated, with respect!

CHAPTER FIFTEEN

After another month of not hearing from Jay, La Vonne finally accepted Craig's offer of going out on a date. When he came to pick her up she was surprised and embarrassed when she walked outside and saw his car. The twenty year old dinosaur looked like it had been across the world several times and back. Craig's car looked so old that she was afraid they wouldn't make the round trip on their date. His car was a far cry from the shiny black BMW Jay drove.

She could tell that his American made car needed plenty of work performed on the smog system because of the black smoke that followed behind them as they drove down the street. The car had a vinyl sunroof top that had dried up from the years of sitting outside in the sun and rain. The sidings on the sunroof had rusted, causing it to no longer open. The only air that circulated from the sunroof came from the cracks that stretched throughout its surface. Craig didn't make a lot of money like Jay did, so taking her to the finest restaurants were out of his budget. He was taking her to a small restaurant that was nice by his standards and within his price range.

While en route to the restaurant, La Vonne made very little conversation with Craig, only answering his questions with one word responses. She tried to make the best of her ride by enjoying the songs on the radio that went in and out of tune due to the missing antenna. The song, *My, My, My,* by *Johnny Gill,* came across the airwaves and softened the mood. La Vonne smiled while reminiscing to the words. Craig also smiled, but aimed his smile directly at La Vonne with hope and love on his mind. La Vonne noticed his silly grin and frowned. She thought, "I know I look good," looking at herself in the side view mirror with confidence, "but I don't know why you're looking at me like that. I sure hope you doesn't think your getting a little somethin' somethin' from me tonight." She looks at him with an evil glare, but remains silent.

Once in front of the restaurant, La Vonne realized that it was far below the standards she was used to having with Jay. She looked around and frowned. "This is nice," she said sarcastically under her breath as they searched for a parking space. The low status of the restaurant didn't have the valet parking privileges she had also grown accustomed to having. Once they found a parking space several rolls away from the restaurant in the full Friday night lot, they had to walk a few minutes in order to get to the front door.

After entering, La Vonne noticed that everyone was casually dressed. She felt over dressed and out of place wearing her silk white pant suit and black patent leather shoes with the purse to match. She knew that Craig was fully aware of her high standards with Jay. Those standards were why she gave Craig such a hard time before allowing him the opportunity to take her out on a date. Therefore, she expected much more from him. She assumed that he would have tried harder to impress her, beginning with renting a car that had class.

Since La Vonne had high expectations for Craig's choice in restaurants, she wasn't in the mood to talk, making her company very poor. Craig sensed her low disposition and tried to make the best of their night, knowing that she was used to much more, along with knowing that he wasn't her first choice in a date. He knew that she was used to the taste and budget of her rich lawyer friend. However, he was happy just knowing that she had finally accepted his offer of going out. He was determined to show her a good time. He was also determined to show her that a man with a low budget was fully capable of being a good date.

"So, what would you like to eat?" he asked, as La Vonne looked at the menu that included a few simple steaks and chicken dinners. She had been used to eating fancy steak and lobster dinners in restaurants that were candle-lit and surrounded by dim lights. This brightly lit restaurant was far from the look, style, or menu selection her taste buds were accustomed to.

"I'm not sure, can I have a few more minutes?" she asked with a sarcastic tone as she continued to stare at the menu. As she sat at the table, she wished that it was Jay sitting across from her instead of Craig. However, she was willing to settle for what she could get, which was a free meal from someone who had begged for her company for months. She almost felt obligated to go out with him since he had begged for so long. She dealt with the situation the best she could.

Craig looked over his menu, but already knew what he wanted. Due to the 'buy one, get one free' coupons that came in the mail, he visited this restaurant regularly and took the free meal home for

Mind Games

leftovers, or for his next day's lunch.

La Vonne continued looking at the menu. It was as if she was waiting for something to jump off the pages and bite her, when Craig finally decided to make conversation, "You look very nice tonight," he told her.

"Thank you," she casually said while still glued to the menu, avoiding him and his conversation.

There weren't many items on the menu to select from so Craig didn't understand why she was taking so long to decide. "Is there a problem?" he asked.

"No, I'm just not sure what I want," she said with an attitude.

"Well, I can help you decide if you'd like." He was trying to be as patient as he could be with her sassy attitude, while still remaining a gentleman. However, her uninterested attitude was making his job very hard.

"I can find something on my own. Just give me another minute will you? I don't see what the big rush is all about," she responded in a very mean and unattractive tone. The restaurant was so busy and crowded that after waiting over fifteen minutes, the waitress had still not come to their table.

After waiting for five more minutes the waitress finally came, "Can I take your order?" she asked with anticipation. You could tell that she was in a hurry and only wanted to do her job quickly, with very little care, while gathering the many tips that would be left behind.

Craig looked at La Vonne to see if she was ready to order. She looked at the waitress and responded, "I'd like a steak dinner, cooked well-done. I'd also like a baked potato with everything on it and a salad with thousand island dressing." She slammed her menu down on the table.

The waitress looked at Craig for his order. "I'd like the same, please," he responded. Their steak and oversized baked potatoes with the works were his favorites.

"What would you like to drink?" the waitress asked.

"White wine please for me and the lady," he casually said with a smile.

When he ordered the wine, La Vonne suddenly saw Jonathan in Craig's eyes and lost it. "OH HELL NO! No wine at this table! I don't drink alcohol and I don't want anyone I'm with to drink alcohol," she fumed out loud while making a scene, then giving him a look that would kill.

Craig's looks often favored Jonathan's so much, that La Vonne often lost it when talking to him when they were at work, which caused her to normally avoid his conversations. But since she was sitting right in his face and relied on him to give her a ride home, made it hard for her to ignore him or walk away.

La Vonne's response and tone caused Craig and the waitress to look at her in shock. "Well, what would you like to drink?" he asked with caution.

"I'd like some iced tea, please." She crossed her arms and looked at him with an attitude to see what he would order.

"I'd like the same, please," he responded. The waitress quickly left their table to avoid any additional embarrassing moments.

After she was gone, Craig looked at La Vonne and shook his head in disappointment. "What's the matter with you? Did I do something wrong?"

"No, you didn't do anything wrong. I just don't like for people to drink while they're in my company. That's what started the drama in my marriage. Drinking played a large part of why I went to prison, that's all." She sat with folded arms and a tight jawed expression.

Mind Games

"Well I didn't know all that. You've never shared the details of your marriage or what put you in prison with me. But now that I know, I can understand and I'll make sure to never make that mistake again. But don't take your bad marriage, going to prison, or the fact that I can't wine and dine you like your lawyer friend can, out on me!" Craig told her with force. "You knew I couldn't wine and dine you like Jay can when you agreed to go out with me. But now you're looking around this restaurant like it isn't good enough for you. Maybe this was a bad idea for us to go out. If you don't want to eat here we can go somewhere else, or if you'd like I can just take you home." Craig was willing to cut his losses before things got worse and take her home to avoid more embarrassing moments.

Suddenly his words shocked La Vonne back into reality, hitting her like a bolt of lightening. "I'm so sorry!" She felt embarrassed by the way she had been acting. She was not raised to act disrespectful. She knew better. Living large and being wined and dined at the finest restaurants in town were not things she was accustomed to, unless she was with Jay, on the few occasions he had time to spend with her. "You're right, I have been rude. I don't know what got into me, but I'm sorry. Let's start over because I do want to be here with you tonight, and I'm thankful that you still wanted to go out with me after all the months I said no. So, will you please accept my apology? Can we start over?" she pleaded.

Craig looked into La Vonne's big brown eyes and smiled, "Of course I forgive you. And of course we can start over. We just got off to a bad start. Let's make the rest of the evening enjoyable."

"Okay, I can do that," she said as they smiled, knowing that the worse was in the past. Their food came and they ate and laughed the rest of the evening while enjoying each other's company.

Toi Moore

****

La Vonne and Craig have grown closer over the last few months. They have allowed their friendship to blossom into a caring and serious relationship. La Vonne appreciates the time Craig spends with her, time Jay never seemed to have. She's happy that there's a possibility for her to actually find true love with Craig. There isn't anything that he won't do to please her or her family. The little money he has left over after paying his bills he gives to La Vonne if she has any additional expenses that she can't handle. He also let's her borrow his car when she has errands to run and if Gloria needs to use her own car.

Craig spends so much time with La Vonne and her family that everyone likes him very much. Gloria looked forward to his visits because she knew that he would fix what's needed to beautify her home. Stacy and Jr. liked him because he treated their mother nice. La Vonne liked him because of the special way he treats her and cares for her family. He cares for her like no man ever cared. When she's with Craig, she always feels special and safe. Since she's been with him, La Vonne has learned that happiness comes in all shapes, sizes and income levels.

Since La Vonne and Craig's feelings have grown very strong, he's always at her house helping any way he can. Over the last few months that she has been serious with him, La Vonne has privately accepted him as her man. However, she hasn't admitted her thoughts to him. She needed to know within her heart that she was doing the right thing before she admitted her true feelings. With all the attention and care she's received from Craig, has allowed herself to fall deeper in love.

Mind Games

After one night after a dinner date, La Vonne went over to Craig's place where they cuddled up under a blanket and sat in front of the television while nibbling on some popcorn. Suddenly Craig began to open up his feelings to La Vonne, "I never told you this, but since we're getting so close I should tell you how I feel." La Vonne didn't know what to expect from his comment so she listened as he continued, "I always felt bad for you when I heard that you went to prison for killing your husband. You never should have gone because he never should have laid a hand on you. In fact, no man should ever lay a hand on a woman to make their point."

As he talked she continued to listen. She was unsure as to why he was bringing up the subject of her past, especially since they were having such a nice evening. She knew that he was aware that her past was something she wanted to forget and didn't care to talk about. However, she remained quiet as he continued, "I grew up in an abusive family. I can still remember the nights when I would lay in my bed and hear my father beating my mother. I was around three years old when the fighting first started. As I got older the beatings became more regular and worse. The police wouldn't even come to our house when our mother called for help. They would tell her to handle things herself. One time the police had the nerve to call our house several hours after my mother's original call and asked if everything was alright. Hell, she could have been dead by then. I hated my father for that, but I was too young to do anything about it until one day when I was in high school. Me and my younger brother came home from school and saw my father beating my mother and we snapped. We pulled him away from her and began beating him like there was no tomorrow. Our two younger sisters held our mother in a corner while we beat him. Me and my brother could hear our mother screaming and pleading for us to let him go. She told us over and over that he didn't mean to hurt her and that it would never happen again. However, we had all heard that story before and had enough of his abuse, along with the repeated apologies he made in the past. So while my sisters and mother watched in horror, we all cried as we gave him a taste of his own torture."

La Vonne could not believe her ears, but remained quiet as he wore a hardened, spaced-out look on his face and continued, "We beat him so bad that we could hear the neighbors in our apartment building cheering us on through the paper-thin walls. Some of them were even peeking through our open front door cheering us on as we beat him down, robbing any manhood he claimed. He screamed and cried like a baby, but that didn't faze us a bit. It was finally his turn to see how it felt to get beat. Ten minutes later, which seemed an eternity, we were done. Our mother had finally broke away from the clutches of my sisters and pulled us away from him. He was bloody and bruised, the same way he normally left her when he was done. Me and my brother proudly wore the blood of our father all over our hands and body. I guess it was a good thing that our mother pulled us apart because the adrenalin that was stored up in our bodies just wouldn't allow us to stop on our own."

"We noticed the visible bruises left on our fist from hitting him so hard, which lasted for at least a week. But the satisfaction of giving him a taste of his own medicine was worth every painful mark we bared. The only thing he could do was lay on the floor and beg for us to stop while calling on the help of God. He called on the very same God he never mentioned in his entire life. The same God he often beat my mother for as she prayed for mercy. If it weren't for our mother stopping us, we probably would have killed him. After we were stopped,

Mind Games

we watched him continue to beg for mercy. The sound of his pitiful voice made us sick. We picked him up off the floor and dragged him to the front door. We opened the door and threw him out of our house like he was a piece of garbage and dared him to return. Yes, he was our father, but we could no longer allow him to hurt our mother.

Craig continued to reminisce back to the day when he and his brother declared themselves the heads of their household. "As our father laid outside the front door of our apartment, the neighbors clapped and cheered. Over the years, they, too, had listened to the many beatings our mother suffered from the powerful blows of his hands. As he looked at us from outside our front door, unable to stand or walk while again begging for forgiveness, we closed the door to block out his cries. Several of the neighbors dragged him down the two long flights of stairs by his arms, allowing his badly beaten body to feel every bump and bang until he reached the sidewalk, where they left him laying alone on the ground. We didn't have a car so I don't know where he went after that. The only thing we cared about was that he was gone. That was the last time we ever saw our father. The saddest part about the entire experience is that we never regretted anything we did to him, nor did we care if he was dead or alive. The only thing we cared about was that our mother was safe, and that we didn't have to see or hear her ever get beat again." After his confession, Craig positioned his head in his hands and cried like a baby.

La Vonne was speechless to his admission. Listening to him cry caused her to cry. She couldn't believe that he had shared something so personal with her about his family. "Why did you tell me this story?" she asked while wiping away his tears with her hand.

"Because I love you and I want you to love me too. I also told you because I don't want you to ever be afraid of me. I want you to know that I would never put my hands on you to hurt you or any other woman. It's just not right! It's not right at all!" He continued to cry.

Suddenly more tears flowed down La Vonne's cheeks as she held his head to her chest for comfort. At that very moment she felt closer to him than she had ever felt to any man in her life. She knew that Craig was indeed the man she'd been searching for. He was the man who made her happy while also making her feel safe. He was also the man who was now a very important part of her life. She knew that he would be there for better or worse. She also knew she could trust him with her life. Over the past few months that they had been a couple, La Vonne learned that fulfilling a person's needs could be simple and not materialistic. She also learned how pure love felt without making love.

After listening to Craig's confession La Vonne knew she was in love. As she held him in her arms he slowly raised his head and they began to kiss. This time the kiss was different. It was filled with more passion than ever before. Their hands became locked into each other's with desire. Slowly, Craig laid La Vonne down on the carpeted floor and continued kissing her with great passion. The thought of making love had laid heavy on both of their minds. Except they vowed to wait until they both felt that it was the right time and the right thing to do. La Vonne did not want to just have sex and get her feelings hurt if things didn't work out, she wanted to make love with someone who would cherish her and her feelings. Craig also wanted to wait until the time was right because he didn't want La Vonne sleeping with him while wanting to be with Jay. He wanted her mind and body to be all his and his alone. With the realization of Jay being history, La Vonne was ready and willing to accept the love and care Craig longed to share with her. She was now ready to admit her true feelings and call

Mind Games

him her man and lover.

As La Vonne raised up from the passion that raced within their bodies, she shared a little news of her own, "Craig, you've been asking me to be your lady for months but I've always refused. Well, tonight I accept. Tonight, I say yes to being your lady and making love with you!" They kissed passionately with Craig smiling like a little kid in a toy store.

After several lonely nights of taking cold showers, Craig was amazed and ecstatic by her confession. He had patiently waited months for this moment to finally come, which marked the first day he set eyes on La Vonne after walking into the dress shop seeing her work with Sandra. Not wanting to waste any more time he immediately began to undress. He pulled his clothes off so fast that one would swear he was running a marathon. La Vonne laughed at his sudden reaction, but understood because she felt the same way. So she followed his lead and began throwing off her clothes as fast as she could.
Together, they were acting like two horny teenagers who were about to make love for the very first time. It had been months since La Vonne had been with Jay in a sexual way. Therefore, she welcomed the soft and warm touches of a man's naked body on top of hers. Now that her passion was truly dedicated to Craig, she was more than eager for what was about to happen. After they were fully undressed, they grabbed each others naked body with enormous desire and began kissing every inch in sight.

"Ohhhhhhhhhhhhhhhhhh, Ahhhhhhhhhh," were the heated sounds that came from their mouths which overpowered the sounds of the television set.

"Ohhhhhhh La Vonne, I've wanted you from the very first day I saw you, you were so beautiful. Now, when I look at you laying here beside me you're even more beautiful than I could have ever imagined," Craig told her as he continued caressing her soft body.

"Well, now I want you!" she responded and laid on top of him, rubbing her naked body softly on top of his. La Vonne caressed Craig in areas where only the softness of a woman could offer comfort. He felt so good from her emotion as she gently caressed his manhood held firmly in her hand. She passionately sampled the juices from his magic wand as they flowed onto his body. He was in heaven as he enjoyed the emotions she was devoting to him, making him feel like a king. He now knew that waiting for La Vonne had been the best thing he could have ever done in his life. Making love to her topped his list of "Things Most Important To Do In Your Life." At that moment, he was finally assured that she was the most important thing in his life.

She took his manhood and positioned it inside of her secret garden. He helped her guide his magic wand to the proper places of excitement, while holding her tightly with all of his strength as they rode the waves of love together. While she slowly and passionately rocked his naked body, he rocked hers with full force wearing nothing but a smile as he enjoyed his ride. This was a journey he had waited a lifetime to travel and she was the woman he had waited a lifetime for. Together they rode with the emotions that were locked deep within, releasing any tension that may have been held deep inside.

La Vonne moaned with great intensity. Making love to Craig was totally different than it was with Jay. She noticed that when she made love to Jay, there was no passion that came from his inner soul, only the feelings of his body being sexually satisfied. However with Craig there was affection vibrating deep within his soul. There was a feeling of togetherness, a perfect oneness. A feeling of knowing that this was meant to be! La Vonne had finally found her soul mate, the man she wanted to be with for the rest of her life. Soon there were no words being spoken, only the sounds of passion that rang in the air as they made love to each other for the very first time.

Craig slowly rolled La Vonne's naked body onto the rug where he gently caressed it with his hands and mouth. Their energy grew much stronger, making her butterscotch body feel like it was quickly melting within his hands. His tongue moistened areas of her body she never knew could ever get wet without her help. He was in no rush, time was totally on their side as they enjoyed the moments of ecstasy. As he slowly positioned her toes inside of his mouth, her body quivered with excitement as his tongue massaged each of them one at a time. His tongue maneuvered itself up her leg, eventually arriving to the inner portions of her warm thighs, where she laid with great anticipation to his motions.

As he began to taste the sweet juices of her nature, he explored every inch of her garden while rolling his tongue in a motion of complete satisfaction. She screamed, "Ohhhhhhhhhhhh hell yeah! I feel so damn good!" she confessed with her head positioned backward where he came up for air and gently kissed each inch. He journeyed back down to her garden, where he explored even more, allowing his tongue to travel deeper, almost to the point of no return. "Ohhhhhhhhhh yessssssss! That feels sooooooooooooo damn good," she moaned to the touches of his tongue.

With her entire body motioning complete pleasure, he continued his journey, putting a big smile of satisfaction on both of their faces. The more he tasted her body, the better the juices began to mature, savoring every enjoyable moment. The more he enjoyed the feelings, the more her body felt one with his soul.

Later, his tongue traveled to her raised nipples where its warm sensation rotated in small circles, tasting every inch, nice and slow. He journeyed to the top of her head and caressed her moistened tongue with his. Shortly after, he placed his manhood deep inside of her body, arousing it in ways she never experienced. "Oh God!" she intensely moaned while totally enjoying every strong and muscular inch of what she was feeling. At this very moment La Vonne felt amazingly good, like she was floating in heaven! The passion within her body made her quiver and cry because she never felt this good before. She could finally say that this was true love because it felt so damn good!

With their hearts racing toward satisfaction and the juices of their bodies melting into each others, they reached their climates and exploded with true ecstasy! "Ahhhhhhhhhhhhhhhhhhh!!!!" they moaned out loud. Their breathe was taken away by the excitement of the experience as they reached a level of passion they never expected. At that very moment their bodies became one, which allowed their love to shine brighter than ever before.

After they finally came up for air, they were exhausted and dripping in sweat. Craig grabbed the blanket that was on the rug and covered their naked and trembling bodies as they laid in each other's arms hugging, happy and content. As La Vonne laid in his arms, they soon fell asleep, both wearing big smiles, feeling totally satisfied.

CHAPTER SIXTEEN

While La Vonne laid in peace, sleeping in the arms of the man she now loves, she began to dream. Her thoughts took her back to a devastating place while she wondered if she actually killed Jonathan or not. She was reliving that deadly night as she tossed in her sleep. "Oh

Mind Games

my God, did I actually kill him or was his death a cover up?" she wondered in fear as her thoughts relived each and every horrifying moment of that night.

Her mind was trying to somehow put an end to the guilty thoughts that had lingered deep inside for years. It was trying to justify whether or not Jonathan was actually dead or alive by again reliving each dreadful moment, step by step. "I took the gun and shot him. I saw him fall off the couch and onto the floor where he was covered in blood. After that, I ran out the house to escape what I had just done. The police showed up, which was something that never happened in the past. The only thing I saw after getting in the police car were my kids crying for me while standing at the front porch of our house as a policeman put his arms around them."

As La Vonne's dream became deeper in thought, she explored more of her nightmare. Her thoughts swayed with fear as she continued remembering, "Wait, wait! I've seen the policeman who was on the porch with my kids before. I saw him a few weeks ago with Jonathan. He brought Jonathan home one night, and before Jonathan got out the car they were talking with their heads close together. I'll never forget that night because it was beautiful. Me and the kids were sitting on the front pouch when they pulled up. The full moon brightened the entire nighttime sky. It was a very clear night and the car was dark, but I do remember seeing the face of that stranger when the light came on inside of the car. When I asked Jonathan who the guy was, he simply told me that it was his friend and quickly dropped the subject. When the guy smiled, I saw his gold teeth in the front of his mouth and his big diamond earrings in both of his ears. He also had a large tattoo on the left side of his arm that resembled a dragon, which is why I remember him so well. I thought that the tattoo was rather large, filling his entire upper arm. He had parked on the wrong side of the street so I could see the tattoo very well."

Her thoughts continued to race as her mind worked overtime, keeping her at the day that changed her life forever. "After the police put me in the car, the policemen on my front porch smiled at me. When he smiled, I could see his gold teeth shining in the night. I also saw the bottom portion of his tattoo that hung below his short sleeve shirt he was wearing. Then he put his hands around my kids and walked them back into the house as they drove me away. Oh my God, oh my God! I was set up! Jonathan is not dead! His friend, who is also a policeman, set me up so Jonathan could get out of our marriage. They didn't want me to reveal all of his dirty secrets of how he sold drugs and to whom he sold them to. His friends wanted me out of his life for their business sake. I made their business difficult and Jonathan threatened, on many occasions, to take my kids away from me if I didn't stay out of his business. And I'm sure he told them everything. He knows that my kids are the only thing in life that I truly care about besides momma. He knew that if he took them away from me I would lose my mind and he was trying to do just that, that's it! He wanted me out of his life for good!" According to her theory, La Vonne was finally figuring out the entire story. However, her mind won't stop at the one theory, it continued, becoming more intense.

"Damn! I didn't even think about the fact that the bullet's in the gun weren't real. I saw him put the gun under the couch the same night he came home with his shady gold toothed friend. He told me not to touch it and kinda smiled after telling me. I bet I shot him with a blank gun with fake blood and not a real gun with bullets. Then he purposely started a fight with me, knowing that I would react after seeing the gun. To make things worst, he knew that if he hit Jr. I

Mind Games

wouldn't put up with his abuse and shoot him with the gun. He already knew that I was tired of his shit and that hitting one of my kids would push me to my final breaking point, which is what he wanted to do! That bastard set me up!" she fumed as she tossed and turned in her sleep.

"I'm sure that his so-called police friend, who was standing on the porch with my kids, took him away from the scene of the crime after the police car drove me away. They probably took me away and charged me with his murder as a favor to Jonathan in exchange for selling them more drugs. I wonder who's body they did find at my house, because I was surely locked up for killing somebody. Jonathan's probably been hiding all this time. When he found out that I was getting out of prison, which wouldn't be hard to find out if he had friends working in the system, and that I had survived without losing my mind, he's been coming around here trying to scare me to cause me to lose it. He's only playing mind games with me, that's all that's happening. He wants me to completely lose my mind so that he can have the victory. But I won't let him do that to me, no I won't! I won't give him the satisfaction of proving that he still has the power over me, even thought he's suppose to be dead. Whether I'm right or wrong about killing him, I have to stay strong for my kids, they need me and I need them and that's what's really important, even if it means that I get professional help. I have to be there for them. I can't let them down again."

It was the next morning when La Vonne's thoughts began to calm down and she faintly woke up. She still didn't know for sure if Jonathan was dead or alive, all she knew was that she needed to get some help. She was ready and willing to get the help she needed to go on with her new life. She knew that she had to put an end to her nightmare that had haunted her all of these years of wondering if Jonathan was dead or alive. She had a good man in her life now, two wonderful teenaged children and a mother who stuck by her through thick and thin. She had several reasons of why she deserved to live a happy and healthy life. She had finally realized that the past had to be left in the past and she could no longer live her life in fear. As she slowly awakened, she was unfamiliar with her surroundings, so she quietly looked around the room and heard a familiar voice.

"Lord, please forgive me! Please take back all the mean things I ever said. It's been over ten years now, please make things better! I'm so sorry, I just want us to be happy again. It's been so long since I've seen her eyes open. Oh Lord, it's been so long since I've held her in my arms and told her that I love her."

La Vonne's eyes were having a hard time focusing. It seemed as if they had been closed forever. Her body also refused to move toward the sound, laying flat and still. In spite of her situation she tried to focus on the familiar voice. The more she awoke, the more her body responded to the words she was hearing. She looked around the room while her body continued to lay still. Her eyes refused to show a clear picture, leaving everything visualized in a gloomy glare. The little she was able to see displayed a horrifying imagine of shock. She still didn't know where she was or what was going on in the room. She gathered enough strength to faintly focus and look to her side. There, she saw a man sitting in a chair by her side with his entire head buried deep within his hands. She assumed it was Craig, so she felt safe and secure. This realization caused her to close her tired eyes and rest once again. Shortly after, as the voice softly continued, she opened her eyes again. This time she saw the man's head rise from his hands. He slowly reached over to touch her soft hand that was resting by her side.

Still confused by her surroundings, but feeling safe by Craig's side, La Vonne's weak body didn't move to his touch, because it couldn't. It felt like it had extra weight stacked on top of it, feeling almost numb. Instead, she continued to lay in silence while feeling the water from the tears he cried. She quickly closed her eyes and peeked out again. She could see and feel that the man had been crying for a while, but she didn't understand why. He put his head back down in his hands and continued to cry, letting his other tears fall to the floor. While his head was again down, she gained enough strength to take a closer look.

After her eyes totally focused on the face sitting in the chair next to her, she noticed that it wasn't Craig sitting by her side, but Jonathan instead. Craig and Jonathan looked so similar that the mistake was justified. Upon realizing that it was Jonathan who was actually sitting at her side and not Craig, La Vonne froze and became deathly frightened. Without saying a word she slowly glanced around the room and noticed a single red rose sitting in a glass vase on the roll-away table by her side. The sight of the rose caused her to become numb with fear. Suddenly her fingers faintly jumped in a defensive manner. The movement prompted a reaction from Jonathan that caused him to raise his head and look around the room, but he was barely able to see through his tears. Since he didn't notice anything different, he put his head back down and continued to cry.

La Vonne noticed his reaction and froze while remaining quiet. She didn't know if she was once again dreaming, or if Jonathan's presence was real. She speculated if he was for real, and if he was the same brutally abusive husband she once loved, or if he could have changed. She became curious as to why he was by her side instead of the man she now loved, Craig. She also wondered why he was crying. Her awakening finally allowed her to hear Jonathan's plea to God asking for forgiveness. "Lord, please forgive what I did and bring her back to us. I promise to be a better man and always make her happy, please oh Lord, just bring her back to us!" Hearing his plea made her leery, but hopeful he was a changed man. "Jonathan, is that you?" she faintly asked with great hesitation.

He looked up through his tears, jumped out of his chair and hugged her as tight as he could. "You're back! Oh thank God, you're back! I love you girl, I just love you!!!" He repeated over and over again. He kissed her on the forehead and all over her face. Without leaving her side he yelled as loud as he could, "Nurse, come quick! Come in here now! Somebody, anybody, she's backkkkkkk!" With all the noise Jonathan was making, several hospital staff members ran toward La Vonne's room. The realization of what they saw amazed everyone, causing them to push him out the way as more staff entered the room. Soon the tiny room was filled with several hospital personnel looking at the miracle of La Vonne's consciousness.

"Oh my God, it's a miracle! It's a miracle!" Many of them shouted. La Vonne became very scared as everyone looked at her like she was a creature from outer space. "What's everybody looking at? What's going on?" she said in a very faint voice while watching them.

"Mrs. Brown, I'm Dr. Bethel Mitchell. Can you hear me okay?" The doctor began shining a small flashlight in her eyes while waiting for her to respond.

She faintly looked at him with a very uninviting expression and answered, "Yes, I hear you. Who are you and where am I? And get that bright light out of my eyes, it hurts," she tried to look around but her head was too weak to raise. After he took the light out of her eyes she was able to focus more clearly on everyone in the room. She froze with shock as she took a better look at the doctor, to her surprise, he looked exactly like Jay and had Jay's full birth name.

"Mrs. Brown, you're in Martin Luther King Jr. Memorial Hospital. You've been in here for over ten years. You were in a very bad car accident and went into a coma. Do you remember the car accident? Do you remember anything that happened to you?" The doctor continued asking questions as he checked her other vital signs.

"No, I don't remember any accident. What accident?"
La Vonne was still confused as she tried to regain her strength and piece everything together.

Shortly after all the excitement, Gloria and her grandchildren came to the hospital for their weekly visit. As they got closer to La Vonne's room they heard several people talking out loud, "I can't believe it. It's a miracle." Gloria didn't know what they were talking about and ignored their conversation. However, the closer they got to La Vonne's room, the more they noticed the crowd surrounding it. Gloria became nervous, "Oh my God, what's happening? Why is everyone in La Vonne's room?" She grabbed her grandchildren's hands and forced their way through the crowd to see for themselves. "Oh my God! Oh my God! It's a miracle! It's a wonderful miracle!" Gloria said when she saw her daughters eyes wide opened.

"Momma, Momma! You're awake! You're awake!" Jr. and Stacy said as they hugged their mother and cried.

La Vonne looked at her children and her mother and started crying. She kinda recognized everyone, but wasn't sure because her children had grown so tall since she saw them last. They were now sixteen and eighteen years old. When she had the accident they were only six and eight. "Jr., Stacy? Is that you? Momma is that you?" La Vonne reached out to touch their hands.

"Yes La Vonne it's us. Welcome back to the world! We've missed you baby!" Gloria said while crying.

"Welcome back? Where have I been? What happened to me?" La Vonne was still confused. However, she was beginning to understand that she had fallen victim to being in a coma. Everything that happened throughout the last ten years had only been a dream. Her mind had been playing games on her for all those lost years. Her mind had decided to finally wake up after La Vonne accepted that she needed help and couldn't fight her battle alone.

Jonathan tried to explain, "La Vonne, like the doctor said, you're in the hospital and have been here for over ten years. You were in a car accident that left you in a coma. We've been very worried about you. But thank God you've come back to us." He said as he held his wife and continued to cry.

Gloria and the kids also continued crying, along with many of the hospital staff members who were witnessing the entire ordeal, and those who had grown to love La Vonne since she had been a patient. "Alright everyone, we need to let Mrs. Brown regain her strength, and she can't do it with everyone looking at her. Only her immediate family can stay," Dr. Mitchell said while everyone began leaving the room talking about the miracle that just happened. "Mrs. Brown, I'll be back later to run some tests on you. For now, enjoy your family and welcome back." Dr. Mitchell left the room and closed the door.

"La Vonne, we've missed you so much! Honey, we didn't think you would ever come back to us. But Jonathan refused to give up on you. He has stayed by your side the entire time, only leaving to go to work, get some sleep and visit the hospital chapel. He even sold your house in order to pay the additional hospital fees the insurance wouldn't cover in order to keep you here. He has been by your bedside everyday, reading, talking and singing to you. He's the one who gave us the added strength we needed to believe that one day you would return home to us. Even the doctors gave up on you, but he never did," Gloria said while Jonathan continued hugging his wife and crying like a baby.

"Yes baby, I always believed that you would come back to me. God told me you would."

"And why is this red rose here?" La Vonne asked with caution and fear.

"I brought it here." Jonathan said. "I bring you a freshly cut single red rose every week. Red roses are your favorite flower. I hoped that the fresh smell would keep you at peace until the day you woke up. I always knew that you would wake up and I wanted you to see and smell a fresh flower whenever that day arrived."

La Vonne felt much better about red roses after hearing his explanation. She was finally able to lay her fears aside about the beautifully bloomed flower. However, she was still confused as to what happened and why she was in the hospital. "What happened to me? How did I get in a car accident? Did someone run into me or what?" La Vonne needed an explanation.

"It was all my fault and I'm sooooo sorry!" Everyone looked at Jonathan as he continued explaining, "Me and you had a big argument and you took off in the car and drove away. I said some mean things to you that day, things I've regretted everyday since. Then I got a call from the hospital telling me that your car was speeding through an intersection, ran a red light, and hit a light pole to avoid hitting an oncoming car. You have been in a coma ever since the accident. Baby, I'm soooo sorry for making you take off like that. Please forgive me! From that day on I've tried to become a better person to everyone. I watch everything I say and do more closely. I've changed my bad habits and become a person that you can love and depend on. I've become the person that you first fell in love with over nineteen years ago. I've also learned that words are very powerful and you can't take them back. Therefore, you must choose them very carefully or you can live your entire life trying to take them back and regretting what you said. So please forgive me!" he begged. Jonathan's guilty conscience is what kept him close to La Vonne's side throughout the years, hoping for a full recovery.

Everyone in the room was crying even more after hearing Jonathan's explanation. "I know you didn't mean anything bad by whatever it was we argued about. We used to always argue. Married people argue sometimes." La Vonne was very understanding to his plea.

"Yeah they do argue, but they should always be careful at what they say to each other because things like this can happen, and someone may never get a chance to say I'm sorry, or they may never get a chance to ask the person they hurt to forgive them. So, baby I'm sorry and I want you to please forgive me!" he pleaded.

La Vonne was finally gaining more strength. "Yes, I forgive you and I'm back!" she cheerfully said. "Now, we can start over from here. Today will be the first day of the rest of our life together." La Vonne cried, hugged and kissed her husband as the rest of the family joined in on the hug. Shortly after the tearful reunion, La Vonne's happy tears dried up as she looked at her beautiful and handsome children. "So, who's been watching you guys while I've been in my deep sleep?" she smiled.

Mind Games

"I've been taking care of them while Jonathan stayed here with you. After he sold the house he moved in with me and the kids, except he stays here with you most of the time. That chair is his second bed. He's never at home with us," Gloria said as she continued, "We always wanted to have someone here to watch over you in case you woke up, and Jonathan appointed himself the guard over you until the big day you awoke. He always believed and gave us hope that one day you would wake up and come back home to us. He always held on to that feeling, even when the doctors tried to convince us otherwise."

As La Vonne listened to everyone, she realized that the lawyer she thought she had over the last ten years was actually her doctor who had been checking on her. She also realized what everyone else knew for years, that she was deep in a coma, imaging everything that had happened to her while her mind played games. "Well, now I'm back! And I'm sure that in time I'll be back to my old self again, whoever that was," she smiled. "Soon, I'll walk out of here to be with my family."

Everyone smiled while Jr. and Stacy continued hugging their mom, not wanting to ever let her go. Jonathan was happy that God answered his prayers and brought his wife back. He knew that everything was going to be alright. He also planned to do all he could to make things up to his wife and children. He was at peace knowing that his family could finally live happily ever after! **The End!**

BOOK COVER ARTIST

Eric Olsen
Professional Freelance Artist

Born and raised in Southern California, Eric Olsen, was made for art. Visual representation of emotions has always been the underlying effort behind his work. From early on he knew that the world of art would be the one he lived in. After graduating from high school, he went on to Brooks College of Design in Long Beach, CA. There he learned various graphical applications from hand rendering and digital imagery, to multimedia and web design. The technical aspects are a must in this ever-evolving computer age, but his focus on traditional mediums still flourishes to this day. The powerful combination of technology and artistic quality is the foundation for his design work.

I'd like to thank all those who are close to my heart and have been there all along. You know who you are. Without you, I am nothing. Without love, this world is nothing. *EO*

Eric Olsen can be contacted at:
TM Publications
PO Box 443
Colton, CA 92324
or by email at:
eosart@aol.com

Never allow the word NO to stop your visions!

The sky is our ONLY limit if we just reach for it!

PUBLICATION ORDER FORM

<u>MAIL ORDERS TO:</u> TM Publications, Orders Dept.
PO Box 443, Colton, CA 92324

<u>Please Print:</u>

Name:_____

Address:_____

City:_____State_____Zip_____

Telephone:(   )_____ fax (   )_____

Email Address:_____

<u>PRICES ARE PER BOOK:</u>

$3.00 S&H for 1st book/ $1.50 S&H for each additional book shipped within the US.

Sales Tax: Add 7.50% for products shipped to California.

<u>*Mind Games*</u> /   Novel   **$14.95** x _____$_____

0-9713221-1-2

<u>*How To Self Publish Your Novel*</u>   **$7.99** x _____$_____

<u>*on a Shoestring Budget! -In 10 Easy Steps -*</u> (Instructional Booklet)

0-9713221-9-8

<u>*Momma, Please Forgive Me!*</u> / Novel **$13.95** x_____$_____

0-9713221-0-4

Shipping Total $_____

Sales Tax Total $_____

Grand Total $_____

**Visit website for discounts: www.toimoore.com
For Multi-Book discounts or Fund Raisers,
contact tmpublications1@aol.com**

Name:_____

Address:_____

Postage

City/State/Zip:_____

TM Publications
ATTN: Orders Dept.
PO Box 443
Colton, CA 92324

Circle of Strength is an organization that sells wonderfully FUN products displaying our colorful logo. Our goal is to share the good and positive message through our products. When you purchase our products, a portion is donated to organizations benefiting women.

Be a part of the Circle Of Strength Strengthening women, and strengthening communities.

CIRCLE OF STRENGTH™

Women's organizations can form an alliance with us by purchasing Circle of Strength products at a wholesale price. This is a fun way to raise money, strengthen your membership while supporting your organizations mission.

To view the entire line of products visit our website:

www.circleofstrength.com

or call us at (909) 242-6934

Tobin & Associates, Inc.

...In A Class By Itself!

Tobin & Associates, Inc. was chosen as the 2003 Supplier of the Year in the "Class I" category during the recent Southern California Minority Business Development Council Awards luncheon. The firm was nominated by Toyota Motor Sales, USA, Inc. for "Superior Performance." Pat is pictured in the middle between John Murray, Jr., president and executive director of SCMBDC and Monetta Stephens, supplier development manager, Toyota Motor Sales, USA. Inc.

Public Relations • Marketing • Special Events • Advertising •
Design • Printing
323.856.0827   Fax 323.856.9510
pat_tobin@tobinpr.com   www.tobinpr.com
6565 Sunset Boulevard, Suite 301, Los Angeles, CA 90028

Always follow your dreams and NEVER give up on your goals!

What People Are Saying About
TOI MOORE

"Leave it up to ***Toi L. Moore*** to keep it real on love, relationships, and accomplishments. She's a dynamic and delightful writer, as well as a hell of a woman!" ***Vivica A. Fox - Actress***

On *Momma, Please Forgive Me!* - "***Toi***, Love the book! With love, ***Mya*"** *- **Entertainer***

"It is always gratifying to meet interested and active young people like you. I extend to you my most genuine best wishes for the future. ***Kweisi Mfume - President and C.E.O NAACP***

"***Mind Games*** is a GREAT book! I love the story! It's never predictable. I also love the dialog you give your characters. People will not want to put it down." ***Michele Mc Dowell - Avid Reader***

"***Toi Moore***, a newly self-published author, is very confident." Author compared to E. Lynn Harris and Omar Tyree on self-publishing efforts. ***Renee Simms - EUR Headlines***

"I am so proud of you. You will do good! I enjoyed *Momma, Please Forgive Me!* so much that I told everyone to buy it! Now, we can wait for ***Mind Games!*** I know you will do well." ***Mary Inell Sterling-Fitzgerald - Student***

"***Toi Moore*** is an emerging African American sistah with a story to tell. She is committed to sharing "real life" situations through the talent of literary writing." ***Lisa Cross - The Sistah Circle Book Club (Dallas)***

On *Momma, Please Forgive Me:* "This story was very touching because there are so many women out here today being abused by their significant others." ***La Toya - Sista Friendz Book Club***

"***Toi Moore*** is such a beautiful individual and has accomplished much in her life, in spite of the fact that she grew up in a family that was affected by domestic violence and abuse." ***Robbie Motter - For You Network***

"***Toi*** is an author who cares about today's issues and I hope she continues in this line of writing." ***Mahogany Book Club***